Published in the United States of America.

FT
Pbk

Terms

Alternate dimension/dimension hop: Each of the seven Pleiades witches possesses the magical ability to travel to a unique alternate dimension where the year is the same but everything is slightly different. Origin of the dimensions: long ago, at the pleading of the Pleiades' father, Atlas, Zeus created an alternate dimension for each of the original Pleiades goddesses to disappear into in order to avoid the unwanted advances of Orion. The ability was then passed on to the eldest female human descendant of each Pleiad.

Death reaper: Human descendant of the underworld god, Hades. Required to shuttle evil human souls to hell at the command of Hades.

Keepers of the Veil: The seven Pleiades witches are the keepers of the veil, or gate, which stands between our world and the afterlife world of their ancestors. The seven must convene at a Confirmation on the last night of Samhain every twenty years to assure the ancestors all is well. If any of the seven miss, the ancestors will cross into our world in anger. Then chaos will ensue.

Pleiades: The seven Greek goddess daughters of Atlas and the sea nymph Pleione, known as Sterope, Calaeno, Electra, Maia, Merope, Taygete, and Alcyone.

Pleiades witch: The eldest human female descendant of one of the seven Pleiades Greek goddesses. Each possesses a unique preternatural power and the ability to hop to an alternate dimension.

Sentry druid: Celtic druid capable of a distinctive supernatural ability. Sworn to protect the Pleiades witches. The Greek gods often choose a mate for the Pleiades witches from the ranks of the Sentry druids.

Chapter One

Shannon squinted into the setting sun's glare in the rearview mirror. *No new cars. Stay alert.*

A minivan ran a stop sign to pull in front of her, forcing her to slam the brakes hard.

"Jesus." She gripped the wheel. Heart pounding, she resumed speed on the two-lane.

A quick recheck of the rearview mirror showed nothing had changed. She expected her bodyguard, Eli, to round the corner in his truck at any moment.

You should be relieved. She wasn't. Deep down, she wished he hadn't accepted the coffee she'd offered him earlier. Given his ability to quick-heal, his body would power through the sleeping potion's effects in no time. She had to do this meeting alone, even though she'd never before bargained with a black market dealer to buy a magical relic.

The Port Royal Bar might be a public place, and one she frequented whenever she visited South Carolina, but that didn't make it a safe zone from those willing to use magic to attack.

The bar's packed parking lot forced her to settle for a spot at the end of a row far from the entrance. Even though not an official spot, no one cared. They wouldn't enforce towing on a Friday night.

Before she unlatched her seatbelt, she studied the lot for auras. Her palm caressed the handle of the Glock in the cup holder. The old Shannon, the one who existed prior to her mother's murder eight weeks ago, would've waltzed up to the front door, oblivious of dangers that lurked in the dark. She rubbed her stomach where the reminder of what happened when she let her guard down festered as a peculiar, sometimes painful, scar.

A predator would stand in the trees at the far end of the lot where shadows masked everything. Leaves rustled as a coastal breeze passed through, but nothing moved in the darkness. No black or red auras swirled in the air.

Her cell phone dinged with a message from her best friend.

Jen: *Harnish confirmed for 8:15. I barely trust him. Don't like that he required you go alone.*

She put the Glock in the glove box and tucked a knife into her jeans before replying: *No choice. Countdown clock's ticking.*

Jen: *Be careful.*

Shannon: *As long as you believe this guy has what he says, then this is a go.*

Jen: *I've only bought potion ingredients off him, but he said he had it.*

Shannon: *I'll text after.*

Heat, typical of a humid July evening, assaulted her outside the car. Usually, she loved everything about the hot summer nights of South Carolina. Not tonight. The instant sheen of sticky sweat beneath her shirt irritated her. She fanned the shirt to promote air flow and angled her steps in a shortcut to the bar's entrance.

Something wild and bottomless, a feral tangle of rage and hate, bubbled upward. It pushed beyond the anxiety and fatigue that had plagued her for days. She would fight to the bitter end to live and to save her family. A surge of energy carried her inside the bar. Maybe it wasn't energy at all, but desperation.

No man of Asian descent sat at the bar. She chose a stool and empty one beside it. Her cell phone indicated three minutes before the designated time. Did protocol dictate she be late to this kind of meeting?

A guy leaned in beside her. "Hey, gorgeous. Here alone? Wanna join us?"

She recognized him as someone who'd been three years ahead of her in high school, but didn't recall his name. The guy nodded his chin toward a table with two other guys and six empty beer bottles.

"No, thanks. I'm waiting for someone." She forced herself to smile.

"If he doesn't show, we'll be over there." He left with three beers.

She scanned for auras, picking up nothing evil. However, she did pick up another person with magical abilities.

Her heart rate sped up. Maybe Eli had caught up with her.

No. The preternatural power came from a tall man in a dark long-sleeved shirt with his back to her, leaning against the wall in conversation with another guy. She openly ogled the hard lines of his worship-worthy body from his biceps, which flexed beneath the shirt as he took a swig of his beer, to the tattoos on his neck and hands.

He was *hot*. And not passingly hot, but more like *I can-make-you-come-with-a-look* hot.

What's wrong with you?

She tore her eyes away to look for the reason she was here. No Harnish yet.

Her gaze drifted back to the stranger. Was he druid, warlock, or something else? No menacing aura colors came off him. One more second of gawking wasn't going to hurt.

His head swiveled in her direction. Caught.

Good Lord. She knew him.

Jason Merck. She'd thought about him a time or two—okay maybe more than a few dozen times—since she'd come down from New York City to her family's coastal estate two days ago in preparation for this meeting. Ten years since she and Jason had...

You don't need this distraction. He must've concurred since he disappeared into the pool hall in the back without acknowledging her. His dismissal hurt, even though it shouldn't matter.

"Shannon?" asked a heavily accented male voice.

She jumped. With a turn she faced the Asian standing less than a foot away. On reflex she accepted his outstretched hand for a shake.

She'd expected someone older, someone with graying hair, not a guy barely out of adolescence with short-cut dark hair and small glasses.

He slid onto the open barstool next to her.

"How does this work?" she asked.

"Buy me a drink. I like rum." He smiled a wide expanse of white teeth but his eyes remained sharp. The smile wasn't for her. It was for those nearby. In the South everyone watched, keen to witness others' business. An Asian in the bar would be the talk of the hair salon tomorrow.

As they waited for their drinks, she drummed her fingers. Small talk with him seemed absurd. Besides, he ignored her to scroll through screens on his cell phone. His body tensed and lips thinned as he read a message. Anger and fear aura hues swirled around him, but then went to gray, which was a color she couldn't interpret. It represented the intersection of many emotions. Only when she knew a person well could she put context and personality together to understand a gray aura's meaning.

What if this didn't work and the item was a fake? She dreaded the disappointment of another dead end in a series of failures. Her family depended on her. They may consist of druids and witches who could protect themselves against humans or magical beings of equal ability, but not against her would-be executioner.

Her reflection in the mirror behind the bar startled her. The wide-eyed woman wasn't her. It couldn't possibly be Shannon Randolph, the adventure camerawoman who filmed documentaries and journalistic pieces in unstable countries. The Shannon she was familiar with had happy blue eyes and an easy smile. That woman liked making people laugh and encouraging others to try new things.

Everything had changed when her mother was murdered and she'd been framed for theft.

Harnish stopped typing when the bartender slid their drinks in front of them. He took a single sip of the rum. "I emailed you the account. Transfer the bitcoin. Once I have the money, I'll give it to you."

A few clicks on her phone and the bitcoin she'd spent an hour last night learning how to purchase had been sent.

His phone dinged.

"Got it. The scrying glass is yours." He removed a small cloth-wrapped item from his cargo pants and put it in her hand. His face scrunched up as he gave her a cursory once-over. "You don't look the type to use this sort of thing. You sure you know what you're doing?"

"Any hints?" The item in the soft cloth emitted a foul energy that alarmed her. Instinct urged she give it back to Harnish and find another way. *This is the end of the line.*

"Not my area of expertise. I sell. You use."

She shoved the small, wrapped item into her jeans and stood. Dizzy, she grabbed the wooden bar counter. Fatigue played a factor in her stress of the past few weeks, but she hadn't experienced vertigo before. Maybe this was reaction to the item?

"You sure you're feeling alright?" He flashed a weird smile before it disappeared.

Crap. She'd been played.

Chapter Two

Shannon moaned and tried to rub her forehead, which throbbed like the morning after a late night tequila binge. Her hands were locked behind her.

Handcuffs? What the hell?

She seesawed her wrists. They'd bruise from the abuse, but she needed her hands free. The handcuffs didn't loosen. Courage abandoned her. Her throat worked, closing tight. She felt herself flying apart, felt her control shredding.

Deep breaths. Don't freak. Look around.

This wasn't the bar. Bookshelves lined the walls, filled with assorted items. Three tables littered with antiques sat to her right. The smell of musty air mixed with cleanser reminded her of an old public building.

"If your wrists are bound, you can't dimension hop to escape, but you can still use magic to protect yourself." Her mother's instruction from long ago blasted through her brain. The concept of jumping from this reality to another, where the people and time was similar and yet not, was mind-blowing and not something she'd attempted.

The only exit from the windowless room was a closed door fifteen feet away, perhaps locked.

Get up. Test the door. Leave before whoever brought you here comes back.

Her neck tingled as if someone watched her.

More Mom words drifted through her mind. "*If captured, don't show the enemy your fear, honey, and don't come unglued.*"

She schooled her expression to reflect blankness. Her best option to defend herself was magic. She wasn't sure how to use the mysterious ability to manipulate elements, which she'd inherited mere weeks ago. Yesterday's experimental attempt to control wind whipped up a tornado that almost killed her. She wished she'd paid a bit more attention when her mother discussed how to control the powers. Too bad the magic couldn't break the handcuffs.

A man stood with his back against the wall in the dark corner nearest the exit. He was taller and broader than Harnish.

She pushed her witchy senses to read his aura, but it didn't work. *No, no, no. Come on. Work!*

Pain throbbed behind her eyes as she swung her legs over the edge of the slatted wooden bench. She struggled upright.

"Good nap, Miss Shannon?" her watcher drawled in a rich Southern accent. His leg dropped off the wall to the floor.

Energy buzzed through her head and resonated deep in her chest. *Uh-oh.* Even if she couldn't see the colors of his aura and gauge his intent, the energy coming off him signified some sort of magical power. He might be another warlock or sorcerer after that which she didn't have.

"Who're you?" Her heart *thump-thumped* piercingly between her ears.

"Does your head hurt?" His deep, rugged voice resonated with concern. His arrogant stance seemed familiar.

"Do we know each other?" She blinked past her head pain to see details. The set of his lips communicated a clear my-way-or-else attitude, but she couldn't make out his face above his mouth. She needed to see his eyes.

"Everyone knows you've come down from New York. The big-city girl visiting the family estate." His tone wasn't taunting or threatening. Only factual.

"Why'd you bring me here?" She jiggled the cuffs, waiting for him to remove them.

He didn't.

This might come down to her need to use magic. Crap.

An HVAC system kicked on. Cold air blew from an overhead vent. She asked the air to pin her captor to the wall. She would exchange his freedom for hers.

Nothing happened. She tried again. Not even so much as a gust stirred the air. Since she got the power, she'd been able to whip up at least a modest breeze.

Whatever drug knocked her out had also stolen her abilities. *Do not panic.* She needed some kind of weapon, anything, no matter how primitive, with which she could protect herself. A piece of broken glass sat on one of the tables. It didn't get much more primitive than that. Next, she had to get him to take off the handcuffs.

"I thought you recognized me in the bar, darlin'?" With a push away from the wall he moved closer. Light filled in all the previously hidden details. She sucked in a startled breath. His face, so familiar, had been created with great care to sharp detail, but injury had wreaked havoc. Linear scars marred his right cheek, the one she hadn't seen in the bar.

"Jason?" Her breath stuck in her chest. "Jason Merck?"

"It's Merck." He didn't smile. Didn't look even remotely pleased. His clothes were simple, a long-sleeved dark T-shirt, bunched up on his strong forearms and jeans. Odd dress for the summer when iced tea and air conditioning were essentials to surviving the sweltering heat. The shirt pressed tight to the ripped muscles she'd ogled in the bar. Colorful tattoos stretched down to the tops of his hands in skeletonlike stylized lines, broken by foreign lettering.

His eyes were so blue they reminded her of Mediterranean Sea pictures.

She'd never forgotten *those* eyes or *those* lips. *Stop thinking about his fricking eyes and mouth. He kidnapped you.* "Why am I in handcuffs?"

A few more dramatic wrist tugs didn't inspire him to unlock them.

"You were hallucinating. I worried you'd hurt yourself."

If that were true, then he would've bound her ankles too. He must know what she was and didn't want her escaping via dimension hop.

No, he couldn't know. She wanted to believe him about the hallucinations. Good Lord. Staring at his eyes, she had a hard time reconciling her memory of the rebellious, yet considerate, teenager she'd crushed on for years and the man before her who'd evolved into something dangerous and dark.

He continued to stare at her as if she were an out-of-control flame he wasn't quite sure he wanted to extinguish but found fascinating.

"Take the handcuffs off. Please."

"How do I know you're in your right mind now?"

She granted him her best squinty-eyed glare.

"There's the Shannon I remember." He twisted the Oakleys hanging on a black neck cord from his front to rest against his back. He'd done the sunglasses rotation hundreds of times while they'd waited for the bus together in high school. *He may not be that guy anymore.*

"The Jason I remember wouldn't have put me in handcuffs."

He smiled. "It's Merck. I've been waiting for you to wake up so I can drive you home. We're going in the same direction, *neighbor.*"

His smile lit up her body like she was still sixteen all over again and at the mercy of a crush on the out-of-her-league, hottest guy in school. No amount of air could steady her heart or nerves, but she sucked in a lungful.

You're twenty-eight, not sixteen and getting kissed by him. He might be your enemy. "Why am I here if you planned to take me home?"

"I didn't know if you wanted whoever was home to see you this way or if anybody would be home at all. Couldn't leave you by yourself like this."

"Right," she said sarcastically.

"Are you visiting down here alone?"

None of his business who may or may not be down here with her. If he'd been acting out of altruism, he would've taken her home. The fact he didn't meant he had an agenda.

"What do you remember about last night?" His smile faded. Furrows creased his forehead. Her gut believed his concern was legitimate. Yet, she was here and restrained. Even if not evil, Merck may be after the same item she sought.

"Did you slip me something last night?"

"I didn't give you anything. I swear. Tell me what you remember."

She jiggled the cuffs.

This time he moved forward and unlocked them, stepping away the moment he freed her.

With a jump, she grabbed the piece of glass off the table and held it toward him.

He didn't look impressed by her threat. "I'm not going to hurt you."

"Tell me how I got here."

"You've been passed out for about,"—he rolled his wrist to view his watch—"fifteen hours."

"What happened?" She glanced around again, her gaze snagging on a gun safe in the corner.

"Are you going to put that down?"

"No."

He shrugged. "I wouldn't want you to hurt yourself. Chad and I were at the bar last night. Remember him from high school?"

She nodded, recollecting Chad's obsession for surfing with his bleached blond hair and signature fragrance of sunscreen.

Merck said, "We were playing pool with some out-of-towners—"

"You two are still hustling?" They'd been notorious in high school. Their post-hustle fights landed them in jail once or twice.

"I wouldn't say we were hustling *per se*. When we do, we simply take advantage of people who equate our accents with stupidity." He flashed a wolfish leer. "It wasn't hard to miss you singing at the top of your lungs. I guess the tone deafness didn't improve."

"I'm not tone-deaf. And I don't sing in public."

"You sing when you're drunk, apparently. I've got it videoed on my phone. Wanna see?" He pulled his phone out of his pocket.

"Show me."

In silence, she watched the minute and a half of her hip-swaying and singing into her cell phone like it was a mike, accompanied by a tinny rendition of a familiar country song on the jukebox. Her face scorched as the terrible off-key performance ran to completion. Who was this woman singing? She didn't do karaoke or anything that involved performance. Ever. He pulled the phone away when it ended.

"I wasn't drunk. I don't remember...that." She pointed at where he'd put away his phone.

Merck's eyebrows drooped low. "You were hanging out with this out-of-towner who got you outside after you serenaded the bar, and then passed out. I can't say you had a graceful lights-out moment, but I figured you weren't on board with whatever the guy planned next."

"Was he Asian?"

"He stuck out like a turd in a punchbowl. You think he slipped you something?" Merck's gaze darkened. He ran a hand through his short, lightly gelled, blond hair, now so much shorter than he ever used to wear it.

"I didn't drink anything."

"He might've used a poison. Did you touch anything he gave you?"

The handshake. "Must've been something because that woman singing...that's not me."

"It could've happened to anyone." His tone was gentle, as if he realized how mortified she was.

"I guess I'm lucky you and Chad were there." Both of them there might not be coincidence. Perhaps, this was an elaborate hoax to get her to trust him.

"Everyone's there on Friday night."

"Did the guy say anything to you?" Such as why the hell he drugged her after she paid him for the scrying glass?

"He said you were drunk and needed a ride home, but I didn't buy it. So I relieved him of you." Something about his tone suggested the *relieving* part hadn't been as simple as a verbal exchange.

"What happened exactly?"

He shrugged, dismissive. She'd have to get details from Chad, if she could find him. She could call his dad, who still worked at the tire store in town. She had to find the Asian to get the scrying glass back from him. She'd purchased the thing free and clear. However, this time when she confronted him, she'd take help with her.

"Most drugs would've knocked you out for maybe six or seven hours. Not fifteen." His tone ended it as a question, not a statement. She wasn't about to get into a discussion of the drug possibly being something magical, a spell or potion. Even though she'd always detected Merck had some sort of preternatural abilities, it wasn't a topic either of them had discussed. Rule one in being a person with abilities was never be the first to reveal.

"Why were you at the bar?" he asked.

"It's none of your business." She finger-combed through a few tangles.

"It's my business when you almost get yourself kidnapped and..." His voice dropped off.

She refused to answer. Alpha males didn't scare her.

He cocked his head. "You've changed. You're different. Tougher."

"A lot's happened in ten years."

"I heard you went into journalism."

"I'm not a journalist. I do camera work on a contract basis. Mostly TV stuff."

"Isn't the camera heavy to haul around?"

"Sometimes. The newer ones are lighter. You don't think I can haul the old ones because I'm a girl?" She encountered this mentality all the time.

"I didn't say that. I was just wondering. Are you visiting down here alone?"

"No." She didn't want to admit yes. Well, other than the well-armed, ex-MI6, druid bodyguard assigned to protect her. Eli was probably having a coronary at her house right now over her missing. She'd be lucky if he didn't call in every druid in the U.S. and Canada to put her on guarded lockdown until her death.

"You have a husband...maybe a posse of kids waiting for you at home?"

She shook her head. "You?" Her gaze darted to his left hand, but she couldn't see his ring finger.

"Nah. Your mother, how is she?"

"Dead." Her mother's parting words had sent her to this hot, humid, mosquito-infested coastal town where she'd supposedly find "help." She needed help for the pile of cow shit she'd landed in.

"Sorry to hear that." His words weighed heavily, as if he knew everything her mother's death meant—the instant promo to head witch in her line and a destiny to lead the other six Pleiades witches. All of it unwanted. He couldn't know all that, though. The information was a guarded secret amongst the Pleiades and their druid protectors, a secret all of them would die—many *had* died—to protect.

"Your brothers? I heard Tom got married."

"Both of my brothers were killed last year." They'd been defending her mom from witch hunters. God, she missed all of them.

"Damn." He rubbed his forehead. "I'm sorry. They were good people."

"Dad is still with us, but since Mom and my brothers are gone, he's not the same." She cleared her throat against the sudden tightness. "Last I heard you'd moved away. What're you doing here?"

"I moved back not too long ago."

"Is this where you live?" She gazed at the relics on the tables representing a mishmash of eras. Magical energy came from the items. They weren't random artifacts but a hodgepodge of mystical items. None of them invited touching.

"This is work." He crossed his arms.

His work involved mystical items. Damn it, he *was* after her for the same reason as all the other magical weirdoes she'd encountered in the past few weeks. She palmed the glass shard, still ready should he attack. "What exactly do you do?"

"I find people."

"Like a private investigator? Or are you a bounty hunter?"

"Something like that." He watched her while moving slowly forward. Six-foot-something of unpredictable, supernatural power, who might be a bounty hunter, intimidated her. Her head carried a pretty high price these days.

She stepped backward. Her legs caught on the edge of the bench and she ended in an awkward sit. The glass piece flew out of her hand.

"You've been here four days, Shannon. Is this a vacation for you, or are you down here for another reason?" His tone encouraged her to talk. Maybe it was a well-practiced skill, or he had persuasive powers.

"Have you been spying on me across the property line?" He was so close now that she picked up his subtle scent. Something clean, like aftershave or deodorant mixed with male.

"I noticed activity next door and figured you were back in town."

"Why would it matter to you why I'm down here? It's our family property. We visit a few times a year."

For an instant, his face scrunched up as if he was irritated. Then his expression smoothed over. He extended his hand to her. "Let's get you home."

She regarded his offer of help, reluctant. He wanted something. Everything about her here at his work after she'd been poisoned was suspicious. Even if he hadn't hurt her so far, he had just tried to grill her, and he had ill-defined magical powers. Right now, she trusted no one who wasn't family.

Before she could decide one way or another on accepting his assistance, his hand closed around hers. The calluses at the base of his fingers rubbed against her palm. She liked his large hand around hers, warm and secure.

No, you can't like it. Snap out of it. As soon as she was on her feet, she pulled free of his grasp. She skirted a few steps out of his reach. "I can take myself home, thank you. I'll get my car from the bar parking lot."

"I had a friend drop the car off at your place. I'll drive you home. Come on." He led her down the hallway of what turned out to be a generic small office building. The rest of the place was better lit and less cluttered, but didn't look to house any other businesses. There was a room full of books and another with a bevy of security monitors flashing images of all angles of the building.

She wanted to trust him, but the desire lay in memories of the kid she always felt got a bad rap from adults, a guy whose mother hated him and who always seemed alone. As an adult, like her, he'd become a different person.

She retrieved her cell phone from her bra while he wasn't looking, the only personal item still on her. Why had he left her cell phone?

It had charge and signal. Notification she had twenty-six voicemail messages flashed on the screen. She thrust it back into her bra moments before Merck glanced over his shoulder at her.

As they passed by an office with an open door, a man yelled in a thick Hispanic accent, "Did Sleeping Beauty wake up yet?"

"I thought you went out, Danny," Merck replied.

"Already back. Just grabbed the mail. You wouldn't believe my last phone call. You've been gazing at Sleeping Beauty so long..." Danny's hazel eyes widened when she stepped into the doorway. His mouth closed against finishing the sentence. "You'd be Shannon Randolph?"

She nodded. The roomy office with two wooden desks reminded her of an off-exhibit storage room at a museum. Countless busts, partial sculptures, pots, and ancient vases had been shoved haphazardly onto crowded shelves. Perhaps, Merck sold artifacts in addition to finding people. If he wasn't after the relic, maybe she could hire him to find it.

Three gigantic, gold-gilded, framed paintings of deities dominated the walls. They weren't prints and she was pretty sure they featured Greek or Roman gods. A chill slithered down her spine. Too much Greek stuff in here. With her of Greek goddess ancestry and in need of finding a Greek God's Trident, Merck was definitely in the *don't-trust* category.

"Shannon, this is Danny Velez," Merck introduced.

Danny stood, coming to an inch or two taller than her five-eight. His muscles bulged, suggesting gym rat, but his carriage and confidence hinted at a history with advanced combat training, only too familiar to her from years of druid bodyguards with such skills. He'd be handsome if it wasn't for his aura of broody isolation. Something tortured this man. A prickle slid between her shoulders. Danny had some magical ability. Not strong like Merck's power, but it was there. Maybe Danny was a dormant druid.

Shannon threw Danny her best smile, the one that could charm any man. Well, except Merck. She'd tried it on him and failed so many times years ago that she'd given up.

She shook Danny's hand.

"You truly are Sleeping Beauty." A flush settled high on Danny's cheeks as his eyes darted down to her chest.

"Thanks. Good to meet you, Danny. This is quite an office you have here."

Danny still stared at her shirt, which was designed to draw attention to her breasts. She didn't think of herself as a flirt, but she enjoyed appreciation from a handsome man.

Merck cleared his throat. He'd crossed his arms and looked pissed. Over harmless flirting with Danny? Maybe it'd been her office comment?

Danny glanced around. "Yeah, we've picked up a few things over the years." He faced Merck. His cheeks flushed a darker red. "Shit's getting real on the water, Merck. Two more bodies washed up down in Savannah this morning. It's all over the news. That makes six. The girls were about..." He cleared his throat. His eyes darted to her and then back to Merck. "Her age."

"A serial killer?" Chills tickled her arms. She might've been the next dead body if not for Merck. Did that mean she trusted him now? No.

"I'm not sure if it's a serial thing." Merck scratched his chin. His gaze was guarded. He addressed Danny, "I'm going to run her home. Call me if you get any new leads on the unusual happenings."

He wrapped his hand around her upper arm and propelled her out the front door.

"What's Danny's job?" she asked.

"He's my assistant."

"What *unusual happenings* is he to be on the lookout for? Serial killers?"

"There've been a some murders in the past few days. 'Round here people don't die unless it's an accident or domestic dispute. Those deaths were strange. They occurred since you've been back, actually."

Was he accusing her of killing? She yanked her arm out of his grasp. "I can get home on my own."

"Get in the damned car so I can take you home." He hooked her arm before she took more than a step away.

She didn't move. Her gut trusted him. Why it did made no sense. One too many red flags had gone up since she'd woken up.

"What can I say to convince you I'm not the bad guy here? That Asian fellow had been hired to kidnap you. I want to know why you were meeting someone like that at the bar."

She should call Eli to pick her up. "I can get another ride."

"Jesus, Shannon. I don't know what've you gotten yourself into." He let go of her and stepped away. "Fine. Call for a ride. But I'm not leaving you alone until your ride arrives."

"I just woke up after being poisoned by a guy who deals in mystical items to find myself in a building filled with similar things. Then there's *you* with whatever kind of magical skills you've got. I need to know what you're up to."

"You're the one with the *special skills*. You arrived in the area and now weird stuff's started happening..."

She crossed her arms. "You've got skills too."

His eyes narrowed. "No, I don't."

"Oh, please. Let's have honesty between us on this. I've known about you since the first time we met. Something spooked my parents enough to pull me out junior year and move north. I think it was you and your skills."

"You're reading into their decision to move. I think it was you who was spooked after we made out that night."

She stared at him, getting conflicting aura readings off him. Hallelujah. Her reading skills were back.

"A little kiss isn't enough to scare me. If I remember correctly, it was you who rushed me off your property and then stayed scarce ever since. Seems to me it was you who ran scared." She pointed at him. "Your aura screams all kinds of complex magical mojo. It always has."

"Okay."

She couldn't tell if he said it sarcastically or out of agreement. "Okay? You admit to having some sort of magical ability."

"Why're you down here, Shannon? Do you have something to do with these murders?"

"Do you really think I'm capable of killing someone?"

"Yes."

She tried to keep her face blank when his aura swirled viciously with part anger, part determination, and part arousal. "All right. I admit I *could* kill someone if I really wanted to. I don't have any desire to attack at random, but you are pushing me..."

Both his eyebrows shot up in challenge.

"What kind of people do you hunt, *Merck*?"

He dangled a round, black glass attached to a golden chain from his index finger. Its foul energy made her back up a step. "I hunt people who use black magic. Like witches with scrying glasses."

Chapter Three

"I'm not a witch."

Like hell you're not a witch. Merck tried not to laugh, but a *yeah-right* snort escaped him.

"What about this?" he asked, giving the scrying glass a shake where it dangled from his finger.

Her eyes narrowed. "Give me back the glass."

"No."

"You're an asshole."

"Won't argue that, but I'm the asshole who saved your ass last night." He liked her angry. It helped him distance himself from how much everything about her pushed him to the edge.

The edge of behaving out of character. Insane. Irrational. Like how much he wanted to kiss her right now. The temptation nearly overrode common sense. Lord, the girl had beautiful eyes. When he saw her blue eyes in the bar and she recognized him, he felt the string connecting their lives draw taut. That instant link hadn't diminished over the years, even though it should've.

Nope. No kissing with her. There's no sort of connection crap. Focus on the scrying glass and why she wants it.

She held out her hand and wiggled her fingers. "I'd appreciate you returning my glass to me."

"Yours, huh? Do you know what this piece is?"

"Of course, I know it's a scrying glass."

"Do you know how it works? What it requires to work it?"

She chewed on her lower lip. "Not really. Do you? I'd appreciate a few hints."

He swiped a hand across his face, relieved she didn't entirely know what she'd acquired. That didn't erase her intent to use it, though.

"This is the Delmindes scrying glass. It's dangerous." For decades, he'd searched for this piece to confiscate it, to put it into his vault of objects best never used again, but which couldn't be destroyed. "It requires death to scry the secret that's being sought."

"Death? What kind of death? Like sacrificing a chicken or something?"

"It's black magic."

"Okay, I'll kill a chicken or a duck."

Surprised, he laughed. "A duck?"

She remained serious. The woman planned to try to power a dark magical item with a duck's death.

"I don't want to kill a duck, but there are plenty of dumb ducks no one will miss. There's one at the house who keeps chewing the landscape lights. She's bound for electrocution since all the lights are hard wired."

He laughed harder. All concern she was one of the black-magic practitioners pilgrimaging to South Carolina vanished. Those who'd traveled here weren't the Mickey Mouse black-magic practitioners. They were the top-tier bad dogs He didn't know why they were swarming here, but guessed it had to do with Shannon.

"Darlin', the tricky part about black magic is what happens to the person dabbling with it. It comes with a price, such as a piece of the caster's soul or a human death. Human death is required to work this piece."

Her face blanched. "I didn't know that."

"Figured you didn't." He wondered what she needed to know desperately enough to make a deal with Harnish. He pocketed the glass.

"It's still mine."

"Not anymore. You should be worried that a top-end witchcraft supplier prioritized kidnapping you over selling you a priceless scrying glass. This glass on the real market would cost far more than money. He lured you on purpose." Harnish had always seemed like a harmless, yet smart, businessman. Not a trafficker in people. Something much larger was afoot.

"I think he was threatened into doing it. Just a hunch based on his reaction to whatever message he got on his cell phone at the bar."

"Why were you purchasing this glass from him?"

She folded her arms across her chest and remained silent.

He'd get the truth out of her eventually. "You'll have to do something else to find whatever it is you're after."

"Your job involves finding a lot of magical things. Perhaps, I should hire you to find what I need."

Not what he'd intended.

"No." His denial was complicated. Years ago, he placed Shannon in the no-touching category. He feared the arrival of the day when what she was collided with what he must do. If she killed people to power magic, he'd be forced to destroy her. He wasn't sure he could.

One glance her way and... nope. He wouldn't do it. He'd never failed his duty as the Enforcer, but for Shannon, he'd neglect responsibility on purpose because he liked her. *Oh, you more than like her. You want her.*

Sex, relationships, and magic were an unhealthy mix. The witch hunter could not date the witch.

His answer was a firm "*no.*" Had to be. *Shit, you're wavering.* If they worked together, he'd break his no-touch rule in a millisecond when she gave him an opening. Their one kiss still haunted him as one of the few bright moments of his life.

"I'll pay you for your time." Her instant buoyancy killed him. Ah, Christ, her eyes were filled with hope.

"It's not about money."

"What's it about?"

"I don't do small-time work." *You're a shitty liar.*

"Guarantee this isn't small-time," she muttered so low he almost missed it.

He pulled the passenger door wide. "Please, let me take you home."

She worked her lower jaw while squinting at him until she finally nodded.

Once they were both buckled in, he cranked the SUV. It turned over several times before grumbling to life with lackluster enthusiasm.

He tried to appear totally relaxed and in control as he pulled onto the road, but he couldn't ignore the roar of stress that'd taken up residence in his head.

In his peripheral vision, she sat with her spine stiff and shoulders up near her ears. Even so, she was just as beautiful as she'd been in high school with her golden hair and sloped nose dotted with freckles. Now she was tougher. Death had touched her, hurt her, and left her to deal with its disagreeable aftermath.

With arms crossed, gazing out the windshield, she said, "There's got to be a way to make the glass work other than killing someone."

"The last person to use this particular scrying glass killed three people to power it and then got possessed by a nasty demon. It wasn't pretty." He glanced over, but Shannon didn't look dissuaded.

"Are you going to take me home or somewhere deserted and kill me?" No hint of fear tinged her tone. The woman could handle herself.

He liked that.

This was bad. Dear God, this was bad.

His sex life had been on hold for months. A year ago, he'd been a one-night-stand *aficionado*, but the empty encounters bored him. The last thing he needed was for his sex drive to wake up, especially for a woman as off-limits as Shannon.

"If I wanted you dead, I would've let Harnish keep you. For the second or third time, I'm not going to hurt you. I'm driving you home, back to your people who might be able to keep you safe."

"What exactly do you do in this job of yours, Merck?" She rolled Merck on her tongue as if familiarizing herself with use of his last name. He liked her saying it.

He shrugged.

"Who do you work for?" she pressed.

"I work alone."

"You work alone with an assistant."

"There's always paperwork and minutia."

"Do you only go after witches?"

"No." He wished she'd desist and wished he could stop answering. What was it about her that turned him into a chatterbox about secrets he hadn't revealed to anyone except Danny?

"Do you chase down all people who use magic or only the bad apples?"

"I hunt the ones who've gone astray, such as those who use this type of scrying glass." He gazed at her, half hoping he'd intimidate her into stopping the questions and half hoping she'd confess whether or not she'd killed to power magic in the past. He needed her in the clear, good-magic category where she belonged. He got visions when someone had performed a death ritual, indicating where and who'd died. He'd never gotten that kind of revelation about her, but Shannon jumbled his mind to the point he might not get normal visions.

"You think I'm a bad apple?" she asked.

"Are you?"

"As if I'd confess." She rolled her eyes. "Why do you think I'm a witch?"

"I've always known about you, just like you suspected I had…abilities."

"Aaha! You finally admit it."

"I'm not admitting anything in particular."

"How would you know about me? It's not like I wear a pointy hat and do naked rituals on Samhain or anything. This is a serious issue if everyone can tell. We're not supposed to… No one is supposed to know about us."

"I'd like to see you dance around a caldron naked."

"I'll bet you would." She whacked his shoulder. "Stop being a jerk."

He grinned and focused on the lines of the highway, not speeding like he normally would down this stretch. He was enjoying himself and regretted how soon this would be over.

"You're not a traditional witch in the sense of covens and rituals in the woods. You ladies were labeled witches centuries ago by those who didn't understand the powers that come from being a Pleiades goddess descendant." He paused to glance at her shocked face. Eons of past life memory as the Enforcer meant he might know more about her descendants than she.

"Who told you that?"

"I know a lot about magic, darlin'. I know who likes black magic and who does only good magic." That was a truth stretch. He only knew when someone killed, thanks to the visions. When close to a person who used magic, he could usually detect what kind they'd practiced most recently. From her, though, he couldn't tell anything, probably because his balls were in a wad.

"I think you like the hint of badness that comes from being a called a witch." He waited, hoping she'd fill him in on how much badness was black magic and how much was sexy wickedness. The latter he could handle and would be a willing participant. Her using evil magic, maybe not a death ritual yet, but still, the darker side of magic, he didn't want to hear.

"So, you're the Santa Claus of the magic world with a naughty-and-nice list?"

"This Santa kills those on the naughty list and doesn't bring gifts to those who behave. Which list do you think you're on?"

She glared, but didn't answer. "You kill people like necromancers? They always use death energy for power."

He wanted to hit his head on the steering wheel. Would she just answer the question? "Sometimes. They don't always need a death ritual, though."

"I guess it makes sense there'd be someone out there designated to keep this in check. I haven't run across very many truly evil magical people. Sounds like a dangerous job. How do you find them?"

He shrugged.

"Why am I not on your kill list if you think I'm a bad witch?"

His heart hammered his ribs to the point of pain. Best to just throw it out there. "Do you and the other six Pleiades witches do evil things that put people at risk or kill people?"

She frowned and shook her head. "We try not to get noticed. Hurting people would definitely get us noticed. However, one of us is an ex-MI6 agent who still goes after the lowest of the low in society. Guess that counts."

She hadn't said she wouldn't do it at some point in the future, but at least she hadn't misused magic yet. His shoulder muscles loosened. "I'm sure you could be a *wicked* witch..."

Her cheeks flushed and she muttered, "Wouldn't you like to know."

Yeah, he would.

"Why do you hunt these people? It sounds like a thankless job, not to mention life-threatening."

Time to get off this topic.

She gazed at him in silence for a few moments. "You don't do this by choice, do you? Like me, you're stuck with some sort of legacy crap."

"Some things we can control and some we cannot."

"I understand an unwanted legacy."

He wouldn't discuss his life of facing off with all manner of evil as the Enforcer, a hell destined to end in a few days when his gods-decreed judgment day arrived. A part of him saw it as a positive to end the endless chase and annihilations. The other half of him wasn't ready to die. He glanced over at Shannon.

She stared out the windshield, her delicate shoulders stiff.

He appreciated her sexy, skimpy dark top and tight jeans. Her eyeliner had run a bit, but it didn't detract. It added a smoky sexiness to the overall package. He had no idea what she'd been up to since high school and hadn't asked those in the area who might know because then he might've tracked her down.

No jumping on the Shannon train. Not then. Not now.

His body didn't give a shit about logic. It wanted on the Shannon train in the first class cabin where there'd be a bed and an overnight trip.

The timing sucked. He resented his life being cut short. Yet another reason to keep his hands to himself around her.

He brushed a stray mosquito off her arm as he braked at a light.

She inhaled sharply.

"Mosquito. Didn't want it to bite." He didn't trust himself to meet her gaze. Why the hell was he explaining himself?

"Thanks." Her voice dropped low, super sexy. "What are you?"

I'm in dangerous waters is what I am.

His gaze darted her way despite his brain yelling, "don't do it." He glanced down her long, lean limbs. *Those* were some serious, deadly curves. He'd always been an ass-and-tits man. Holy hell, this woman delivered on that fantasy. He wanted to kiss her so hard she'd melt, like she'd done on the night in the woods long ago.

She meant his abilities and job, of course. His clouded brain detected the subtle transfer of energy. Magic. "Did you try to use some sort of coercive crap on me?"

"If I did, it didn't work." Her seductive smile disappeared.

Good. At least he wouldn't worry she could sway his mind by use of magic.

"Why're you down here in South Carolina, Shannon?"

Her gaze met his, but she didn't answer. There were depths and shadows in her eyes that made him wonder what she left unsaid.

Her here now, mere days before his Greek gods' judgment day, was suspicious. The gods could meddle all they wanted in his life, but he refused to play their games. Maybe her presence was a test. Throw the most tempting yet off-limits woman he'd ever met back into his life and see how he handled it. Admittedly, it was good play on their part if they wanted him to screw up again. His only clue to avoid a death sentence was he needed to be found "pure of heart," whatever that meant.

She moistened her lips. The movement might not have been intentional, but his gaze locked onto the moisture now there. Not feeling so *pure of heart* right now.

Yep. The longer he was close to this woman, the more convinced he became they'd end up in far more than a lip-lock. And he didn't care about the gods' opinion of it.

His cell phone vibrated inside his pants pocket. He shifted in his seat to retrieve it and answered, "Yes?"

"Hey, it's Danny. I think I found your master warlock."

"Where?"

"An abandoned property north of town on the edge of a cemetery. I'll text you the address."

"I'm still on the way home with Shannon."

"There's a problem, which makes this a can't-wait situation. Sleeping Beauty can stay in the car."

"What kind of problem?"

"I think he took Chad's little girl."

Merck's visual field blurred. "What? His daughter is missing? You're just telling me this now?"

"I found out a few minutes ago when Chad stormed in here. His daughter went missing from school earlier today. No one even knows how it's possible, but they didn't notice she was gone until lunch. Chad went to the school and the bespelled Hexenspiegel you gave him went nuts vibrating when it picked up bad-juju magic. Based on the information you gave me to find the master of the bastard who tried to take Shannon, I looked for somewhere abandoned and found it."

"Keep Chad there. I'll find his daughter and bring her back to the office. Text me the address." He clicked off the phone. A text appeared seconds later. The address was in a familiar area just north of here.

"Damn it. We're going on a detour." He couldn't take Shannon with him, but if Danny was right then there wasn't time to run her home.

"Everything okay? Chad's daughter is missing?" Her eyes filled with worry. He'd forgotten this about her. Shannon could go from spitting fire to hugging in a split second, always concerned for the welfare of those around her. Big heart, big emotions. It was why people gravitated toward her. How could he have believed her an evil magic dabbler?

"I'm going to make it as okay as it can get."

"Can I help?"

He didn't reply since his answer was *no*.

Minutes later he pulled into a rundown convenience store whose only indication of its open status was a flashing neon lottery sign. A nineties black Ford Taurus with a dented bumper was parked on one side. The old gas pumps were almost rusted out and obviously nonfunctional. "I need you to wait here until I'm done."

"What? Here?" She rotated to look out the window. "I want to go with you. I can help."

He got out of the car and rounded to her side, opening her door. "Go on inside. Matt's a bit grumpy, but he's a good guy with a big gun. Just tell him I dropped you off for a few minutes. He can keep you safe until I get back. Where I'm going will be way beyond anything you've ever dealt with. Trust me on that."

"Here's safer? This is the bumfuck middle of nowhere."

He scanned up the road. "I'm sorry I can't get you home right now. Maybe you should call one of your people to pick you up."

"This sounds risky for you too. I can call for help." Her forehead creased.

"This is what I do, darlin'."

"What is it you're going to do exactly? At least tell me what you're about to deal with since you're dumping me here."

"A warlock."

"What're they like?"

I don't want you to know. "The best plan is for you to get a ride home and text me when you get there. I don't know how long I'll be." *Or if I'll be coming back.* As he shifted to give her space to get out of the car, she caught his hand in hers, holding it there.

"Jason...Merck, be careful," she whispered, her gaze darting up the paved two-lane in the direction of the dirt road and abandoned house. "This feels really dangerous."

Her soft touch trapped him, like a caught wild animal. He shouldn't imagine kissing her, not right now. Shouldn't even go there. Something about her concern melted every ounce of his resistance to her. He wanted. Christ, he wanted. He hadn't felt this kind of all-consuming desire since the last time he ignored his rules to kiss her.

Her eyes widened and she withdrew her touch. "I'm sure you'll be careful."

"Always am." Tempted beyond endurance, he captured the back of her head and put his lips to hers. He coaxed her mouth open with his tongue. She deepened the kiss with a groan of surrender and gripped his arms.

She wanted him. The knowledge was more intoxicating than any high-inducing drug or enticement spell. This was what he'd remembered about her, but had convinced himself was no more than the product of fantasy. Kissing her wasn't just a kiss. It was a full-body, mind-altering experience. It blocked out the rest of the world and all of reality.

His brain nudged him about the warlock. Yet, this...*this* was so much better than whatever sickfest he'd find inside the house. He wanted her, this, and everything that came next. Hell, he'd wanted it, dreamed of it, and run away from it for over a decade.

He pulled away and forced his brain back on the job at hand. The drive to finish what he'd started with Shannon warred with responsibility.

This was about a little girl. She wasn't just any little girl, but Chad's princess. He had to hurry.

Hoarsely, he rasped out, "I gotta go."

Her already flushed face turned a deeper shade of pink. "I didn't mean to distract you. I'm so sorry. You need to get to Chad's daughter. Go."

His smile was hard to smother, but she'd probably slap him if he showed an ounce of humor. "I don't think you're entirely to blame."

He grabbed his tactical vest out of the backseat and zipped it into place, removing an amulet from the front pocket. "Take this. It's a crystal talisman from Colombia that's enchanted to provide protection. Wear it around your neck. There's foul magic at work up the road. If for any reason it strays here before your ride arrives, this should help."

She accepted the talisman and followed him to the driver's side. "If you're in trouble, call me. I can help."

He wanted to say *okay,* but he wouldn't allow her anywhere near the vile creature he expected to face. If he didn't agree to her, though, he had a bad feeling she'd follow him. "Give me your cell phone number."

She rattled it off while he plugged it into his phone.

The air temperature dropped a few degrees. He hoped he wasn't too late. Temperature drops happened when a death ritual was close to completion.

No time for more delay. "Put it around your neck. Stay put or get a ride home."

He hopped in and left. Her reflection in the rearview mirror watched him as he drove away.

He shouldn't have left her alone with a measly talisman as her only protection.

***

The SUV disappeared down a dirt road less than a quarter mile away. Him alone bothered her. No one should go up against evil by himself.

Shannon's gut urged her to follow Merck. Everyone could use back-up, but the evil emanating from up the road scared her. She didn't have the skills to face off with a warlock. She didn't even know the capabilities of a warlock who used black magic.

The warlock was probably here for the Trident. If Merck failed or got himself killed and she followed without her bodyguard, then she'd be in the same situation she'd almost been in last night. Dead.

Her safest bet was to call for a ride. She pulled out her cell. No signal. Crap. How was Merck supposed to call if she had no signal? Maybe there was a payphone inside and she could call for a ride.

A blue sedan circa 1980-something roared down the road. It screeched to a halt just as it passed her, backed up, and pulled into the old gas station. The car was as large as a mid-size boat. It could probably run over a high curb with the driver feeling little more than a slight rocking motion. A Smart car would fit on the hood of the giant vehicle.

The driver hand-cranked to roll down his window. He said something, but she couldn't hear over the roar of the car's screechy motor belt.

She shook her head and pointed at her ears. She walked closer. "Can't hear you."

He cut off the car. "Where the hell's Merck? I know he didn't take you home last night after we were at the bar. So he must've dumped you here to wait while he..." He stopped as if realizing she might not know what Merck did.

This had to be the grownup version of the lovable-but-obnoxious, rotund blond who as a kid she used to trade homemade pie for his Little Debbie cakes in elementary school. "Heavens to Betsy. Chad, is that you?"

"Yeah, that's me."

"It's been ages since I've seen you. High school. God, you look just like I remember. I heard the guy Merck went after might have your daughter. I'm so sorry. I mean, Merck will get her out. He has to." She rubbed her arms against an unseasonably cold breeze. It felt like fifty-something out here when a typical July midafternoon should be uncomfortably hot and humid.

"Where'd Merck go?"

"I think you should let him do his thing. Sounds like whatever he's going up against isn't something we can help him fight."

"Not when they've got my daughter. Now which road did he take?" He scowled. "If you won't tell me, I'll drive down every road until I find him. He can't be far. This was the general location I saw on Danny's map before he shut down his computer."

"Let me hop in, and we'll go together." *Distract him. Give Merck time to rescue his daughter.*

"He wouldn't want you there."

Or you. The passenger side door creaked as she opened it and slid into the vinyl bucket seat. "This door weighs a ton. Why does it smell like fish in here?"

Chad pulled the car back on the road. "My brother sells shrimp out of here on weekends. He spilled one of the coolers in the backseat on Saturday. His idea of cleaning is to get all the shrimp off the floor."

"I think Merck turned here." She waved at the dirt road on the left, even though it wasn't the road he'd taken.

Chad gunned the car down the pothole-rich road. It rocked through the small holes but caught a large hole and sailed upward for a few seconds before its front fender landed on the road in a metal-crunching crash. She whiplashed forward and gripped the oh-shit handle as he sailed through another large hole, throwing her back in the seat. He ground to a stop at the end of the drive, which dead ended at a mobile home.

"He's not here," Chad announced.

"Maybe I was wrong."

He glared as he hit *Reverse* and subjected her to the return journey through pothole hell. Another ten minutes and three dirt roads later, Chad released a litany of curses.

He turned onto the right road, not that she confirmed. Coldness seeped into her body as if in warning to turn around. Adjusting the air conditioning vents to point away from her didn't help.

The road ended at a dilapidated house. An unnatural fog obscured the edges of the house and treed areas surrounding.

The car stalled out not far from Merck's SUV. Chad turned the engine over and over, but it wouldn't catch. He hit the steering wheel. "Damn it. I just had the battery replaced."

Evil energy, which reminded her of the one who gave her the non-healing wound on her stomach, shrouded the area. Chills slithered across her shoulders. Perhaps they'd driven into a death trap. The car dying might not be a simple mechanical problem.

She whispered, "We shouldn't be here."

"I'm getting my daughter." Chad jumped out of the car, brandishing a gun like he was James Bond on meth. She pushed open the bulky door with two hands, ran forward, and caught his arm when he took a few steps in the direction of the house.

"We don't know for sure whatever's in there has her. What's that?" She pointed to a shadow in the mist. Her heart jumped into her throat. A human shape stumbled. Its gait was stilted and unsteady. It didn't have an aura. Not living. "Shoot it."

"What? You sure?"

"Yes. Shoot it."

Chad targeted the staggering form. He pulled the trigger. Nothing happened. "What the hell?"

"Safety's on," Shannon said.

He rolled his eyes, clicked it off, and fired two rounds, not hitting anywhere close. "Damn it."

The staggering human-like creature wasn't deterred.

"Give it to me." She wrenched the gun out of his fist instead of waiting for him to hand it over. Deftly, she shot two rounds, hitting it center chest. *Yeah.* Weekend target practice, a mandatory activity in the Randolph household throughout her younger years, had paid off. The creature shuddered but kept moving. Grabbing Chad's arm, she pulled him around to the back of his car and to a kneel, not that the car provided much cover.

"What is that thing?" Chad peered around the car at it.

"I don't know. A ghoul or zombie? I'm pretty sure it's not alive. There're more coming from around the house." Her legs felt weak, her body shook. She grabbed the bumper to steady herself.

Run! Her instinct was to bolt. She couldn't die right now, not from a zombie attack.

"We gotta get out of here." Chad peeked around the car again. "Oh shit, the one you shot is closing in. Get in the car. I'll get it started somehow and get us out of here."

"They're coming from behind us too. They'll trap us inside there."

She fished her cell phone out of her jeans, praying for signal. It had one bar. Great. She dialed Jen.

"Jen, I need a protection spell."

"Oh, thank God, it's you. Where have you been? Everyone's freaking out."

Shannon tried to interrupt, but Jen continued, "I've been a mess. If you're in trouble, I'll be there. Well, I'll try to be there. I'm the worst at the dimension-hopping business. I can't promise I'd be there fast, but I'd be on my way. Eli…I can send him. He's at your house."

"Calm down. I was out last night and slept at a friend's place. I'm fine. I'm calling because I need a protective spell to ward off zombies. I'm needing it pretty fast."

"Zombies? That doesn't sound like you're doing fine. I'm on my way."

"No, please don't. It's not safe. Maybe I'm not exactly fine right now, but I'm fine from last night. You're the spells guru. I need your best protective spell. I'll tell you more in a few minutes once there aren't zombies."

"Can't you use your other powers, like wind to blow them away? I'm worried about you trying a spell. You're not good at them."

"I need to try. I don't trust my abilities. These undead things are the product of black magic or voodoo or something like that." She shot one of the zombie-type creatures that got too close. It fell backward and didn't move. Maybe they could be stopped if she aimed for the head. The zombie she'd just shot twitched. Oh, no. It was getting back up.

She put her hand over the phone and asked Chad, "Got more ammo?"

He shook his head.

"None?"

"Didn't think I'd actually need to shoot anyone. The threat of shooting someone is usually enough to stop them. Merck might have more in his car." His terrified gaze never left the corpse on the ground whose fingers were still moving.

"What caliber is this gun?"

"8mm."

"Merck had an ammo container in the backseat. Let's go. Here, you take the gun and hold them off with the few rounds that're left." As she jogged for Merck's SUV, she asked, "You still there, Jen?"

Shannon balanced the phone between her shoulder and ear while yanking open the back door of the SUV. Score! Ammo can...but no ammo inside. There was a gun, though. She checked and it was loaded.

"Anything?" Chad asked.

She flinched, not realizing he'd moved directly behind her. "Just a gun."

Chad pushed her aside to grab a discarded tactical vest. He patted pockets and took out a second gun.

Jen yelled in her ear, "Pop away from there. Go to another dimension. Gunfire, zombies...this is *not* you being fine. Get out of there."

"I can't leave right now. Will the spell work for two? There's a guy here with me."

"It should. Do you have some salt?"

"No. I'm outside a car with a gun and a cell phone. That's why I'm calling you."

Chad fired five rounds into a new approaching undead thing. Good for him, hitting the thing this time. Her ears echoed as if everything was now down a long hallway.

"Did you say something? I couldn't hear you," Shannon said into the phone. She turned up the phone's volume.

"I said draw a circle around yourself."

"Hold on." She pulled Chad a few feet away from the SUV's bumper. "Don't move." She grabbed a rock and etched a rough circle around her and Chad in the sandy soil. "Okay. Circle drawn."

"I'll give you a spell, but when you say it, you have to believe it'll work. You have to feel it deep in your soul. Say this three times:

Great goddesses of day and night.
Protect us with all your might.
Let all who venture near feel your might's burn
Until none are left to make us squirm."

"Squirm? Did I hear you right?" Shannon asked. "Is this a real spell?"

"I'm not good at creative spells under pressure. You can do this. You have to do this."

"Give me clear direction to make it work, please."

"When you cast it, you must find something to focus on which you believe in with all your soul. Something powerful. Think about it while you say the words. I can say it with you, if you want. On the count of three."

"Yeah, that'd help." She didn't hear Jen counting from the other end. "Jen? You there?"

Nothing.

Then the phone flashed: *Call lost.*

Crap.

She shoved the phone into her pocket. Something she believed in? The Greek Gods, perhaps, but she didn't like any of them since they seemed to like mucking around in the lives of their descendants. Her mind skirted through images. Her mother. Jen and the other Pleiades witch ladies. The image that popped into her brain and stuck was him. Merck. Inexplicably, she believed in him. He'd do what needed to be done inside the house to win. Focusing on him, she intoned the spell three times.

A walking corpse closed in. Chad emptied what was left in the gun into it, knocking it down with a head shot. A second corpse reached for them. Chad released an earsplitting scream. He tensed as if to move.

Shannon grabbed his arms. "Stay still. Don't step outside the circle."

"It's going to touch me." His body bowed away from the dead hand reaching toward them.

"Stay. Still." She wrapped her arms around him to keep him in place.

He grabbed her tight and screamed again, causing her ears to ring.

The necrotic hand hit the circle boundary and ignited into flames that consumed its entire body.

Holy cow, the spell worked.

"So long as we stay inside the circle we should be okay." She wasn't sure he heard her through his terror.

Fifteen burnt corpses later, the remaining zombie-esque creatures fell to the ground like someone had unplugged them from their energy source. None moved. That could be good or it might mean something worse would come next.

"I think you can let go of me now. It looks like the zombie-things stopped." She shook Chad, who'd gone from screaming to frozen.

Chad blinked rapidly a few times. "It was like *The Walking Dead,* only we were in it. What were those things?"

"I'm not sure, but there don't look to be any more coming at us. We should leave. Perhaps, we go back to the gas station and wait for Merck there." She wanted to get as far away as possible from a being that could conjure zombies.

Her phone buzzed against her hip. She wiggled to dig it out. "Hello?"

"Oh, God. I was so scared. I lost you and I thought the worst. Thank goodness. You're okay?"

Shannon tried to cut in, but Jen's babbling didn't stop. "I didn't know what to do. I can't dimension hop well and—"

"The call got dropped. Sorry. I'm fine. Your spell worked. So, thanks."

"Why are zombies trying to get you?"

"Long story..." She stopped talking when Merck emerged from the house carrying a small girl who couldn't be older than five or six. An almost painful relief seized her insides.

"Merck's coming." Crap, she hadn't meant to reveal his name to Jen.

"Who's Merck?" There was a pause.

"I think he might've eliminated whatever controlled the zombies, at least I hope he did. I gotta go. We'll talk later." She shoved her phone back in her jeans.

Chad ran to Merck and grabbed the little girl out of her arms. "Is she...?"

"She's sleeping."

"Time to wake up." Chad jostled her.

The girl's eyes popped open. "Daddy? Uncle Merck?"

"How're you doing?" Merck asked.

"I had a weird dream. There was this bad sorcerer who took me..."

Merck touched her cheek. "You know I'd never let a bad sorcerer take you or hurt you, Princess."

"I knew you'd rescue me. You're my knight." She smiled a toothy grin.

"In a previous lifetime I might've been a knight. Not now."

The girl put her hand on Merck's cheek. "I love you."

"I love you too, Princess." A gentle smile transformed Merck's face, one that hit Shannon mid-gut with a serious case of the *awws*.

Over the top of her head, Chad said, "Thanks, man. I owe you one."

"Couldn't let the warlock...er, sorcerer get our princess."

Chad smiled in gratitude, but his grin fell as he glanced around at the dead bodies. He pulled his daughter against him to keep her from seeing.

"What are you two doing here?" Merck's expression shifted to fury and targeted her. "I told you to stay put."

"No, you said to get a ride home from someone else after dumping me. Guess what? There wasn't any cell phone reception at the gas station. Then Chad showed up with a firecracker up his ass to find you. I delayed him as long as I could."

Chad scowled at her.

"Sorry, Chad," she said. "Then we had to deal with zombies."

"Zombies, huh?" Merck met her gaze.

"I handled it." She stared at the no longer animated bodies.

"That you did." Merck nodded, glancing at the chaos around them again.

Shannon chewed on her lower lip.

Merck asked, "Can you can get home okay, Chad?"

"I don't know. The car stalled."

"Mine too, but it was part of the deter spell on this place. Should be fine now, but we'll wait until you get her started."

"You and me are going to talk about all this later, Merck. I want to know how they got her and what we can do in the future to prevent that."

"All right." Merck pulled a knife out of his pants and placed it into one of his tactical vest's pockets.

"I never saw anything like these things before. We're going to have to review how to deal with them." Chad pointed to the corpses and shook his head.

"Here." Chad handed Merck the empty gun. "Borrowed it, man."

Chad glanced at the circle in the sandy driveway. "She did some sort of spell. I don't know if it qualifies as the type of magic you wanted to know about, but it kept those things away. Saved our asses." He cast her a narrowed-eyed glare. "I'm pretty sure she still thinks you're hot. Just thought you'd want to know." As he marched past her, he whispered, "Now we're even on delaying me. I never forgot you used to pump me for information on Merck in high school. Figured you still got a thing for him."

Merck's eyebrows shot up.

Shannon's face scorched. She ducked her head and scooted around Merck's SUV.

He removed his tactical vest and threw it into the backseat. "You think I'm hot?"

"I might've had a crush on you in high school, but I'm long over that. He was spewing crap to get back at me for not telling him exactly which road you'd taken." She clicked the seatbelt.

"Uh-huh."

Shannon cleared her throat, jittery with need to clarify she *wasn't* into him. *Even though you are.* "Chad totally freaked out. You shouldn't have invited him here."

"I didn't. He must've gotten our location out of Danny."

"I'm surprised Chad works for you. He needs target practice. He didn't handle the zombies very well. He squealed until I hugged him. "

"He squealed?" A snort of laughter shot from him. He wiped the corners of his eyes.

"I find it hard to believe this is the first time he's seen something magically weird, if he works for you."

"I've kept him out of the heavy situations. He's solid. He'll get over it and do great next time. You didn't freak out, did you?"

She emitted a harsh *as-if* grunt. "I've seen bizarre things my entire life. Freaking out never helps. There's plenty of time to freak afterward. I'll admit I had to phone a friend to get the right protective spell. But I took care of it."

"You did." His gaze didn't deviate from the road, but his tone was filled with respect. Pride bloomed inside her at earning his approval.

"Are you okay?" She pointed at a scratch on his right shoulder, which peeked through a tear in his T-shirt. More scratches littered his lower arm. The way he held it stiffly against his thigh suggested it hurt. The scratches, although deep, had already stopped bleeding. Maybe had some sort of speedy healing ability.

"Side effect of the job. Nothing new. I'll be fine."

"You don't look okay, but...all right. What happened inside?"

"Standard warlock shit."

"I don't know what that means."

His lips curved into a smile that was part evil joy at whatever he'd done to destroy the warlock and part humor. "I took care of it."

His expression grew serious. "He's not the only one down here after you."

Chapter Four

She thought he was hot.

Hot damn.

Not that he would be taking whatever pinged between them to the next level. The kiss had been a mistake.

Her hugging Chad...nope, not jealous of Chad. The guy adored his wife, who'd cut Chad's nuts off if he cheated.

Merck's priority needed to be to figure out why magic-wielding deviants like the warlock he'd just deep-sixed wanted her. If he tried to ask her, she'd want to discuss what happened with the warlock. He didn't want her knowing about that or the death stench inside the house. He wanted her to remain innocent of the filth he dealt with as a part of being the Enforcer.

There'd been no question the warlock had caused more than a handful of deaths over the past few days. This was an unfortunate and common sight when dealing with those who practiced black magic, but he wished he could forget visions of the bloody aftermath of the death rituals. The demented being hadn't been interested in explanations, and Merck hadn't the time to wrangle from him what his presence here had to do with Shannon, not with a child's life on the line. He worried the warlock kidnapping Chad's daughter from school wasn't a random coincidence. The warlock might've known he had Shannon and knew Chad's connection to Merck.

Several miles down the road, he asked, "What's rolling around in your head?"

"Nothing." She clenched her hands together, but he hadn't missed their trembling.

"It's over. The warlock is dead and gone."

Her gaze darted to his. "Maybe I'm not as *okay* as I thought I was. It'd be nice to forget rotting dead things trying to touch me. I've seen weird stuff, but that was disgusting."

Not as disgusting as what was inside the house. "I find the best way to deal with this kind of thing is to force my brain to move on. I dealt with it and now it's over."

"Aren't I supposed to think happy thoughts like teddy bears and rainbows?"

"That's bullshit. If rejecting it doesn't work, try pot."

She giggled. "Seriously? Getting high is the ultimate temporary out."

"Worked for me in high school." *Before I got used to it.*

"You have some here?"

"Nah. I haven't smoked in years. I know a guy, though, if you want me to give him a call..."

She shook her head. "You're a badass. Hunting warlocks, saving kids, getting tattoos..." She grinned at him. "You were a badass in high school. I'd never seen anyone our age smoke anything, but you were always lighting up."

A smile nudged his lips, but didn't quite happen. "I'd just started this type of stuff—the chasing black-magic people—in high school. Drugs and smoking helped me handle things." Back then when they'd ridden the bus together, she'd been a gangly teen much too young for him and too easy to shock. They'd waited for the bus on the porch of an abandoned house at the end of what used to be a dirt road between their properties. He'd been riveted by her from the first moment he met

her because beyond any drug or alcoholic drink, only *she* made him forget the vileness he'd been forced to contend with.

"I didn't realize you were doing this kind of thing. I knew you
had some sort of after-school job, but never imagined... That must've
been awful. Back then I was worried about school and clothes, whereas
you were dealing with all this?" She touched his arm. "I'm sorry. It's
no wonder you were always cramming homework before school and
studying on the bus."

He shrugged. "It was what it was. My life didn't hinge on my ability
to graduate high school, although I did. Barely. I appreciated your
help."

"No kid should have to deal with this sort of thing. I wished you'd
told me. I would've... I don't know what I would've done, but maybe try
to make your life better."

Her smile killed him. Shannon had always been a do-gooder for
anyone in need. She would've tried to help him, if she'd known. And
gotten in big trouble. Her father had forbidden her to speak with him,
an edict she violated at the bus stop and on the bus. He wondered if she
told her father they rode the same bus. Probably not.

She asked, "What about your mom? Didn't she care what you were
up to and why you were smoking?"

He snorted out a sarcastic laugh. "That woman only cared that I
was scarce when she brought over a boyfriend or had one of her pot
parties. Me gone to do whatever...well, it worked for her. I always wondered why your parents let you ride the bus with me."

"I never thought about it. Not sure they knew. There was a good-
sized group of kids. Maybe they figured it was safe. I pitched a fit about
how uncool it was to have a bodyguard on my tail at all times in high
school. That's probably the only time in my life someone wasn't loom-
ing behind me, ready to take a bullet or kill a witch hunter."

"They were overprotective."

"There's always someone trying to kill us. It's understandable, but my parents compromised and placed a teacher at the school who was an undercover druid. He had cameras on me at all times. So, still under lockdown and highly annoying. My only free time was the bus. I'm sure someone put a spell on the stop to guarantee its safety."

He pulled down the quarter-mile dirt drive to her family house. "You're really visiting down here alone?"

"My bodyguard's around somewhere. Since my mom died, Dad's been insane about my safety."

"Your guard isn't very good at his job if he let you go off alone last night. Where was he?"

"I didn't invite him along."

"What's the point of having a bodyguard you can send away at whim?"

"You try being locked down your entire life like you're some sort of princess. We all have an expiration date. Some of us are shorter dated than others. I have things to figure out and having him around isn't always convenient." Her face went red. "Sorry. Forget it."

She worried about dying soon? Anger slid through his brain. This was probably why she was after a scrying glass. Were the gods playing with her life too?

"How do you ask a trained bodyguard, who's probably got some magical ability, to let you go out on your own?"

"Who said I asked?"

"Sometimes it feels pretty good to take fate in our own hands and flash the gods the middle finger, but last night you would've ended up dead if I hadn't happened along."

"I'm lucky you were there. I know."

He rolled down his window, drawing in a deep, calming breath of summer. He loved the smell of the ocean nearby mixed with humidity and heat, both of which heralded the coming of the hot August days. The winding road ended in a circular drive around the front of the plantation's Colonial-style house. The house could use a good power-wash and a roof sweep to get the pine needles and leaves off, but it still captivated him with its antiquated majesty. His house on the neighboring property, which had probably been the servants' quarters, might still be Colonial era, but it came off like the poor step-cousin.

"I've got to get going," he said after he opened the car door for her.

"You have to go? Won't you come in? I made ice tea yesterday." She gazed up at him, so hopeful. "I make good tea."

"I'll bet you do." He wanted tea and was tempted.

"Bloody hell, Shannon, where've you been?" a British-accented male demanded, his big boots crunching gravel toward the car. The Brit targeted Merck with an assessing glare. Stats were catalogued and probabilities weighed. No question this was her bodyguard. A north-to-south scar went from the guy's forehead to cheek, adding a deadly air to his *don't fuck with me* vibe.

Shannon's face lit up with a huge smile. "Eli. I'm so glad to see you."

Eli's unblinking gaze narrowed on Merck. "Who the hell are you?"

Merck stepped forward, hand extended. "Jason Merck. Neighbor." He tossed his chin toward his property. "She slept off last night on my sofa. I brought her home from the bar."

"Eli Morgan." He extended his hand.

They shook briefly. He caught the hint of magic from Eli and catalogued him as a druid. The joy of being the Enforcer was instant recognition of exactly what kind of being he faced.

Eli's brows snapped to a glower, which he targeted on Shannon. "On his sofa, huh?" There was a whole lot of *yeah right* oozing from the words.

"I'm fine. I can take care of myself. You're not my keeper." Her gaze darted to Merck. Guess she didn't want Eli knowing the full story.

"Damn it, Shannon. I swore on my life to your father that I wouldn't let you out of my sight. That was the only way he'd allow you to come down here without an army of protection. You have to let me do my job." Eli shook his head and blew out an uneven breath. "I told your father you're a thrill seeker who's too wild for any of us to follow you. Always have been. The nightclub shit in New York...drugging your guards up there to go out and do whatever..." He rubbed his hands over his eyes.

"A thrill seeker? Who're you to judge me Mister I-bolted-from-my-duty-to-join-MI6? You were gone for six years." Shannon put her hands on her hips. Energy swirled around her, and the wind picked up, ruffling the trees.

The hairs on the back of Merck's neck rose, charged by ambient static electricity. Her energy had stirred up the air, even though she didn't seem aware. The power surrounding her awed him with its beauty and ferocity. He'd seen plenty of magicals have this much strength invoked by a death ritual, but never from pure, innate ability.

"You drugged me." Eli advanced to tower over her, clearly unaware of the dangerous potential within her.

She poked him in the chest. "Back off."

"You went to a bar? And picked up the first random bloke for a night of crazy like you always do?"

Merck's brain tripped over the thought of her and random guys. He buried the rising jealousy. Her personal life wasn't his business.

Her eyes widened. "First, he's not random and I don't do one-nighters or crazy. I knew him in high school. Second, it's not your concern what I do on my own time, especially when it involves figuring shit out."

"What about us as in you and me?"

"What?" She stepped backward.

What? The exact one-word question detonated in Merck's brain. She didn't have a boyfriend. No, she'd said she wasn't married. They hadn't gotten into a boyfriend discussion. He'd assumed. And been wrong.

Although he had no right to feel territorial, he didn't like her being attached to Eli. Or, going on wild nights in New York City.

"Sweetheart, I only followed your attractive ass down here to patch up things," said Eli in an syrupy tone.

Shannon folded her arms. "Oh, my God. You're something else. There's you posturing about protecting me and me doing what I need to do. This is low even for you." She met Merck's gaze. "There's nothing between me and Eli. I've known him since he was seven and still peeing in the bed."

Eli glared, promising retribution for the peeing comment later.

She squared off against Eli again. "I know all your embarrassing little secrets. Don't push me."

Eli scowled. "You think I don't know your secrets?"

She leaned forward and hugged Eli's stiff body. "I love you and every one of you irritating bullies who try to dictate my life and security. Relax. I'm fine. We're all going to be fine." She pulled away and chewed on her lower lip. "Is the cavalry on its way down here?"

"Yes." Eli's lips thinned.

"I didn't want them here."

"Too late. Your dad went nuclear when he called to check in last night and you weren't around. Then he couldn't reach you on your cell phone. I told you not to turn it off."

"You could've covered for me," she said.

"I would've if you'd actually told me where you were going and what you were up to instead of poisoning me."

"I didn't poison you. If I had told you, you'd have been glued to my ass."

"You're goddamned right I would've been."

Merck pushed the passenger door shut with a loud slam. "Well, it's been great to catch up, Shannon. I've got to get going. Seems like you've got a good guy here to watch over you against...whatever. You should let him do his job."

Merck unclamped his locked jaw as he strolled around the SUV. Her hugging Eli and using the L word while doing so didn't sit well with him. This woman always pushed him to extremes. He had to get out of here before he did something he'd regret later or that she'd never forgive.

Where did this craziness over her come from? He didn't think *mine* when it came to women and then go caveman. Sure, he appreciated women and enjoyed them on occasion, but never with this level of possessiveness.

She met Merck on the driver's side of the SUV before he shut his door. She touched his hand and whispered, "Thanks for last night. Be careful."

Her eyes tempted him to test her lips again. How he wanted a brief touch to gauge the softness of those pink contours. He'd prove they had so much more between them than she'd ever experience with Eli.

As if she sensed the direction of his thoughts, her lips parted. It took every ounce of his self-control not to pounce. He could press her against the car and slide his hands beneath her shirt and up her ribs. She wouldn't protest. Her body was already leaning toward him, drawn by the inexplicable magnetism that drove him wild whenever in her presence.

"We're not going there. I mean it," he choked out. Oh, he wanted to. So, so much. But he'd already broken his don't-touch rule regarding her once today. She belonged with someone like Eli. Someone of her world who could keep her safe and away from the evil assholes who occupied his life. Someone who had longevity potential.

He was going to pass the "pure of heart" test with regard to Shannon, damn it. He'd fucked up so many times in his life that if this was his last chance at redemption to prove to the gods judging him he could be "good," then he was staying away from her.

He said, "Earlier? I was just reassuring you. You seemed worried I couldn't take care of myself."

Her eyes widened, and he almost regretted his words when he saw the hurt she quickly hid. "Going where? Do you mean us as in you and me? If so, totally agree."

He almost flung *liar* in her face, but he wasn't fifteen.

"Hey, you done yet, Shannon?" Eli yelled. "Because I've got to get you on the phone with your father."

"Yeah, we're good," she replied.

"Far from it," Merck muttered to himself as he scooted into the driver's seat. He still wanted her more than his next breath.

Chapter Five

Merck powered his boat a few miles offshore until the boat's tossing on the angry waves reached capsizing-risk critical. He cut the engine and swallowed against nausea, but not from motion sickness. His insides had been as choppy as the ocean ever since he'd driven away from Shannon a few hours ago. The wrongness of not helping her, of not finding out why exactly the warlock had tried to kidnap her, ate at him. Regardless of how ignoring his attraction to her drove him nuts, she was in trouble.

He was no one's knight in shining armor. She had her own people who didn't want him around, especially her father, who hated his guts. The moment her father found out where she'd been last night there'd be an angry druid on his front steps with a shotgun and no questions asked before blowing a hole in his chest.

Far off, the sky loomed with gray clouds. Details of the horizon were hazy where the rain had already started. Wind plastered the windbreaker against his body, carrying the smell of approaching rain. Two pelicans clung tight to a rocking buoy a few hundred yards away.

He leaned over the side of the boat to dip his hand into the choppy water. Instantly, information on the chaos below the churning surface swamped his mind. Animals were confused and panicking. Environmental conditions were unstable—fluctuating temperatures, salinity off, and algal blooms along the coastline. Energy from deep within him revved, demanding freedom to fix the chaos. On an exhale he released the surging power. Everything for miles around became stabilized. Even though still windy and choppy at the surface, the stability below relaxed him. He might've inherited some water abilities from his water-god father, but he couldn't control the weather.

The animals in the ocean's depths had been his companions through the toughest moments of his childhood—a selfish and sometimes abusive mother, an absent father, drug addiction, and his tendency for fights. The water healed his wounds, and the animals soothed his emotions. He'd do anything he could for them.

He'd have to return tomorrow, if he expected his stabilizing session to hold. Healing the whole ocean wasn't possible. Just little patches. Why were things out here and on land so out of whack?

The darkening skies gave the illusion of an early dusk.

As he returned to the wheel he heard clapping.

He whipped around, reaching for the knife on his belt.

A familiar ichthyocentaur reclined on one of the boat's white benches. The creature had shed his part-merman, part-horse form to appear human, dressed in a Hawaiian shirt and white silky pants. The shimmer in his purple eyes hinted at the masked inner god, but the outdated long dark hair and beard gave away his ancient-Greek origins.

Merck yelled to cast his voice through the wind. "Bythos. Why're you on my boat?"

Merck tensed for an attack. Most times he saw this creature, it was coming at him with a big-ass sword in the name of "training." A demand the mythological water creature take a flying leap back into the watery depths, back to Poseidon's side as his right-hand man, might end up with them in a knife fight again. Given he had a six-inch blade and Bythos usually swung a huge sword, odds weren't in his favor to win the matchup. Although Bythos looked unarmed today.

Bythos placed a dramatic hand over his heart. "Why the hate?"

"Maybe because the last two times you visited me, you tried to kill me?"

"Not true."

"Attacking with intent to cut off my head qualifies as intent to kill."

"I needed to ensure you knew how to defend yourself. You're still alive, aren't you? Had I wanted you dead, we wouldn't be conversing. I don't need to kill you. Your stubbornness will do the job for me."

"What did *Dad* feel was so important that he'd send you above water?"

"You need a reminder of your impending judgment."

Four days. "As if I could forget."

"You're doing all right at your on-land..." Bythos glanced around as if searching for the right word, "purpose. Now you must be judged if you are worthy of an ocean purpose."

"I didn't ask for this. Any of this." An ocean job too? Shit. Maybe death as the outcome of the gods' judgment was preferable. He could barely manage to take care of everything required of him as the Enforcer. In the hundreds of times he'd been reincarnated as the Enforcer this was the first lifetime he'd also been a first-generation Greek god's child.

"None of us request our fate. We learn to live up to it."

Merck folded his arms. "My life's about to be decided upon by a bunch of power-tripping gods on a whim."

Bythos showed no ounce of humor. "Do you not remember what I advised on how to improve your judgment?"

"*Strike the path to become pure of heart.* By the time you tossed that ambiguous pearl at me I'd already fucked up my life enough. I figured I'd be deemed death-bound regardless of what I do. I'm not a Medieval Templar knight, and I'm sure as hell not a religious fanatic who worships the Greek gods. I'm good with death."

Bythos's brow drooped and eyes narrowed. He gave a slow head shake. "Your little beloved ocean you oversee will go to hell without you. You'll be shuttled to live with Hades when you succumb to your human-bound death."

"Hades will U-turn me right back into my next reincarnated life." Then he got the pleasure of remembering everything about being the Enforcer in his teens. That's eons of bad memories of tracking and killing magical shits. He'd remember again the one and only time he had a family. They got tortured and executed by a coven of witches.

Merck said, "This time I might discuss a deal with my uncle to stay in the afterlife and give some other schmuck Enforcer duty. Poseidon can take care of the ocean. I just put a Band-Aid on it when she's hurt. If having an active Enforcer is important enough, then the gods can find someone else."

"You want to die?" Skepticism oozed from Bythos's words.

"Hades and hell don't sound so bad."

Between one blink and the next Bythos stood next to him. He fisted Merck's windbreaker and pulled him close. "Accept your destiny."

"I thought I was by destroying deviant magicals as the Enforcer." He stayed still in Bythos's hold and glared. "Maybe my destiny *is* to die and leave this world over and over as the cursed policeman of the magic world."

"You have a purpose and it's not to spend time with your uncle. I'm sure Hades would find you entertaining though. Your dual purpose in this world involves be the Enforcer and...Let's just say yours is a great destiny."

"What is this shit about a great destiny beyond being the Enforcer? Me, the by-blow of Poseidon? I'm a half-human bastard who can do some water tricks and talk to ocean creatures. And the gods negotiated to shuttle me into the lifeline of a man cursed to fight inhuman evil for all eternity. So far, this destiny sucks."

"Who said anything about being half-human?" Bythos's face scrunched up. He released Merck.

"Oh, right. I'm pure god?" He rolled his eyes. The boat rocked between several large waves. He grabbed the rail, catching himself before he smacked into it. To his disgust Bythos stayed upright without seeking stability, riding the rocking like a pro surfer. Merck cleared his throat and resumed. "I don't think so. *Jason Merck, son of Poseidon god of*... hell, I'm not a god. Jason is a ridiculous god name."

"Jason isn't your birth name. That's the name the human selected to raise you decided upon."

"Then what's my real name?"

"I'm not allowed to tell." Bythos crossed his arms.

"Because you're nothing more than the spineless dick peon of my father?"

"I'm not a dick peon. I liaise with all ocean creatures, primarily the sea nymphs. I am the son of Cronos, King of all Titans." His arms rested on his hips and head was thrown back with his chest on display.

Quickly, Merck snapped, "Oh, great one, what's my real name?"

Bythos's lips scrunched into a clear, "*Really?*"

"Please. I need to know my real name." God, he hated begging.

Bythos released a long sigh and gazed upward. "Thanos."

Merck's mind whirled. *Thanos?* "Shelly wasn't my real mother?"

"I can't discuss this with you."

"She says I was the product of a one-night stand with some guy she picked up in Savannah. She even remembers his name, but I assumed he was Poseidon in disguise. I'm the cursed bastard child of an affair Poseidon's real wife didn't approve of, which would be the reason for my impending life judgment and death sentence."

Bythos scowled. "Memories can be altered, as were those of the woman who raised you. Poseidon would never lie with *that* woman."

"He foisted me off on her? He gave up his son to a cold-blooded bitch. He made her think I was her real son. Who's my mother?"

"You got all the family history you're getting out of me today."

"Why does Poseidon care what happens to me at this point? A real father would show up when his son goes through...shit." Like when his mother—not his mother but the bitch who raised him—tried to sell him when he was ten to some pothead in exchange for drugs. He was tough enough at that time to scare the hell out of the pothead and stop the idiocy. What kind of mother sells her kid?

"It matters not to me if you live or die a human life, but it matters to them."

"What *them* are you referring to?"

"The ones judging you."

"So everything—my life—is all some sort of test?" How he hated being at the mercy of otherworldly beings. Who gave them the right to judge him? Resigned, he said, "Just tell me why you're here this time."

"To unlock your future and for you to be found pure of heart..."

How?

Bythos's lips curled into an amused grin. "How? Ah, the tough kid isn't quite so ready to die, now is he?"

"Stay out of my head. And, fuck you."

After a slow, lascivious scan, Bythos smiled. "You're not my type. Don't take offense. You're all right to gaze upon. Now that fine lady ashore you keep avoiding... She could be my type. Blonde, busty." He ran his hands in the hourglass figure of a shapely woman.

"You're not her type."

"I'm a god. Humans love me. I'm always their type."

"Stay away from her. Just tell me whatever it is you need to tell me. Let's get it over with."

Bythos rubbed his hands together as if preparing to start a delightful project. "Good to know you're not so apathetic about death. Get back to shore and make sure nothing kills the answer to your problem. I suggest you bind your life to hers."

"What?" Laughter bubbled from deep within Merck. Inappropriate at the moment, but everything about matrimony when he was about to die felt ludicrous. He doubled over as the hilarity erupted. It actually felt good to laugh this hard.

"What's so funny?" Bythos demanded.

Merck held up a hand, struggling to rein in his amusement. He swiped his weeping eyes. "You want *me* to marry Shannon?" He belly-laughed again. "In order to be found *pure of heart* you suggest I marry someone who you guys must deem to be so trying, so tedious, that I would be seen as a martyr?"

"I didn't say that."

"She'd be a handful, but...damn." A solitary snort shot out of him. He shook his head and waggled a finger at Bythos. "That's a good one. Cold, but a good one."

"Those nameless dead girls washing ashore weren't human. They were Pleiades."

What? Amusement fled. "As in the goddesses? No one can kill a goddess."

"They can if they stole *Deus Mortem* poison from Circe. All the deities have a purpose. With the Pleiades murdered their human descendants become critical. Someone wants to wipe all trace of them out of existence." Bythos disappeared.

Merck stood there, frozen, staring at the vacant spot Bythos had occupied moments ago. Someone murdered Pleiades goddesses? Six were dead. One remained alive. He tried to remember the exact purpose of the Pleiades goddesses but couldn't other than there was a constellation named for them.

Shannon was in bigger trouble than he thought.

A few drops of rain hit his face. The wind shifted direction, plastering the thin windbreaker against the other side of his body.

The wind blew harder with rain pelting from above. He cranked the engine. It turned over, but didn't catch. Damned battery was low. He bent over in the pouring rain whose droplets felt to be the size of oranges and hooked up the engine to the backup battery. Two cranks and it rumbled, but sputtered out.

"Oh, come on!" he shouted. He didn't want to call Chad for a tow. Twice in one month was humiliating. He cranked once more. The motor rumbled to life.

He would help Shannon with whatever brought her down here, but he wouldn't deceive himself by thinking doing so would solve his judgment-day problem. It was the right thing to do if her life was in danger. It'd be the first step in what promised to be a complicated, painful scenario the gods mapped out. He despised being manipulated but, apparently, she too had been sucked into their plan.

Chapter Six

"Until we arrive you are not to go anywhere. No popping to an alternate dimension. No visiting old friends. No bars or restaurants. Don't even go outside," Shannon's father ordered over the cell phone.

Ha! I'm already outside. She shifted on the bench in the private cemetery near the house where she'd placed a towel to cover the dampness left from last night's thunderstorm. The nearness of her mother's grave, and her brothers where they'd been laid to rest under the old oak, gave her strength to get through this conflict. She loved her father. He wasn't a bad person, just overprotective, more so when his ex-CIA faculties kicked in.

"Are you listening to me, Shannon?"

"*We* arrive? You and who else is on his way down here?"

"All of us who are available."

Great. A mini-army of super Sentry druids were boarding her father's plane in New York to fly here.

"Dad, I can't find an answer to all of this sitting in the house on lockdown. I need to go out and do research. I won't find the right people inside. You know this. Mom told me to come here to find answers."

"Shannon. Desist."

She complied instantly. His tone reduced her to a little girl. "I'm sorry. I don't mean to speak out of turn. I swear I'm not doing this to sass you. It's just... Why can't you understand if I don't get this figured out, we're all going to die?"

"I've been more than lenient with you, but that time is gone. I understand the importance of answers, but now we're going to do this my way. We've sent our best out there to research the problem. They're questioning experts in Greek history. I've got others consulting specialists on magical items. I've got an archaeologist at Yale who's also a druid who I want you to Skype with tonight. We'll find the answer to stop this. We always do. It's not the first time one of you Pleiades ladies has been under a mortal threat. You're not alone in this, and we have resources. You cannot disappear like you did last night without so much as a text. Do you care so little for me that you want me to suffer your death too? I've lost your brothers and your mother. I can't lose you too."

Swallowing the lump in her throat, she expelled a long sigh. "Tell me honestly you're coming down here to help me figure this out and this isn't about you being controlling. Hiding me in the house isn't going to keep a god at bay when he comes to get the Trident back. We don't have it."

"*Yet*. We don't have it yet. We'll find it. There're protections on the land and the house."

"They're not going to stop a god." Didn't her father understand this?

"Until we arrive, Eli is in charge. You'll stay put and listen to him."

"Dad... Dad?" She glared at the phone that read: *Call Ended*.

She shook the phone and cursed.

Indoors didn't work. Countless hours on the internet last week revealed nothing. Reading through her mother's library of handwritten research notebooks had proven useless. No druid had any knowledge of Poseidon's Trident. Help wouldn't be inside the house or on a superjet scheduled to arrive in a few hours. The archeologist might be helpful to translate ancient Greek artifacts, but a human wasn't going to find Poseidon's stolen Trident. She needed to consult with someone who knew about powerful magical items.

Like Merck.

Her mother's whispered words moments before she'd died two months ago echoed in her head for the millionth time: "*Go home. To South Carolina. Help will find you like he always does.*" Her thoughts had immediately flown to Merck, but none of them had known he'd moved back. Maybe her mother had known. She'd had an eerie knack for foretelling things. What other "he" was here who could help her or would find her?

How she missed her big-hearted, stubborn mom who'd died right before the Poseidon ultimatum rained down on her with gloom, doom, and assured death. *Find my Trident or I'll kill you and every Pleiades descendants.*

What do I do, Mom?

Wind rustled the trees, fragmenting the early-morning sun into small shadows, but no answers arrived.

She expected something. Maybe her mother's ghost would walk from her grave. A sign. Anything.

The ancient oak trees with Spanish moss swayed in the wind. The gentle breeze soothed her. Images whipped though her mind. Visions, sounds, and smells. And Merck. Was this her sign? Probably not. He always dominated her thoughts when she was in South Carolina.

She dwelled on the intricate tattoos now covering Merck's hands and up his arms, wondering what prompted him to get so much ink. Maybe it'd been some sort of rebellious phase, or maybe they had meaning. It made him mysterious in a risky way. Gracious, she was a sucker for ink. More than the tats, she liked his arms. Muscular arms that offered refuge from both threats and the terror of what may happen in the near future.

She'd never gotten over her crush on him. The man was the embodiment of every wild fantasy she'd ever had. He was the reason anything with other guys never lasted long, although she'd never admit it to him.

Perhaps, he was her destined guy, the guy chosen by the gods to be her soul mate. The one she was fated to have children with and spend however long she had before she died.

Nope. She'd been over this ground countless times before. If he had been, he wouldn't have been able to stay away from her for a decade. Based on chitchats with the other Pleiades women and their men, once they met their soul mate, they couldn't deny their connection, even if they wanted to. There was a magical draw between the two that made him as nuts about her as she was of him. As well, they were supposed to have amazing chemistry. Okay, check, she and Merck had the zing factor. That didn't make them destined to be together. If so, he shouldn't have been able to resist her last attempt to get him to kiss her outside his car.

The wicked-witch part of her teased he could be stubborn to the point of mulish. If he'd decided he wasn't pursuing the attraction between them, then he might be tough enough to ignore it.

Mosquitoes hovered around her bare legs near the edge of her khaki shorts. Some of the flying demons braved attack and some floated in wait. She batted a few away from pale skin that could stand a few days in the sun and contemplated going back inside.

The curtain at the corner window moved. Even out here, Eli watched. She should find it comforting but instead felt stifled. Mosquitoes were preferable to Eli's glowers, which were part betrayal she'd given him the slip the night before last and part eagle-eye supervision. She'd pursued a career as a contract cameraperson, taking short jobs on documentaries, a few reality TV shows, and on occasion traveling with a reporter for the sole purpose of freedom. Freedom from a druid lurking nearby as her assigned protector. On jobs to the more remote locations, like a few months ago when she went on *Extreme Survivor* as a request from Jen, a bodyguard couldn't go because he was too obvious. What kind of cameraperson needed a bodyguard? Her father hated those jobs. In her mind the risk outweighed the benefit to have a few days of not being watched.

Her mother's headstone read a rather generic: *Do more than listen. Understand. Do more than exist. Live.*

Unhelpful. It'd probably been chosen by a local engraver.

Unlike her, her mother had lived without regret—vibrant, even if strong-willed and always moving forward. Shannon wallowed in regrets, most of which revolved around her mom. The biggest was being the cause of her death. If Shannon hadn't signed on to be a cameraperson on the *Extreme Survivor* reality TV show, even though Jen had needed her in that godforsaken jungle, then her mom wouldn't have sacrificed her life to save Shannon when a producer went crazy.

I'm sorry.

She opened her eyes and wiped tears from them. A shadow stretched in front of her. Her head snapped around, irritated by the intruder.

"What're you crying about?" Merck moved to stand in front of her. He clenched two white camellias by their small stalk in his right hand.

"Nothing. Why're you here?" Her heart stuttered and tumbled over itself as her gaze drifted across his cheekbones to his lips.

"You visiting with ghosts? Do they talk to you?" He nodded his chin toward the headstones a few yards away beneath the large oak. The question didn't carry a hint of sarcasm, only curiosity. He seemed genuinely sad for her. He'd believe her if she said yes. How many men would even consider ghost-talkers believable other than him? The trees swayed hard with gusts of wind as if reacting to the emotion on Merck's face.

"They don't give me any answers. Can you talk to them?" she asked.

"Wouldn't know. I haven't run into a ghost yet. Here. These are for you." He thrust the flowers her way. His hands fidgeted, a quirk so at odds with the exterior toughness he presented to the world.

"Thanks." She inhaled their powerful fragrance, flattered that he'd come all the way over here to bring her two flowers. "They're beautiful."

"I've got them all over my property. You feeling okay after yesterday?"

"I'm fine. Are you spying on me?"

"I just thought I'd check on things on my way in to the office. See if anything odd is going on over here."

"Check on things?" She glanced around. "Did you pick up something not right around here?"

"Nah." Although the denial didn't carry conviction. He squinted toward the house and scanned the yard before returning to the headstone.

Then he nodded to her legs. "You're welting up."

"I'll live. There's no way they can suck enough out of me to kill me."

"The bites will itch like hell in about ten minutes. Come with me."

"Where?"

"I've got something in the car that'll help the itching."

She hadn't even heard his car pull up. She gazed up at him, heart pounding. Damn her traitorous body, feeling things for the man standing in front of her that she hadn't allowed herself to feel since she was a naïve high-school girl back when she'd wished to have this particular guy see her as more than a kid. He did, eventually. The memory of their first kiss replayed in her mind. She didn't know what she expected from him. For him to kiss her again? Touch her? She was surprised by how much she wanted it.

Snap out of it. You're going to die. That's where your mind needs to be right now. Get him to help you.

Merck had to be the "he" who her mother said would help her. If he wasn't, then he might know someone or something safe she could use to find the Trident, maybe something from his collection of weird items.

"I promise if you come to my car I won't cuff you unless..." his voice dropped to a sensuous tone, "...that's what you want." His lips curved in a wicked half-smile that did funny things to her insides. She swallowed, her throat devoid of moisture.

"No cuffs. It might be nice not to have the itching." She gripped the camellia stalks tight between her fingers and followed.

He opened the front seat passenger door and waved for her to hop in. She watched with fascination as he removed an unlabeled brown bottle from the glove compartment. He emptied a bit of beige ointment into his palm. An astringent smell burned her nose, drawing her back to days when they had horses down here. She missed the ornery Quarter Horse she'd ridden every day after school.

She tucked her legs away from him when he neared with a dab of the stinky concoction. "Horse liniment doesn't work on bites."

He laughed low and shook his head. "Secret concoction from a friend good at remedies, but it's not horse liniment."

"I think they're pulling your leg, then." She didn't get a chance to argue further before he cupped the back of her calf and rested her sandal on his thigh. Her foot looked tiny against him. He examined the bites and applied a small amount to each welt. Amazingly, the itchiness disappeared within seconds.

She tried to think of anything other than the intimacy of her foot on his hard thigh. So close to... *Don't look.* Of course, her gaze went there. The hard bulge between his thighs signaled he wasn't immune to what bounced between them.

His gaze swung upward. The intensity in his eyes was thrilling. With a frown, his capable fingers left her leg and touched her neck. "Mosquitoes got you there too?" He rubbed softly over a welt.

She couldn't answer, hypnotized by his touch on her skin. Her body remained frozen and her breathing shallow as he explored her neck and upper chest for more bites. His fingers dipped beneath her neckline, finding a welt. He slipped his hand into her shirt and applied the concoction.

"More?" he asked.

She swallowed hard. "I'm good."

"You sure?"

She nodded. "Where'd you really get this stuff?"

"It's a potion from a Wiccan woman who lives down near Savannah. She's a sweetheart and likes giving me stuff like this when I visit. She's also a great cook. Her biscuits and grits are incredible."

"Is she someone you like for more than her biscuits?"

He chuckled. "Don't go sounding jealous, darlin', or I might think you like me."

A bird cried out while flying overhead. Another answered. Egrets. They sounded irritated. He gazed in the direction of the ocean.

"No jealousy here." She hopped out of the car.

The birds cried out once more. Alarm traveled down her spine.

He caught her arm before she could move away. "Do you feel it?"

"Yes". She batted at a mosquito on her arm.

"Something's off. The birds... Put the flowers on the seat." He slammed the car door and grabbed her hand in a tight, painful grip.

At a jog, he pulled her toward the side of the house and down to the creek bed. It wasn't a short walk, but at the speed he was dragging her through the damp forest, they made it to the water in minutes. He squatted next to the twenty-foot wide creek and placed a hand in the water.

"Yeah, it's infested with monster mosquitoes down here. Worse after the rain." She batted a few away from her face. With a kick she flicked wet debris off her sandal-clad feet. The shoes weren't intended for marching around damp forest. She plucked out a leaf caught in her left shoe and flicked a tick off her leg.

"There's something out here far worse than bugs. I don't know why you're attractive to the shittiest of the scary shits, but they're here."

"The land is protected by an old spell. Only those of nonthreatening intent can get on the property."

"Unless the trespassers are far more powerful than whatever your people laid down." His arm wrapped around her waist and yanked her away from the creek, into the thick woods and behind a tree. Something smacked into the bark above their heads. He whispered, "Ericthonians."

What? Shannon sensed a strange power around them, something simultaneously slithery and forceful. How could someone with an evil purpose get through the protections on the property? "What are Ericthon—"

He put his hand over her mouth and whispered into her ear, "Shhh."

Clouds drew in overhead, darkening the forest until only flickers of light peeped through the leaves. The temperature dropped several degrees.

"No sounds or we both die." He removed his hand from her mouth and led her to the left. He halted behind another large tree and gestured with a finger against his lips to keep silent.

The threatening presence marched nearer. Not one, but many.

She whispered, "Who's out there?"

"Not one hundred percent sure yet, but if it's what I think, then we're both up shit creek." He gazed at the rapidly moving water. "Too exposed for us to try to get across."

"It's too deep after the recent rain."

"Maybe it is, maybe it's not. Depth can be varied."

She liked his closeness and the heat of his breath on her cheek. She glanced up, far too aware of him. Put her in heels and she'd reach his chin. His essence seeped deep into her lungs. He smelled of danger and...something mesmerizing. Her heart, already pounding, went into a bongo rhythm. Wrong time. Definitely the wrong place for attraction to kick in.

Do not stare at him.

The slashes of his eyebrows drew low. "We have to get out of here. We'll have to run for it. Better cover for us in the darker forest."

She blinked a few times to break her fixation. He hadn't unwound his arm from her waist. The gentleness of his touch was at odds with the threat in his stance. Something hot and dangerous glimmered in his blue gaze, which cried out to her.

"Pray to whatever you believe in that they don't send the snakes."

"Snakes? I hate snakes." She shivered.

He grabbed her hand and dragged her into a sprint. Bark exploded around them. Must be suppressed gunfire since she hadn't heard the expected crack of a gunshot. A glance up saw six small knives lodged deep into the tree bark. Not bullets.

Merck shifted positions, pushing her in front of him. A few paces later he stepped on her heel, catching the back of her sandal. She stumbled. He slammed into her back. Her side whacked against the rough bark of a tree.

"Sorry," he grumbled, catching her before she nose-planted into a new tree.

Yelling echoed from behind them in a foreign language she didn't understand.

She refused to stop. She fixed her shoe, grabbed his hand, and pulled hard.

Something burned into her back and side. She stumbled again and hit the ground, her face landing on wet leaves and pine needles. He fell to his knees next to her, clutching his side.

"The snakes are here," he announced.

Her neck hair stood on end as the air around them cooled. She scanned the terrain for movement, snagging on something in the shadows near a tree. A serpent the size and look of an adult cottonmouth slithered their way. Her nightmare—chased by a cottonmouth. It'd happened when she'd been about ten or eleven. They were vindictive snakes that didn't run from people, at least not in this area.

"Don't let them strike you." He jumped up and kicked the closest slithering serpent against a tree. Its thick body fell, unmoving. Dead? Or stunned?

She froze when the mother of all snakes reared up in front of her face poised to strike. The creature was anaconda gigantic. The opaque fangs oozed clear fluid. Time went into slo-mo. She could hear it breathing and see the coiled base tense.

In a whirl, Merck tossed his knife at the snake. It fell, decapitated.

Her back screamed as if she'd been bitten. She twisted to find two knives lodged deep into her skin. Her heart rate soared as she tugged and seesawed them out, which hurt. Wow, it hurt.

Merck darted around the perimeter of the small clearing in which they'd fallen. She couldn't see what he was doing, but suddenly he pivoted and tucked a small vial into his shirt pocket. "That should keep at least the snakes away for a while."

"What was that?"

"Special potion." He squinted toward the house and scowled. "Shit."

He retrieved his knife and dove for another snake, cutting its head, and landed on his side a few feet from her.

"They're resistant to the deter potion. Damn it." The pain hazing his gaze indicated probable knife hits, maybe a snake and who knows what else. Him dying wasn't an option. He had to be the person who'd help her, the one her mother referred with her dying breath.

She curled her small hand around his. "Please don't die. I think I need your help. I think that's why I'm here."

"I am helping you. I'll distract them. Go wherever you go when you Pleiades witches disappear." He wiped debris off her face.

"How do you know that I can..." *Jump dimensions?* she added silently. She should leave. She could pop away to her alternate dimension and, even though she hadn't tried it since she got her magical powers, she was guaranteed to arrive somewhere not surrounded by demonic snakes and whatever else was coming for them. Her chest jerked at the thought of leaving without Merck.

His eyelids drifted closed for a moment.

She shook him. "Don't you dare pass out or die on me. You have to help me or the world will end."

"Who told you this?"

"A Greek god threatened me."

"Is that why you were after the scrying glass?" In the scant light peeking through the foliage, she made out his skyward eye roll. "We're both descendants of Greek gods. They like to sell that crap about end of the world scenarios to get us to play their games. Do you think they really want the world to end?"

"Right now, it sure feels like they do." She traced the jagged scratch-like scar on his cheek. The old damage incited her need to soothe, which made no sense.

His gaze met hers, so intense her breath caught. Then his eyelids drifted shut. "Damn it. It's too late."

"What? Are you dying?" Her hands roamed his chest, neck, and arms.

"I wish. Please get out of here. Go." He grabbed his knife and pulled himself up using tree branches. "These guys are particularly nasty. Don't let them touch you."

He faced a horrific creature that was the size of a man and shaped similarly to one, but its head was narrowed to a point and covered in dark scaly skin. A few slits of skin composed its nose. Rows of sharp teeth gaped open as the creature panted. Bulbous eyes locked on to her. It jumped for her, but Merck tackled it. The creature's clawlike fingers slashed down Merck's side.

The snake creature was fast.

Merck was faster. The snake man fell to the ground, its neck gaping open from Merck's knife. Its body still twitched as Merck attacked a second snake man. She saw only a blur of motion while they parried into the woods.

Stay or go?

She couldn't leave him. She should attempt her newly inherited elemental magical skills to help him. No water or fire nearby to draw upon. Wind. *You'll botch it and might hurt Merck.*

A third snake man appeared and stalked toward her. It almost seemed to be leering, although emotion with the toothy mouth was difficult to interpret. She crab walked backward until her back hit a pine tree.

On instinct, she reached for wind, hoping to whip up enough of a gust to throw the snake man away from her. A strong blast pushed against the creature, keeping it at a distance from her, but not powerful enough to toss it away. She needed the wind to be fierce.

I can't do it. Crap.

The wind died. The snake man caught its balance and headed her way.

Merck attacked the snake man threatening her, jumping onto its back and slashing at its neck before it could react.

"You okay?" he asked while pivoting as if in search of the next one.

"Yes."

"More are coming. You can't get scratched. It changes people into one of them."

"Will it change you?"

"No." He waved behind her, toward the creek. "Get out of here. I don't mean run for the house. I mean go wherever you can go that's not here. Disappear."

"It's not safe for me to take you with me."

"I didn't ask you to take me." He crumpled to the ground, gripping his side where she'd seen him get slashed.

She couldn't take anyone to the other dimension who wasn't her soul mate or a child. Explicit details of the consequences remained unclear, but her mom had implied serious badness.

She chewed on her lip. Screw risks. Her only lead to understand what was going on and potentially save everyone she cared about would not die today. "Why did you help me today and yesterday?"

"Seemed like the right thing to do."

"Just being a gentleman? Right." She leaned over him, gripped each of his biceps, and stared into his eyes.

"If you're taking me with you, then head for water. I need the ocean."

The world dimmed and swirled. Wait. She wasn't ready to change dimensions yet. She hadn't visualized their destination. She was so new to this. Pain clobbered her skull.

Badness.

She whispered, "This might kill us."

Chapter Seven

Shannon felt as if she'd been compressed into a jewelry box and squeezed out a toothpaste tube. Just when she thought her head would explode from internal pressure, everything ended with her plastered, nose-down, against Merck's chest. She rotated her head outward to work her jaw, desperate for her ears to pop.

He moaned in complaint. She rolled to get off him. When her back hit the ground pain lacerated the inside of her skull. Any movement was excruciating. She swallowed over and over to suppress the vomit pushing to break free.

Freezing wetness saturated her clothes. Sandals and shorts weren't appropriate attire for wherever they'd ended up. A test squint to see her surroundings failed. She wanted to bypass the temporary blindness—a side effect of dimensional travel.

Finally, her vision changed from cloudy to details. The trees were unfamiliar, devoid of leaves and covered in snow.

Snow? Where are we?

Her breath fogged as it came in *oh-shit* pants. The cottage a few hundred yards away wasn't familiar. There wasn't a body of water in sight. On the upside, there weren't snake men here. But... Crap.

"Need water. The ocean," Merck wheezed.

"I don't know where we are. I messed up. I don't think there's an ocean around here."

She scooted close to him, her mind whirling with agony at the subtle movement. After a few deep breaths to block out pain, she closed her eyes to concentrate for another dimension hop. *Come on, come on, take us somewhere near an ocean.*

"Nothing happened when I tried to get us out of here."

"S'okay," he slurred. A soft noise came from him when he tried to push up onto his elbows. He crumpled and blinked upward into the skeletal, snow-laden tree canopy. Finally, he rolled his head to the side to meet her gaze. No blame or disappointment met her in his brilliant blue eyes. He stared as if hazed out. She glanced down his side to where he'd been hit. His dark shirt looked darker and wet. Redness tinged the snow beneath him.

"I'm sorry we're wherever we are. I'm new to this kind of travel." She reached for his hand, finding it cool. He weakly clasped back. "Will the ocean help you get better?"

"Yes." His eyelids drifted closed.

She squeezed his hand. "Please, hang in there. I'm going to make this work." After a quick prayer to her Pleiades goddess ancestor for help, she envisioned the Hawaiian beach where she wanted to land. Image firmly in her mind, she took several deep breaths. The compression started again. Yippee, and... Holy crap. This time the travel hurt ten times worse than before.

Shannon came to awareness, but kept her eyes closed against the bright light all around her. The sun burned through her eyelids as it blazed overhead. How long had she been passed out?

Her hands fisted into hot dirt. Not dirt, but sand. Waves crashed nearby. She hoped for an ocean, although her mind tormented her with the vision of being at a water park lying next to the wave simulator.

It was hot, but not unpleasantly so, which was a stark contrast to their last destination. The air wasn't thick with the humidity of South Carolina.

She didn't hear anything from Merck. Not even breathing. Did he make the jump with her? Oh no, she might've left him in those frozen woods. She'd never find him again to get him help before he died. She squinted against the blinding sun and rolled her head. He lay a few feet away, unmoving.

Maybe he wasn't just passed out, but dead. Blood stained the white sand beneath him, suggesting they'd both been unconscious for longer than a few minutes.

No. No. No. He's not dead. Can't be dead.

A roll to crawl to him sent her mind whirling. Too weak.

"Merck?" She'd aimed for a shout, but it came out a hoarse whisper.

His chest moved once. Not dead.

Water. He needed water. She gazed at the ocean on the opposite side of him. So very far away. With a hand wave, she drew a pitiful cupful of water toward him through the air and dropped it on his face.

On the wow side, even though drained she'd gotten her ability to manipulate water to work. But overall, it'd been a pretty lame performance.

Merck gasped and rolled his head toward her. His startled gaze met hers.

"Ocean." She pointed toward the lazy waves of the Hawaiian shoreline. At least she hoped it was the shoreline in front of one of the houses her mother owned in this odd otherworld.

He stared at the ocean, then dragged himself to the edge of the water and flopped in the wet sand.

Now what?

She tried to crawl to him, but her shoulder and back screamed in protest. Darkness closed in on her brain. *You will NOT pass out.*

Although the tide looked to be going out, water crept toward his fingers, as if pulled by an imaginary force. It swirled up his arm. A huge wave reached high above him and swept him into the depths of the ocean.

Then everything was peaceful again with the ebb and flow of small waves.

The water had reached out for him and swallowed him. Now *that* was impressive water manipulation. He must be a water-god ancestor.

Questions swirled in her brain. Her mess revolved around Poseidon, the king of all water gods, which was too coincidental with Merck having water powers.

She stared at the ocean so long her vision blurred, worried about Merck.

Her eyes flickered closed as she fought dizziness. Even though next week Poseidon might execute her, it no longer mattered because right now she was about to check out. She hoped her death here would end the Trident quest and keep her Pleiades witch sisters safe.

Splashing jolted her awake. She gazed toward the ocean, wondering if her last view would be of him. Not a bad last view. He walked thigh-high in the water, and he'd lost his shirt. There was no residual damage to his skin. No blood. No bruising. All had been healed.

He had the body of a top-class athlete. To say he was movie-star stunning didn't cut it. Neither did drop-dead gorgeous. He was heart-thudding, ahh-maz-zing, and then some with those sexy tattoos that streaked from his shoulders to his hands. More tattoos spanned his chest and abs. His short, sandy-blond hair wasn't wet when it should be dripping.

His eyes, now so light a blue they looked almost shimmery, seemed to swirl. She forgot to breathe, but not because he was beauty incarnate. Power oozed from him like a second skin in a way she'd never seen before. It made him intimidating and scary as hell. If descended from a god, then his godly parentage wasn't quite as far removed from the tree as hers.

He knelt next to her. "This is not the world to which I was born."

"Dimension," she whispered. "Not world."

"What is this place?"

Her mouth worked to answer, but nothing came out. She squeezed his hand, although her grip was weak, hoping he'd understand she regretted stranding him in a foreign dimension.

"Hold on." He lifted and held her tight to his body.

Power swirled around him in various aura colors, beautiful whirls. She'd never seen such energy. The converging colors of his aura stimulated a giddy, punch-drunk high.

She pressed her face tight against him, seeking heat against the chills wracking her body. Water licked at her skin as he waded deep into the water.

She ran her finger along his bare chest, unable to resist touching.

He halted, now chest-high in the water.

"You lost your shirt," she mumbled. *Oh, my God. You're dying and losing your mind.* She giggled.

"I did." His body seemed to tremble when she traced the contours between his nipples.

"Why do we have this connection?" She needed answers before she died.

"I don't know."

"You sense it, too? This whatever it is?"

"I'd have to be dead not to," he muttered.

Then she was wet. She bowed away from the stinging salt water. "Hurts."

He didn't acknowledge he'd heard as he continued into deeper water, now cradling her head above the water.

"I think I'm dying," she announced.

"Not today, darlin'. Take a deep breath. We're going under. Now."

"No—" Her denial was lost by sudden emersion.

He pulled her far under. The water turned cold and dark. Had to be very deep. Now she'd die. Drowning hadn't been a way she'd conceived of ending.

Need air. Need air. Don't breathe.

The stinging of the areas where she'd been hit by knives worsened until reaching a critical peak of *holy hell that hurts*. She thrashed. *Must get free and out of the water. Make the pain stop. Oxygen...need oxygen.*

More flailing, this time with kicks and hits didn't break her free of his hold.

Suddenly, he broke the surface and held her head above water.

"Breathe," he ordered as he swam with her in his arms.

After a few gulped breaths, she realized the water didn't sting her skin anymore. She also didn't hurt.

"After this we're almost even on life saving." He didn't look happy about it. He stood, now at a depth that had the water hitting him mid-chest.

"You tried to drown me."

"No, I didn't."

"Can we get out of the water, please?"

"Not yet." He held her to him with one hand and reached out his other hand. Dolphins broke the surface around them. She'd only seen ones in captivity this close. One nosed his hand. A smile transformed his lips, which gentled his entire façade as he touched the animal. He whispered foreign words to the dolphin. His aura swirled with those stunning colors again, but nothing dangerous or menacing. She recognized love, caring, and something authoritative in his aura.

The dolphin bobbed and made noises. Another dolphin touched his hand with its head. Several other dolphins touched him as well.

She'd never witnessed anything so poignant. So beautiful. The dolphins dove under and disappeared.

"That was incredible. Did they speak to you?"

"Dolphins are the correspondents of the ocean. They inform the water gods of happenings and problems. They also communicate to other creatures of the primary water god's intent. Here there's no primary water god to provide stability for their world. They were relieved to speak with me of their troubles, even though I'm not their god."

"Doesn't the lack of an imposing god make them free to live as they wish? Why would they want to be enslaved by a water god?"

His eyes softened. "So naïve for one descended long ago from gods. Enslaved? No." He gazed toward the horizon. "Poseidon may not be a benevolent god, but he's necessary. Sea creatures, like all animals and even people, need his existence, or at least firm standing belief of his existence. People may no longer worship the Greek gods, but most have faith in something larger. Poseidon gives water creatures comfort of certainty and of control. If there's no certainty in belief of the entity who oversees the world around them, then there's but existence without meaning. The sea animals are here in this dimension, but they have no certainty, which leads to chaos."

"Deep thoughts by Merck." She smiled. "They picked up on your water abilities?"

He nodded.

"Could you be their god?"

"That's not my fate."

"What's your fate? What exactly are you?"

He continued to stare across the ocean. "I don't know. I thought I knew, but things changed. Can you take us back to the regular world now?"

She closed her eyes to concentrate, envisioning her house in South Carolina. Nothing happened. Not even a sputter of magical energy. Apparently, his healing didn't extend to magic rejuvenation. "Not yet. I think I need some time to rest. Sorry."

He looked so alone, so far away as he gazed out at the ocean.

"I'll try to get us back," she reassured him.

"I know."

"Can we at least get out of the water now?"

His expression hardened. "Tell me why you're being attacked by Ericthonians. Why a warlock tried to kidnap you. And what you're doing in South Carolina."

"I'm wet. I'm not a huge fan of being wet when not in a bathing suit." She plucked at the top now plastered tight to her skin and cast a glance at the beach. Thank God it was the right beach. "Let's go inside the house, shower, and change."

"No." His jaw tightened. "I need some answers for what the hell is going on."

"I'm not discussing anything out here when you can drown me at whim."

"I'm not going to drown you."

"You almost did once already."

"I didn't. I saved your life. I deserve a bit of gratitude."

"You did make everything better somehow. For that, thanks. But you pulled me underwater. In my book, that's a clear almost-drowning."

"I didn't try to drown you."

She pushed at him to get free without effect. "A little warning before dunking me would've been nice."

"I told you to hold your breath." He released an agitated snort. "You'd been hit by poison knives. There was no other way."

"I didn't know you had some sort of magical water healing ability. That would've been useful information before being dunked." She wriggled against his grip. "Let. Me. Go. Don't make me hurt you."

His eyebrows rose in a clear *Give it your best shot.* Eagerness sparkled in his eyes.

Ugh. Typical alpha-male bullshit. He enjoyed this game. His grin pushed her with the insane need to win. She couldn't overpower him. Tactic-change time.

She gripped his head and kissed him, making sure to graze his lower lip with her teeth. As expected, his mouth parted. She pressed her tongue inside.

Wowzers, he tasted amazing. His *oh-yeah* groan signaled he thought it pretty darn good too.

The kiss shifted. His large hand cupped the back of her head. What had been all her became more him. She opened for the bold thrusts of his tongue. She couldn't get close enough to him. His hand cupped her ass, rotating her body and pressing her tight to his ready-to-rumble down south. Guys taking charge wasn't usually her thing. She liked control, but with Merck she melted beneath his touch and felt wild to the point of almost woozy.

Her legs automatically wrapped around his hips. A violent shudder wracked through her. God, she wanted this man.

Uh-oh. Don't let your plan backfire.

But good Lord, this man could kiss. Her brain shut down all argument against stopping. Sensation sucked her into a desperate desire to get naked. She wanted to see him completely, without clothes, and have her hands on him. On his tattoos, his skin, his muscles, and everywhere else.

No. Not naked. Definitely not naked.

She needed to get away. The second his other hand started roaming, she'd make her move. His hand caressed from her ass up her back. His touch was far gentler than expected, yet provocative and addictive.

His mouth dominated again. Her resolve to escape wavered. This was so, so good.

She couldn't follow through with him, not when she didn't know what exactly he was after the revelation of his water powers. He may be after Poseidon's Trident, and maybe that was why he was hanging around her, except it didn't ring true. He seemed genuinely as surprised by the snake creatures as she was, and saved her life.

She pulled her mouth off his and shot him a glance she wished was a lot less *oh shit* and a bit more *gotcha*. With a strong push off, she broke free of his hold and swam for the shore.

As she stomped up the beach with him close behind, her mind whirled with confusion. What had she done? She hadn't experienced an *oops, shouldn't have done that* moment with a guy since, well, maybe the last time she'd kissed him next to his car.

Be a big girl. You played with a fire you could normally control and got burned. Or, more correctly, she got betrayed by her own body. It'd been too long since she'd been with a guy. Yeah, she tried to convince herself that was the problem, but the effort failed. With guys, she could always detach and remain in control. With him, he retained control, now and in the past. Maybe it was whatever god powers he'd inherited that made him irresistible to her. She wished she wasn't so attracted to everything about him.

Maybe he was destined to be her soul mate.

Impossible. She'd already been over this and dismissed it.

Great. Now she'd have to convince him to help her locate the Trident, perhaps by using one of the magical items he had at his office, and avoid the urge to do *that* again. She hoped he wouldn't try to use sex as a bargaining chip. He didn't seem like that kind of guy, but she didn't know much about who he'd become. He might be a player, but he didn't come off as a user. The fiendish girly-girl side of her danced around while screaming, *"You won't forget kissing him."* If he put sex on the table she might not be able to say *no*, at least not easily.

She stood at the front door and stared at the numeric front door lock for several long seconds while her mind tried to remember the code. Her birthday. It worked.

She faced him when he entered. "I'm taking a shower. Then I'll make us something to eat. We can talk before we pop back to the regular world."

"Showering alone?" Innuendo laced his tone.

Oh, God. He was putting it on the table. *Be strong even though that small taste had been so good.*

"Yes, alone. By myself. That, out there... I just wanted to get out of the water. It worked."

"Mmhm." His eyebrows slowly rose.

Her face heated. "I should apologize, but a girl's got to do what she must when faced with someone like you. You can use the guest bathroom. I think it's stocked with basics." She pointed up the hall. "Look in the closet for some clothes. My father's stuff will probably fit you."

She'd have to pilfer through her mom's drawers for fresh clothes. Her heart clenched. It hurt to think about her mom who'd first brought her here long ago. They'd talked about dimensional travel over a game of checkers. She hadn't understood most of the discussion and barely paid attention. Her mom had tried several times over the years to discuss it more in depth, but Shannon thought if she allowed her mom to finish the discussion, to tell her everything about inter-dimensional travel and her future abilities, then it paved a path for her mother to die, which was an inconceivable possibility prior to two months ago.

What would her mom have done about Merck to get out of the water? She'd have probably kneed him in the balls and sent a huge wave to pull him away. Shannon should've thought of that.

"What's wrong?" he asked.

She chanced meeting his gaze. The concern in his eyes startled her. She choked out, "Nothing. I need a shower and then I'll make us some food."

His eyes narrowed for an instant. He didn't buy it. The tension of his jaw and swirling colors in his aura indicated he wanted to push her to get the truth. "I don't eat seafood."

"Wasn't planning on cooking any." Her eyes started an admiring scan down his naked chest. *Stop it.* No more appreciating how incredible he looked since he'd ditched his shirt.

She swallowed and realized he might be totally freaked out about being here, maybe even about the concept of alternate dimensions. "I'm sorry I can't take you back to your dimension right now. I want to get home too, but..." She chewed on her lower lip. "I'm zapped and need some time to recharge. Please don't be mad at me for bringing you here. I didn't see another option."

She pivoted fast and almost smacked into the wall in her haste to leave.

"I'm sorry about us being here, but we're somewhere safe," she shot over her shoulder without looking back.

***

Mad at her? No.

Stunned by this place? Yes.

His brain could barely wrap around the concept of multiple dimensions. That and the fact she could travel here at whim. Now that was a useful skill.

He glanced out the window into what looked like a perfect beach day. If she hadn't brought them here, she'd be a snake girl after they scratched her, a state that wasn't reversible, and he might be dead.

He was tempted to follow Shannon into the shower and make their trip to this bizarre alternate reality memorable. This time, kissing with clothing off.

His entire body grew hot.

He resisted going to her. Something had scared her out there on the water during their kiss. Whatever it was hadn't been about him. Maybe it was because the kiss hadn't gone the way she'd planned. She'd clearly initiated it to distract him. It'd worked. He respected the hell out of her for using whatever she could to escape. But their connection had burned so hot they'd both been lost to it.

Her kiss was no longer that of a virgin teenager. Today's kiss had been that of a woman who'd sampled and knew how to enjoy sensual pleasure. The urge to hunt down and kill every other man who'd ushered her into advanced kissing surprised him. Their chemistry was real and unique, not something he'd experienced with another woman. No one could fake that kind of mind-boggling attraction.

Jesus, the gods had set a daunting test in front of him. How as he supposed to protect Shannon when he could barely keep his hands off her?

Although he hated being manipulated by gods, Bythos was right. He wasn't ready to die. Battling evil filth might be exhausting, and as Shannon pointed out, a thankless task, but he worried what would happen when the black-magic deviants were left unchecked by his absence. That meant he'd keep his ass glued to Shannon's and ensure her safety.

Chapter Eight

Shannon watched cinnamon buns cool on top of the stove. Her mom used to make sure all freezers remained stocked with a ready-to-bake pan. Thank goodness she'd found one in the freezer today and frozen frosting. Ingredients to bake the buns from scratch, which she could do, required grocery shopping and time. This wasn't a vacation stop over. Fresh food would spoil if she left it. There was no guarantee she could get back here again to use the food or that she'd even be alive to return.

The heavenly smell of sugary cinnamon reminded her of hundreds of breakfasts with too much food, a lot of laughing, and family. There hadn't been any family get-togethers since her mom died and no laughing. Without her mom everything was broken.

The responsibility to cook the buns now fell to her. She'd been so wrapped up in finding the Trident that she'd forgotten the importance of this, not just for herself, but also for everyone else. The druids needed her. Her father needed her. Her fellow Pleiades ladies needed her. They needed her to remain strong, bake buns, and save their lives.

Ask Merck to help.

Frosting the buns relaxed her. She wanted Merck to like the food. He deserved buns for risking his life for her and then healing her, even if his method involved almost drowning. The memory of him in action, fighting the snake creatures, amazed her. He'd been cool, relentless, and totally in charge, whereas she'd been a mess. She prided herself on her ability to deal with magical weirdness, but one ensorcelled snake and she'd lost it.

Give yourself a break. It was a monster snake that wanted to kill you.

She felt Merck's presence before he entered. Her heart beat in her throat, leaving her breathless. The spatula fell to the floor. A few kisses, saving her life, and now she fell apart when he appeared too?

"Tea or coffee?" She recovered the spatula and faked busyness by cleaning droplets of frosting off the stove.

His gaze darted to the percolating coffeemaker. "Coffee works. Black."

The kitchen shrank when he swung the door shut behind him as if circumventing any plans she had of making a break for it.

"I'm sorry I don't have much to offer. I've got cinnamon buns, though."

"That sounds nice, but Shannon..." Merck's low voice sent chills down her spine.

"Yes?" She moved the cinnamon buns to the table and handed him his coffee.

"We need to talk."

"You're right." She placed two plates on the table and served each of them a bun. Jittery, she took the seat across from him. *You have no reason to be nervous.* There were things to talk about. Big things. Yet, she wanted him to like the buns.

He sipped his coffee in silence, eyebrows raised. She fought not to squirm.

"What?" she finally said, pushing her still-damp hair away from her face. "Do I have frosting on my nose or something?"

A grin split his face. "Frosting? Were you sampling before you used it?"

"A good chef always tastes the food before serving. It's good frosting."

Her stomach flipped when he laughed, low and quiet. Humor fled his eyes. The somber man now evaluating her was an entirely different person than the one who'd just grinned.

She crossed her arms.

"Tell me what's going on." He didn't ask. He demanded.

"About what specifically?"

"Let's start with what attacked us. You truly don't know what they were?"

"No."

"Ericthonians. They're the minions of Athena. She sends them out whenever she wants something or she's mad. Does she have a reason to be angry with you?"

"The goddess Athena?"

He nodded.

"You said those creatures could be after you, not me."

"I had a run-in with Ericthonians a few years ago over an item I acquired. She hasn't sent them after me since then. So, their appearance this time must be about you. Why're you interesting to her and a lot of other magical shitheads? Are they after you to get the scrying glass?"

Great. Now Athena was after her too. "I hoped to use the scrying glass to find an item. Athena and the others might think I've got it already, but I don't have it. I swear I don't. I need it, though. The glass might've helped me find it, but I didn't know it required killing someone. I wouldn't have done that. Maybe I can find one that doesn't require something evil to power it."

"What does Athena think you have?"

"Poseidon's Trident."

"What?" He put both hands on the table and leaned forward, eyes wide. "Are you shitting me?"

"He thinks I stole it."

"Poseidon...this is the water god we're talking about? He threatened you?"

"Yeah."

"Do you have it?"

"I just said I didn't."

"Why would everyone think you do?"

"Everything about this is ridiculous." She buried her face in her hands. "No, it's worse than that. It's fricking catastrophic."

"And deadly. Athena's minions will be back. There's nothing she'd like better than to have the power of the water world. She's not a goddess who likes to lose." He leaned back. "Why don't you start at the beginning. Explain what's going on."

Shannon released a frustrated breath. "A creature who works for Poseidon appeared to me a few weeks ago. He said if I don't return the stolen Trident by next week, they'll kill me, every other Pleiades descendant and wipe out all evidence of our bloodlines."

Merck took a sip of coffee. He didn't seem impressed by her revelation. "That's interesting."

"What's interesting about everyone I know getting erased?"

"I'm not talking about your people dying. I'm pretty sure Poseidon doesn't want to wipe out your bloodline. I refer to them thinking you have the Trident. No one can waltz into Poseidon's underwater fortress and steal it. I'm not sure anyone other than Poseidon can touch it. Well, Zeus or Hades probably could, but it's not as if either would care enough to get off their golden thrones to steal it. I think the Trident's power can only be controlled by Poseidon or another very powerful god."

"Like Athena?"

"Maybe. You've touched the Trident, though, and it didn't kill you, but you're not a god."

"I just told you I've never seen it. That means I've never touched it. I don't have it."

"Its essence is..." He waved his hand her way. He stood and moved around the table to kneel by her, his hand hovering over her midsection. "I don't understand how it's possible, but Poseidon's power feels as if it's here somewhere."

She flinched when he touched her stomach over the ugly scar. She pushed his hand away. "How would you know that?"

"Hard to explain, but it calls to me as I suspect it would other water creatures or powerful gods."

"Are you a powerful god?"

"I'm not a god. Let me see." He tugged up the edge of her T-shirt.

She yanked down the shirt before he saw anything, face flaming. "Please, don't."

"Why not? What're you hiding?"

She released a shaky breath and exposed the magical scar, which although healed into a tangle of mutilated skin, still burned off and on.

"What did this?" He traced the edges of the scar, gently probing.

Heat flared through the scar as if someone poked her with a hot skewer. She gasped, grabbed his wrist and jerked it away from her.

"It burns?"

"Yes," she choked out. "Don't touch it. When people with magical powers touch it, it hurts more. Our healer tried to fix the scar, but he couldn't."

"What I did couldn't heal this. Usually, I can heal almost anything." He touched the side of his face over his scars.

"What did that to your face?" She put a finger on the scarred scratches, still not finding them at all a deterrent from his hard, dangerous appeal.

"It happened the first time I faced off against Ericthonians over that item Athena wanted. The thing scratched the shit out of me, and it turns out if I don't get to the water in time, I scar."

"Did you scar today?"

"No."

"Good." She cast him a small smile.

"Tell me how you got the thing on your stomach." His hand hovered over the scar as if he could feel the heat, which simmered from the inside out as if revving up to a power burn again.

"Someone shoved a sword through me a few weeks ago."

"A sword?" His hand hovered above the scar again. "Not many go for swords these days."

She squirmed against the softness of his touch. "The blade must've been cursed or poisoned or something. Doctors said I should've died. It went through my liver and intestines, but I didn't die."

"The sword must've left something inside you when it went through. Something that prevented you from dying. Maybe a piece of the Trident or the whole thing. Did you steal the Trident or do something to miniaturize it and store it inside yourself?"

"I didn't steal it. I'm not a sea creature who can hold her breath long enough to reach Poseidon's home, brave whatever scary things guard it, and then tiptoe in, steal it, and get out. I have no powers to miniaturize."

"You could get in and then do your dimension travel thing to get out. Or maybe even pop into Poseidon's domain from here, this other dimension?" His eyebrows shot up.

"It doesn't work like that. Even if it did, I suck at it. Look at today. I'm clearly not good at ending up where I want. It's a miracle we ended up on this beach after that snowy place. Also, I didn't have the ability to move between dimensions until *after* my mother died, which was after I'd been run through with a blade."

"Why are you in South Carolina when you're under some sort of gods' ultimatum?"

"Mom told me to go to South Carolina right before she died. She said I'd find help there." She narrowed her eyes at him. "What exactly are you aside from a hunter of evil magic people? Whoever you're descended from has water powers." Gut instinct told her his water god ancestor was a direct relation, maybe a parent or grandparent.

He resumed his seat and crossed his arms.

She leaned forward. "Which Greek god do you come from? You owe me at least this much."

"Poseidon."

"That's a weird coincidence." Super jackpot? Maybe not, considering the gods liked to muck around in the lives of her and the other Pleiades ladies. This might be a complex game, and they were the pawns.

"Don't look at me like I've got answers. I've never met him. I've never seen his Trident other than pictures, which are probably wrong since that's human guesswork."

"You're related to Poseidon. Poseidon has me under an ultimatum. My mom sent me down here for some reason. Any thoughts?"

He shrugged.

"You can get answers, I'll bet. You're not as far removed from him as I am from my descendants, are you?"

His face closed down. "What do you want from me?"

"I have to find the Trident and give it back to him within the next week or—"

"You die, everyone you know dies. Scary death shit and end-of-world scenarios. Standard gods Armageddon crap. You said that before." He shook his head. "I don't have a clue how to find it."

He grabbed the cinnamon bun off his plate and bit into it. His eyes drifted closed. "These are really good. Really, really good."

"Thanks." She grinned. Now to get him on her team to help. "Why did you come back this morning?"

He finished eating the bun and took a swig of coffee. "I don't think I've had cinnamon buns as good as this. What happened leading up to when you got stabbed with a sword?"

"Good Lord, you're annoying. Can't you answer a single question?"

He snagged another cinnamon bun and bit into it. He stared at her in silent demand of an answer.

After a sip of orange juice, she said, "I'll tell you the rest of the story if you tell me in what way Poseidon is related to you and your thoughts on the Poseidon coincidence."

He continued chewing on a bun without commitment to the bargain.

"I signed on to a reality TV show as a cameraperson two months ago. It was last minute. I did it to help a friend, the one I called to get the right protective spell against zombies—"

"Zombies don't exist. They were revenants or animated corpses."

"Okay, revenants. Once on the TV show, there was a lot more going on than the nightmare of being in a South American rainforest for a few days. The guy who stabbed me was a producer named Rick Holloway. He—"

"What?" Merck's entire body tensed. He sat upright. "Rick?"

"You know him?"

"My mom dated him for a while. It's why she moved to California when I went off to college. He's a real asshole and also of Greek gods descent."

"I know. He's dead."

"How'd Rick die?"

"He stabbed me and then to make sure he finished the job planned to shoot me, but my mother stepped in the way and took the bullet. Before she died she killed him."

"Are you sure he's dead?"

"He was smashed by a boulder. Pretty sure. Rick descended from Orion. Apparently, his family is obsessed with killing all of us Pleiades."

"Reality TV...I assume you mean *Extreme Survivor*. Was Owen Campbell hosting the show?"

"Yes. His fiancée was killed in the ordeal as well."

"Owen had a fiancée?"

"Ana something. She was pretty scary for a necromancer, not that I've met one before her."

"Anaïs?" His eyes widened.

Shannon nodded.

"You should stay away from her. She's not only vicious, but also smart. Are you sure she's truly dead?"

"Her soul was removed by a death reaper. Come to think of it, you and my friend who's a death reaper should meet and commiserate over your shitty destinies to chase evil people."

"He goes after regular people who're evil. I go after deviant magical shitheads. Him removing her soul doesn't mean the necromancer is dead. Unless... Did you remove her heart and burn the body? I'm not sure if it'll work since I burned her once before and she rose from the ashes. My new theory is if I remove her heart and dispose of it elsewhere, then burning the remains of her body might work."

"I have no idea what happened to her body. I passed out."

"Let's assume she's not dead, then. She likes to absorb multiple souls. Giving up one soul to a death reaper isn't a big deal."

"Did you know Owen is Rick's son?"

"Yeah. We crossed paths a few times. Owen collects friends who practice black magic, but we've never picked anything up about him being intent on wiping out all Pleiades. He's caught up in Hollywood bullshit most of the time."

"What do you think Poseidon's Trident has to do with them?" She sipped coffee.

"It promises unlimited power. I'm sure that's the necromancer's goal. She may not have counted on you to survive Rick's attack, definitely not to take the Trident's power with you. I wonder how they harnessed its power. Or maybe they didn't know about the Trident until after you'd been stabbed."

"You said no person could touch the Trident. Why is it possibly in me?" She ran a hand over her stomach, disturbed.

"Told you, darlin'. I don't have answers. Wish I could help."

You can help. "Do you have something at your work that could help me find the Trident?"

"Nope."

"Not a single thing in all that junk you have sitting around, which reeks of magic?"

"It's all confiscated items. They're relics best left alone."

Time to push Merck a little bit. "If you've got nothing, then it sounds like I need to pay Owen a visit."

"Stay away from him and Anaïs."

She shot him a challenging glare.

"The world of black magic is pouring into South Carolina in search of you. Let's assume Owen's friends are interested in you for the same thing. Anaïs will kill you if she thinks it'll grant her more power."

"How are you related to Poseidon?"

He slid his chair back and took his dishes to the sink. "He's my father."

"What?"

The gaze he cast her clearly indicated that was as much information as he was willing to dish out on the matter.

Merck was a demigod. Oh my. The strength of his power now made sense.

"Can you talk to Poseidon for me?"

He shook his head. "I don't know him. He's never wanted anything to do with me."

So far, the recruit-Merck plan was tanking. She cleared her throat and slid her chair back. "I'll do the dishes and then see if I can get us back to South Carolina."

"I can do my own dishes."

They both washed and dried dishes, and placed the leftover buns in the freezer.

After the plates had been returned to their place in the cabinet, he said, "Don't go after Owen."

"You can't help me. So I need to talk to people who might know something."

"You have no idea what you'd be up against."

"I'm fully capable of dealing with whatever comes my way. I'll do whatever I need to in order to get this situation resolved. Sounds like Owen or his undead fiancée may be my only leads." She pushed to get past him.

He caught her arm, spun her, and caged her against the refrigerator. His palm supported her chin and fingers wrapped her jaw. "Anaïs is as strategic as she is cunning. She targeted you. It's not over with her, not so long as whatever has to with the Trident still involves you. The stupidest thing you can do is seek her out, whether you go alone or with your druids."

She struggled against his hand until he released her face. She bucked, getting herself locked tighter between him and the refrigerator. "Get off me."

"Not until you promise you won't do something reckless like fly out to California."

"Since I'm on my own, I'll decide my next step. I'm not even sure if you and I are on the same team or if you want to be enemies. We could be on the same team..." She stared at the temptation of his lips. Was she above a little seduction? Naughty witch time. With a smile she leaned in and kissed him hard.

Her body trembled with the force of emotions swirling in her brain. Control slipped away as she fell victim to the mad addiction to succumb and let him take over. For days she'd been wound up, frightened and tangled, needing an outlet. Now it presented itself. Those emotions eagerly funneled themselves into her kiss.

He pulled back. "You're not seducing your way out of this." He leaned forward, his lips inching close to hers, but then he ducked away. The tip of his nose brushed her jawline.

He tipped her head sideways and nuzzled down her neck. "I'll give you what you what right now, but you'll swear to me you won't go after Owen." His hand skimmed down her side, teasing the edge of her breast.

She moaned. "Okay."

He kissed her neck, quick and brief. Then he nipped her skin, followed by his tongue sweeping over the nip, erasing the sting.

Air wouldn't move through her chest. She had to breathe or she'd pass out in a few moments from lack of oxygen.

He demanded, "Okay to what?"

She sucked in air. "I promise I won't go after Owen without you."

He kissed her again. This time his tongue sneaked past her lips. She got lost in the feel of his warm, smooth lips against hers. She slid into a world where everything was about feeling. A noise, deep and guttural, escaped her.

He lifted his head. The fire in his gaze awed her. It promised a satisfaction she'd never achieved with a man before.

He said hoarsely, "I want you. But I don't want some confused moment when we're both unsure of who's using who to get what we want."

He didn't return to kissing.

"I don't get you. You want me. I want you. It'd probably be pretty good right now."

"It'd be a damned sight better than pretty good. But no."

She glared, so confused by mixed messages from him.

He rubbed his eyebrows. "All right. I know someone who might be able to help you, but it won't be easy and probably dangerous."

Chapter Nine

"You know someone who can help me find the Trident?" Shannon ducked out of his arms.

"Maybe." He didn't want to be involved in a quest that had to do with his absent father, but he also didn't want Shannon running to California. *You must protect her. Damn it, the gods are fucking around with us.*

"What does *maybe* mean?" The hope blossoming on her face pushed him to help her.

"There's someone. I don't know if she can tell you anything new."

"Is she a witch?"

"She's something else, but at least she's local. Well, not local to here, wherever we may be."

"You'll take me to see her when we get back?"

"Let me see if talking to her is the right way to go." He pulled out the small black pouch of runes he'd stuffed into his pants earlier in the day. He'd taken them on his last trip to Europe weeks ago and intended to return them to the office.

Runes only worked if the user asked the right question. The questions dominating his brain revolved around *his* impending death in seventy-two hours, not her. *This has to be about her and how to find the Trident.* After a gentle shake of the bag he reached in with his left hand, pulled out four stones, mixed them in his hand, and placed them on the table with the symbol side up.

A yew came up. *Oh, shit.*

It doesn't have to be negative.

"Runes? You hunt witches, hate them, and yet you use their magic?"

"Never said I hated witches." *Definitely not your type of witch.* "This kind of benign magic can be useful."

He tried to remember the question he'd asked before drawing stones. He should ask again and draw new stones, but that was bad luck. The last thought before he'd drawn had been about his judgment day.

She nodded to the stones. "What does it mean? Does it tell us what to do? I've never tried runes."

"They don't give exact answers, but they can give hints." He pointed at the two stones on the right, which were the symbols of Ansuz and Othila. "These are past and present influences. They represent gods and genetics. No surprises there." His finger hovered over the third stone, the symbol of Inguz, which stood for true love and harmony. Did it mean him with Shannon for the next three days? Or longevity with some woman beyond his judgment day?

His finger moved to the fourth stone, the yew, which was bad, although it could be a symbol of a departure from the past. He met her gaze. The only words he could force out were, "The last one tells of future influences."

"What does it mean?" A frown creased her brow. "It's not good, is it?"

Death. He'd asked the stones about himself instead of her, damn it. Now he'd confirmed he died. He grabbed up the stones. "Makes no sense."

"I don't believe you. It's something bad. Tell me." She scowled at him, waiting for an answer.

Finally, he said, "It suggests something not good may happen."

"Not good as in death? Or does it mean don't visit your witch friend?"

"I think this has nothing to do with seeking advice. It may have to do with the gods. We're in the middle of one of their games. No matter what we may want to do, the scenario they designed has to be played out."

"I hate deterministic crap," she muttered. "What's the bottom line on what the runes said?"

"Based on the runes something big is about to change. I don't know more than that." His shoulders lifted and dropped. "I gave up figuring out the gods' plans the second time Poseidon's right-hand man tried to kill me, even if he did claim he'd done it in the name of training."

"You know his right hand guy? Maybe you could ask him about the Trident for me?"

"I have no idea when I'll see him again. Maybe never. It's not as if I can ask him to appear. He's a god. A lower-level god, but still not something I can control." Actually, he didn't know if he could request Bythos's presence. He'd never tried. However, he distrusted the god enough not to try it, even for her.

"Would you mind asking him, if you do see him soon?"

"Sure." He was pretty sure the next time he saw Bythos he'd be about to die, and that might not be a moment conducive to a chitchat about her issues. *Tell her about your death date.* The words wouldn't come out. Vocalizing it to her would confirm his impending death as reality. Even though he'd spent years knowing of it, judgment day seemed unreal. He functioned by avoiding it and focusing on the current day. If he didn't speak of it, then the horror of it couldn't own him.

"Since that guy isn't a certainty swear to me you'll take me to your witch person when we get back to the other dimension."

He blew out a long sigh before he nodded. He'd help her. It'd be the last thing he'd do in this world, but he'd figure out her mess.

She motioned for him to follow her as she walked through the house, turning off lights and then out the front door. "How'd you end up as both the son of Poseidon and a hunter of those who use magic to kill people?"

God, she was full of questions. He didn't answer.

"Why can't the son of a god do whatever he wants? Why be forced into a dangerous job?"

"Seems not to be the case. Maybe it was a coincidence."

"A coincidence? When gods are involved?" Skepticism dripped from her words.

"Probably not. I don't know why I'm the son of Poseidon. I subjected myself to an eternity soul-binding ritual in the Dark Ages in exchange for help from a warlock to save my family who'd been captured by a coven of evil witches."

"You remember back that far?"

"Yeah." His family had died despite his vow.

"Can't you undo your soul-binding ritual? It's been hundreds of years. They've got to understand you're ready to pass the duty on to someone else."

He shook his head. "I've consulted with everyone—magical experts, occult specialists, religious gurus, and even a few lower level gods."

"How do you know who's good or bad and who needs hunting?"

"I get visions. Intuition, I guess you could call it, on what's going on."

"You weren't sure about me. Did you have some sort of vision?"

"No. But you met a black magic relic dealer to buy a dangerous piece."

"True. Thanks for putting up with my questions. This is all a bit overwhelming." She scanned the horizon over the ocean. "Sure is beautiful here. Even so, we should go back."

"Is the return as nauseating as the journey here?"

"Yes." She took his hand in hers.

"That sucks." He took a deep breath and readied himself for the painful squeezing.

***

The world narrowed and compressed until there was no room for breathing, movement or thought. Seconds later it ended.

She squeezed Merck's forearm, not to reassure him, but to confirm to herself he'd traveled too. One of his arms wrapped her waist and gently squeezed.

"Can't see," he muttered.

"Me either." Hot, muggy air caught in Shannon's nostrils. Humidity was good, but it didn't mean this was South Carolina. A rainforest in South America would be humid. So would Jamaica.

Her ears strained to catch a familiar birds call, but all she heard was leaves rustling and crickets. They might be cicadas or frogs and not crickets.

Finally, her eyes agreed to work again. She recognized the massive oaks framing the gravel driveway in South Carolina. Merck's SUV sat a few hundred yards away.

Thank, God. Perhaps she was getting better at the movement between dimensions.

Oh, no. Her stomach plummeted. Her father and six tough-guy druids, including Eli, marched up the driveway toward them. For a few moments she was reduced to a teenager about to get yelled at for making out with the tennis team captain in the driveway.

"Ah, a welcome home party. Fun, fun," Merck murmured. No fear came from him. Considering the magical weirdoes he must encounter on a day-to-day basis, a couple of druids with miscellaneous skills probably didn't register on his scale of scary. Even so...

"I won't let them hurt you," she said.

"It's not me I'm worried about." He chuckled and tilted her chin to meet his gaze. The confidence in his eyes melted into something more intense. "Darlin', you concerned about me?"

She nodded, mesmerized by his penetrating blue eyes. No man had ever looked at her like this. Hot. Sexual. As if he couldn't wait to lick her from head to toe. Okay, that might be her imagination reading into his look.

"I'm not worried." His tone warmed her with assurance he could handle himself and he'd keep her safe. She'd never been a girl who thought she'd like being treated as a protected woman. Until right now. Well, until Merck.

She wished he'd crush his lips to hers again in a hard kiss. Something in his eyes said he wouldn't go there. One glance at their rapidly approaching company reminded her why.

A wicked smile curved his lips. "You want me."

She cleared her throat. "I *want* you to help me find the Trident."

He whispered into her ear, "I'll help you, if you admit since our first kiss you imagined us together so many times that the images of us haunt you at night and sour the touch of any other man."

How'd he know? Sounded like he spoke from personal experience. To think he might've dreamed of her, might've even wanted her for years, made the girly girl who'd been in love with him for all of high school rear her giggly self. It wanted to wrap her arms around him, lean in, and let him possess her.

He warned, "If you don't answer, I'm walking in five seconds because a shitfest train is storming our way."

She released a shaky breath. "This, whatever it is, drives me nuts. It's driven me crazy for years. Is that enough for you?"

"That works." He turned to face their audience.

"Shannon Elaine Randolph. What the hell are you doing with *him*?" her father blasted at her. He'd lost more weight since the last time she'd seen him, making his tall frame thinner but no less intimidating.

More gray highlighted the dark strands around his face. Grief wasn't a good companion. Her heart ached for him.

Merck's hand around her waist clenched tight. He'd turned glacial with his eyes fixated on her father.

She said, "He's here to help."

"He'll never be able to *help* you." Her father glared hostility at Merck, the two of them in some sort of silent pissing match.

"Why the hell are you back?" Eli's gaze narrowed dangerously onto Merck.

Her father's mouth settled into a severe line. "Jason Merck. I thought I made myself clear with regard to you and my daughter years ago. You stay on your side of the creek. We stay on ours. Step away from her."

Seeing her father this worked up broke her heart. Even though bristling like a cornered hedgehog he appeared fragile to her. Perhaps only she could see the signs of him crumbling on the inside. Outwardly, he still appeared to be the warrior he'd always been. Even so, he didn't get to bark at Merck. He wasn't the enemy.

"Brian Randolph. It's been a while, sir." Merck's jaw clenched. His entire body was ramrod stiff against her. The arm around her tightened. She'd bruise where his fingers curled into her waist, but he probably didn't even realize he was doing it. Merck's aura swirled with dark colors. Protective. Possessive. Dangerous.

Her turn to protect him. "Back off and leave him alone."

The six druids halted several feet away from them.

She demanded of her father, "What exactly did you say to him *years ago*? When did this discussion happen?"

"Get away from him." Her father took another step toward them. She knew his tactics well. He planned a stealth approach and grab.

She turned to Merck. "What did he say to you and when?"

"That night when I helped you back across the creek, I followed you. Thought I'd ask you out."

Shock exploded inside her chest. It hurt so much she could barely move air. A decade ago she'd been a naïve girl believing she'd found Prince Charming after one kiss. Dead wrong assumption. Merck's kiss had been no more than a tease, as if he'd been testing how much power he could wield over her with his magic sexual mojo before dumping her like a hot potato. He'd escorted her across the creek and never sought her out again.

Now to find out it might not be true? He'd come after her? He'd considered making them into something real? Their kiss hadn't been fleeting to him—a forgettable, one-off kiss with a desperate girl.

Barely able to speak, she rasped out to Merck, "What did Dad say to you?"

"He told me you never wanted to see me again. That your whole family didn't want to see me and to stay on my side of the creek." Her father was notorious for blowing his top over boys who got near her. He'd probably gone off the deep end with a whole lot of expletives.

"I never said that." She'd been confused and scared when a guy a year out of high school with far more life experience turned her world upside down. Who knows what she would've said to him, but it wouldn't have been an outright no. From an experienced perspective, she saw her father's point of view. Merck could've probably written the advanced sex playbook back then. That didn't give her father the right to make decisions for her.

"It's in the past." Merck didn't release her, no hint of forgiveness in his tone or scowl.

Her father reached in as if to yank her away. "Get away from him. He's sucked you into his bullshit. You don't even know what he is."

She flinched away from her father's grasp. "I know a hell of a lot more about him than you do, apparently."

Her father straightened with the glower of a warrior mentally browsing weapons to determine which might best smother the enemy. "He hunts witches like you. And kills them."

"Only bad witches. He hunts the ones who practice dark magic."

Her father rolled his eyes. "The guy is slick as shit and a criminal. Don't believe him."

She glanced at Merck. A flash passed through his gaze. Hurt? Deception? She'd always relied on her father and the Sentry druids. Their whole existence was built around a life vow to protect her. They'd die for her. Her gut trusted both them and Merck. There'd been too many opportunities for Merck to kill her or harm her. He'd saved her, laughed with her, and kissed her. Nothing hurtful.

Her father was being overprotective around a guy he didn't like for some reason. It wasn't rational.

Her father signaled. One druid went left and the other right. Her father and Eli headed down the center. Instinct took over. She stepped in front of Merck. "Everyone back off."

Her father jumped forward and grabbed her arm, yanking her away from Merck. He tucked her close to him. "Leave," he ordered Merck. "Or I'll kill you this time."

"No." Power poured from Merck. His aura swirled all kinds of vicious. "The last time you spoke for her, I let you intimidate me because I wasn't thinking clearly. This time, you're not her best bet. Shannon and I are caught in the middle of something. I'm not sure what yet. I know all about her being a Pleiades descendant. I probably know a lot more about the Greek gods than any of you. You can't save her from this by keeping her holed up in a room."

"I will keep her away from people who might kill her. Like you."

"Brian..." Merck blew out a long sigh. "Think beyond your need to be the helicopter parent. She's in deep shit."

"Exactly. You're no good to her right now, witch hunter."

Merck cast his eyes heavenward. "The night before last a warlock's minion drugged Shannon after she, in her desperation brought on by your confinement, tried to purchase an ancient scrying glass. If the warlock hadn't killed her, then the scrying glass would've. I took care of the evil shit, confiscated the glass, and let her sleep off the drug in my office. When I confronted the master warlock, he was willing to risk death in order to get what everyone thinks she has. These guys don't risk their lives over something that doesn't promise supreme power. This tells me your muscle and diminutive powers are nothing against the creatures coming after her. Fighting black-magic users is what I do. Shannon's a big girl. Let her decide who she trusts to help her."

Brian scowled. "My daughter does not get involved with criminals."

"You've got to let it go. I was a teenager on Halloween. I could've used spray paint or something worse on your car, but I didn't."

"You and your gang vandalized my car...a dozen cars. I'm sure it was the tip of the iceberg for what you've done over the years."

"It was me and Chad. No gang."

She wiggled away from her father and waved her hand. "Enough. I have news." She forced a bright smile.

"What kind of news?" Her father asked.

"Merck has agreed to help me. As he just said, he knows a lot more about black magic and magical items in general than any of us. Quite a resource." She feared her father would interpret this as a declaration of independence and shift in loyalty, although she hoped not. She moved next to Merck again, nervous about her father's impending explosion.

Her father's face tightened. "That's not happening."

Eli's said, "I don't even know what he is. This is insane."

Her father pointed at Merck. "He's sucked you into his bullshit, maybe hexed you or something. Snap out of it."

Shannon faced Merck. "Between fighting Ericthonians, almost dying, and breakfast, did you hex me?"

Merck pinched the bridge of his nose. "I don't do this kind of fucking drama. It's been a long morning. Way too long. Shannon and I have somewhere to be."

Eli pierced her with a glare. "You're not going anywhere with him. I don't trust him."

She snorted out a frustrated breath, rolled out of Merck's tight grasp on her waist, and advanced on Eli. Wind picked up in the trees, and she detected a power flare around her.

Eli stepped backward, glancing around.

She said, "How can you not trust me and my choice? Seriously, Eli? We've known each other since we were old enough to talk. Sure, we fight. But I've covered for you so many times over the years, especially to your father when you were in high school. Remember when you guys were visiting back then and you wanted to sneak out every night to see Melissa Calvin in town for a..."

Eli held up a finger, warning her not to finish that.

"Melissa, huh?" Merck chuckled. "She still lives off Southside."

"Enough." Eli's cheeks flushed. "We don't know this guy, Shannon. This is me telling you I'm worried."

Her father chimed in. "How do you know you and Eli aren't destined? Why're you running all over with this guy when Eli may be it for you?"

"Did I ever say Merck and I were destined? No. This isn't about finding my soul mate right now. It's about all of us surviving." Her father's stubborn look said he wasn't giving this up. "Eli and I? We're not."

Eli's eyes narrowed and he crossed his arms.

Shannon purposely licked her lower lip and gazed up at Eli, giving him her best sultry half-mast eyelid gaze. Eli's gaze didn't deviate from hers, not even to watch her tongue. He stared at her like an annoyed older brother, a look she knew well, having had two of them.

"Eli, do you lose your mind every time I'm nearby, with need to...you know." Her eyes darted to her father. The graphic word she needed to use got tangled in her throat when she caught her father's pinched look. She focused on Eli again. "Or is there only a need to protect me, like a big brother?" She poked Eli's chest with a solitary finger, feeling none of the heat that drove her nuts around Merck. One finger into Merck's chest like this and he'd have her pressed against the side of the car, taking her challenge and one-upping it, no doubt. She'd be fully into it, hoping Merck would finish it this time.

But Eli? No. She glanced at her father. "You want me to kiss Eli and prove this isn't ever going to work with him?"

She'd puke if she had to kiss him. When a druid wasn't destined for a Pleiades, there was some sort of cosmic deter spell that made anything with the man disgusting.

Eli leaned away. She could tell by Eli's wary gaze it was a no-way.

"Don't do it." Merck's words froze her.

He'd moved directly behind her. The godlike power he kept under wraps poured off him. His aura swirled with threat.

"We're leaving. Don't follow us," Merck said, striding toward his parked car with one hand on her back, gently pushing. He helped her into the passenger side and closed the door.

Eli yanked open the passenger door seconds after it'd shut. "Get out of the bloody car. Don't make me force you."

Merck climbed into the driver's seat and cranked the SUV.

"I need to go with Merck right now."

Eli shot her a wounded gaze.

She leaned out of the seat to touch Eli's cheek and said softly enough her father couldn't hear, but Merck could, "I meant what I said before. I love you like a brother. Would I kill for you, if I had to? Yes. Would I do what I needed to protect you? Yes. I understand where this attitude is coming from, but you need to trust me. I'm going right now to do something about my problem. I'll come back. I promise."

"Everything's trying to kill you. You're running all over with this guy who we know nothing about who hunts witches. Be reasonable."

"Get out of the car, Shannon," her father thundered.

"Shut the door. Now." Merck levied a feral gaze on both men. Her father's eyes widened. Eli backed up a step. Nothing that she'd ever seen scared Eli or her father until now.

"What the hell are you?" To Shannon Eli asked, "Do you really trust him?"

Doubt plagued her. She couldn't control Merck like she could other guys. That meant she had to trust in him. Did she? *You have to trust someone right now.* "He's faced off with some dangerous creatures attacking me and... Yes, I trust him. I'll be back in a few hours. We can discuss whatever plan you guys came up with then."

Eli closed her door.

"Sorry about all that," she said as he pulled away.

"You can avoid, but you can't run away from your father. That's something you'll have to deal with."

"I know. First I'll let him cool off. Where does this witch live?"

"West of Savannah. She's a voodoo mambo, not a witch."

Chapter Ten

"Voodoo? I thought that was only in New Orleans and mostly urban legend designed to draw tourists. The dolls, the blood sacrifices and all that stuff. There's someone around here?"

Merck hoped this consultation didn't go south, getting one of them hexed or possessed. He wouldn't let it happen. He could handle a voodoo mambo.

"It always seemed so dark in the movies. What should I expect?"

"I can't be sure with Lola. Sometimes it's spirit conjuring. Sometimes spell casting or reading various signs. Depends on her mood and how much she wants to show off."

"She's reliable?"

"She's given me good information in the past, but I don't trust anyone who uses any sort of death to power spells, even if Lola only uses animals."

Shannon crossed her arms and hugged herself, staring out the side window.

"I won't let anything happen to you."

"I know you won't," she whispered.

The trust in her voice kicked him in the gut. He'd get her through this. Smarter would be not to take her at all, but she wouldn't go for being dumped somewhere close by, but safe, twice.

Merck hummed along with the country tune on the radio to fill the awkward silence that settled between them. Last week his life had been under control. He'd been captain of a sinking ship scheduled to wreck soon. He convinced himself he was fine to go down with the ship. He even had a night-before-death plan, which involved a lot of alcohol with Chad and Danny. Now, he'd lost the captainship. He'd become a passenger clinging to the rails in a hurricane.

His mind kept going back to the rune symbol of love and harmony. It might mean Shannon. Maybe Bythos really did mean his best life-saving scenario involved tying the knot. He hadn't said a clear no to matrimony. He'd only indicated Merck needed to protect Shannon.

Sweat trickled down his back. The thought of the commitment, to honor and *protect*, one woman scared the hell out of him. It wasn't that he couldn't commit if he survived beyond this week. He feared he couldn't ensure her safety from the evils he was eternity-bound to chase. He couldn't opt out of being the Enforcer. Should he marry, word would get out in underground black-magic circles that he now had a vulnerability. Her. If there were kids the threat was ten times worse. He couldn't risk the possibility of his little one in the hands of a warlock, or worse, a necromancer. He'd seen what they could do. Eons ago when he'd vowed his soul in order to save his wife and son, he remembered the torture done to them by a warlock. He might've freed them with his eternity bargain, but they'd never been the same and ultimately took their own lives.

Then there was Brian Randolph's bomb. He'd lied to Shannon all those years ago. She didn't know about the first, and only, time in this lifetime that he'd attempted to be a stand-up guy. One kiss and he'd lost his mind and forgotten about consequences. Getting shut down had been for the best. Even if he had the chance at a do-over of that night, he'd allow himself to be intimidated by Brian again out of fear he couldn't keep her safe long term.

Was she really any safer with him right now than with the druids? Probably not, but at least he knew the full scope of capabilities for each nasty magical she might encounter. He never should've offered to take her to Lola, but something about her made him unable to say no and move on. That and Brian had pushed more than a handful of his hot buttons.

Enough. He would ensure her safety. That was his job. Protect humans. Remain level-headed, vigilant and prepared. *I'm the Enforcer.*

"We're not far now," he said to break the silence. The car bounced along the rough two-lane for another mile before he turned onto an unmarked dirt road. He sped over the washboard surface to the next unmarked turn onto a sandy road.

"Do you still have the protective crystal I gave you yesterday?"

She removed it from beneath her shirt where it hung around her neck.

"Keep it on. It'll ward off spells. Lola should behave, but you never know."

Lola's one bedroom house had been built on the edge of a pond. She'd added a screened in back porch since the last time he visited several years ago. Even though it looked better kept than most of the houses in this area—clean with a fresh coat of paint and a mowed lawn—it wasn't a welcoming place to him. Too many spirits had been called upon here. Too many spells had been cast and animals killed to power magic than he cared to imagine.

"Be alert." He scooted around to open her door, barely making it before she hopped out.

She glanced up, her eyes wide with unease.

He squeezed her hand and held on. "I got this. You're going to be okay."

"I'm glad you're helping me." She gazed at a stork strolling through the cattails. "This is quaint."

"Don't let it fool you. This isn't the type of voodoo practiced in Haiti where they do it as a way of life to achieve cosmic harmony or something like that. Here, it's become twisted with a focus on want and need rather than mastery of the divine." He lowered his voice as they walked up the path to the front porch, "Don't look directly into her eyes."

"What?"

He shot her a quelling look as the porch door opened.

"Jason Merck. Had a feelin' you'd be by today. And ye brought a special friend to visit." The petite Haitian's lips widened to reveal white teeth with a gold crown on a lower canine tooth. The smile stretched the maze of wrinkles on her dark skin. Although ageless, he guessed Lola to be in her seventies. The hem of her sky blue dress flapped in the breeze. "Come on in and we'll get you and your lady friend sorted."

As they passed close to her through the door, the smell of rum and cigars assaulted his nose. She'd been conjuring spirits today who'd probably foretold of their arrival. One step inside and his stomach lurched at the fetid odor of barn animals, putrefying blood, and incense. He stared at Lola's eyes, violating his own rule. Yet, he pulled away before he became entranced by her cloudy, pale blue irises. The eyes were disconcerting next to her dark skin and Haitian heritage.

"You been communing with Papa Ghede today?" Merck infused calm into his voice.

Lola cackled. "You's a smart one. Papa Ghede does love his rum. He be telling me abouts you and the lady, he did."

Great. Just what he needed was the voodoo spirit of death to be talking about him. "Guess he's looking forward to a meet-and-greet soon. He say anything useful to you?"

She laughed her shrill noise again. "He's a fickle one, that Papa Ghede. I take everything he say to be only half true."

Lola waved at her dining table, which she probably never used for meals, but only to invoke spirits and cast spells. "You two sit at the table. I made us tea."

"Don't drink," he whispered to Shannon as they sat.

Her throat worked as she glanced at the table of rotting severed heads of dogs, snakes and lizards—fetishes used in spells ranging from the simplest libido enhancement to the darker rituals. Three skinny, hobbled roosters lay on the floor near the kitchen table ready to be used as sacrifices. On a side table an altar to a goddess was decorated in flashing Christmas lights, flowers, and mini liquor bottles.

He tried to convey reassurance with a small smile, but feared it came out stressed.

Lola placed a cup of tea in front of each of them and nudged at the sugar bowl in the center of the table suggestively. The tea smelled herbal with a splash of something extra that most likely helped push people into "the spirit."

Lola rubbed her lower lip with her index finger as she stared at Shannon. The excitement in her eyes wasn't good. "What brings you two all the way out here?"

"We're searching for something."

Her gaze snapped to Shannon. "You don't think you have it? Many think you do. 'Course Papa Ghede told me you thought you didn't. You want me to help you find it?"

Merck said, "I think we need to clarify what *it* refers to so we're all on the same page."

"Poseidon told Papa Ghede he's very angry. He don't like being angry with his son, ya know. But his son is helping the one who stole." Lola clucked and shook her head. She rubbed her hands together. "Maybe I call on Papa Legba and see if he has anything to tell you about the staff of Poseidon."

"Is he a more reliable spirit than Papa Ghede?" He distrusted all voodoo spirits. If they didn't receive the perfect offering and proper veneration they were apt to lie to the conjurer.

"I have a price for asking."

Of course she did. He gave her a *go-ahead-and-name-your-price* nod.

"I want the scrying glass that she tried to buy off Harnish."

"That's not really your style, Lola."

"It's what I decided this be worth."

"Don't make me have to hunt you."

A slow smile spread across her face. "Not your business what I do with it. If I use it, then we be seeing who's got better magic. If a friend uses it, I'll warn her you be vistin'." She crossed her arms. "It's the price."

He didn't want to give up the dangerous piece. Shannon chewed on her lower lip and looked at him with a mixture of hope and apprehension.

He wasn't going to win the argument of not giving it to Lola. If Shannon said please or shed a single tear, he'd do it.

Merck said, "Okay. You want it now or after?"

Lola waved her hand dismissively. "We'll get around to it."

She placed beans and rum in small dishes in the center of the table as offerings. Then, she began weaving from side to side, humming. Eventually, she broke into song:

"Legba, open the gates for me
So that I may go through.
Upon my return I shall greet the Iwa.
Voodoo Legba open the gate for me
So that I can come in.
Amen."

Lola seized a hobbled rooster off the floor and cut off its head with a dirty knife, draining its blood into a calabash bowl. The annoying humming she'd maintained throughout the rooster's death stopped.

Her eyes rolled upward until only the vein-ridden whites were visible. Trembling starting in her arms and overtook her body. Energy stirred in the small kitchen.

Lola's eyes popped open. Her dilated pupils obscured the pale irises making her eyes appear black. Her body shakes ceased. Silence descended with only the sound of their breathing in the room.

Her gnarled hand reached toward Shannon. "Let me see your hands, honey."

Shannon stared into the black eyes, mesmerized.

"No." Merck grabbed Shannon's hand as it reached toward Lola.

Shannon's gaze snapped to his, startled and apologetic.

"Lola, Legba, or whoever you may be right now, if you touch her, I'll cut off both your hands. If it's worth losing limbs and you hurt her, I'll ram this knife into your heart." Merck slammed his black-blade knife on the table. "Are we clear?"

"We's good." Lola smiled and folded her hands together on the table. She gazed sightlessly above their heads for several long seconds. Her eyes focused on Shannon. "You must survive to thrive."

Silence rested between the three of them for several dramatic seconds before she turned to Merck. "That you seek is not ahead of you but now."

With a headshake, Lola's head rolled forward onto her chest where it stayed. End of spirit possession. Show over.

All this for two bad lines he could've gotten out of a fortune cookie? What a buttload of worthless crap to have suffered the stench of this place and be cheated out of the scrying glass. Usually, Lola provided better information.

Moments later, Lola blinked. "You get what you needed to know?"

Merck pushed away from the table and grabbed Shannon's hand, encouraging her to stand. "Yep. As always, it's been an experience. I'll get the glass out of the car for you."

Merck pulled Shannon outside. Questions loomed in her gaze.

"Not now." He retrieved the scrying glass from his duffle bag, walked it up the steps and handed it to Lola.

Lola palmed the piece and laughed. "Nice doin' business with you. Stop by for tea again."

He paused on the lower step to face her. "Behave or I'll be back sooner than either of us would like."

"Of course, Mister Enforcer." She fake saluted him.

Shannon didn't unfold her arms until they were back on the washboard road. "What'd it mean?"

"No clue." *That you seek is not ahead of you but now.* Confirmation he had no future.

"I can't get it to make sense for anything to do with finding the Trident. And, I feel grimy."

"Sometimes Lola isn't helpful, like today. It's rare she has nothing to offer, but she's not a guaranteed answer. We need to go somewhere with lots of people right now. A tourist trap works best. I usually hit Seaside Papa's after a Lola visit."

"Why do we need a place like that?"

"We need somewhere friendly to erase the darkness voodoo leaves."

The restaurant's dirt lot had few spaces remaining, and that was with good parking technique. Tourists didn't excel at make it into the narrow spaces. The rectangular one-story building had retained its homey feel, which he enjoyed, even if it'd been overdecorated with crafty, country shit.

As they entered, the busty brunette hostess lit up. He stifled the *oh shit* on the tip of his tongue when the thirty-year-old with whom he'd spent a disappointing one-nighter a year ago scanned him from head to crotch. He'd forgotten she worked weekdays.

"Merck, how ya doing, sweetie? It's been a while." The hostess's eyes narrowed with promised payback for not calling or texting afterward.

"We're two for lunch, Mariah." He slung his arm around Shannon's waist and pulled her against him. Her head collided with his chest.

Shannon glanced up with wide eyes. He didn't know if her look was in reaction to Mariah's behavior or his. She rose onto tiptoe and pressed her soft lips against his. This was taking it farther than he expected, but it worked for him. Oh, Lord, it worked.

Curtail it or you'll end up getting kicked out for indecent exposure.

Shannon pulled away with a wicked smile that insinuated all kinds of badness.

He was hooked on Shannon. How he hated being a predictable part of the gods' plans. If everything continued to be as mind-boggling as it'd been so far every time they touched, then what the hell. He'd stay on the bus and see how far it went.

When he glanced back to Mariah, she'd turned several shades of scarlet. Guess she'd received the message he'd moved on.

"This way." Mariah led through the busy restaurant to a four-seater with a window view of the ocean. He moved around to get Shannon's chair for her.

As Mariah set a menu in front of Shannon, she whispered, "He might be pretty good in the sack, but he's not a stayer." Mariah cast Merck a saccharine sweet smile and left.

Shannon nibbled on her lower lip, but the twitch of a smile creased the corners of her mouth. She glanced up at him. His face heated.

"I never knew you were such a gentleman. Car doors and chairs. Of course, you are a ladies' man sometimes, aren't you?"

"My mamma would box my ears if I didn't hold a chair for a lady." The Southern charm came easily. The bitch who'd raised him might've resented him, but she'd instilled manners from the moment he could talk.

"You and Mariah, huh?"

He glanced toward the hostess station. Stepping into this conversation with Shannon was a bad idea.

He busied himself with the menu. They placed their orders.

"So, what do you think Lola's answer meant?" she asked.

"I don't know. I'm sorry I suggested her. Total waste of time."

"It's okay. Had to try something. Any other suggestions?"

As the waitress returned with their drinks she glanced up at the TV screen overhead. "That girl kind of looks like you. Bless her heart, I can't believe she was attacked on *Extreme Survivor*. I mean, she was just doing her job, and then someone on the staff went nuts on her with a knife. Weird that the couple who was also attacked on the show disappeared too." Her tone left the sentence open-ended, waiting for Shannon to comment.

He didn't miss the dread in Shannon's gaze when she glanced up at the flash of her image across the screen with the headline: *Mystery camerawoman disappears. New lead.*

"Maybe the show paid them to all disappear," Shannon offered.

"She was stabbed while working on the show." The waitress gazed at Shannon again. "You do really look like her. Are you...?"

"Do I look like someone who got stabbed on a reality show in the jungle?"

"Nah. I guess not. That poor woman." The waitress shook her head and wandered off.

He sipped tea and stared at the TV, which had now changed to a different news topic. "How exactly did you get hired to work on the show? Did they seek you out?"

"It was last minute. Jen got into her head she had to be on the show. We later found out she'd been hexed to do it, but we weren't sure who cast it. The producer, Rick, seemed focused on killing my mother and me as a way to wipe out our bloodline. He might've been involved with my brothers' deaths last year. He's the one who got me with the sword, which must've somehow transmitted the Trident's essence to me."

"What about Owen? Other than hosting the show how exactly was he involved?"

"Owen convinced Jen he would only date her if she went on the show. She was convinced he was her soul mate. Again, ridiculous, but when we have a chance to find our once-in-a-lifetime guy, we've gotta do whatever needs to be done. Jen was convinced. Later we realized it was because Owen gave her a hexed necklace. The good news is Jen's now husband agreed to be her fake boyfriend for the show and turned out to be the right guy for her. I don't know how Owen or Rick knew if they got Jen on the show that I'd try to get on as a cameraperson. In the end it seems Jen wasn't their primary target. It was my mother and me."

"They could've consulted with a fortune teller to find out how to get you on the show. I'm sure Owen knows a few."

"You mean someone with precognition?"

"Sure. You still think Owen Campbell is the key to understanding what's going on?"

She glanced at the TV, which now flashed sports scores while cradling her cheek in one hand. He noticed the delicate bones of her wrist—so fragile. She said, "He's the only lead I've got...the only person alive who played a part in me getting run through with a sword, but I agree that he's dangerous. He was involved in Jen's hex, but it's unclear if Owen cast it or his fiancée."

"The necromancer isn't dead."

"You don't know that."

"I don't believe she's dead. Confronting either of them is a bad idea. They may not know where you are, but once they do, they'll come after you if you're important to their plans."

"I'm not sure I have time for a wait-and-see approach."

"You don't need to find them. They'll find you."

"Within the next few days?"

"Probably."

"Sounds like a reunion. Can't wait." She pushed her silverware around. "Maybe Lola wasn't talking about me. Maybe she meant you."

Damn it, he thought so too.

Chapter Eleven

"The Enforcer? Is that what you're known by in the world of bad magic?" Shannon picked at the edge of the paper placemat.

"Yes."

"Why would Lola give information that had to do with you, and not me?"

Merck tented his hands on the table and gazed at them.

The voodoo ritual with the blood, the stench, and the dark energy had scared her until Merck threatened Lola with death. She didn't doubt he'd have killed Lola, if she crossed the line. Her heart shuddered all over again at the magnificence of protective Merck. Yet, something ate at this man. If she knew, maybe she could help. Whatever bothered him was a big enough issue for a spirit to comment on *it* rather than her being framed for stealing something from a god.

Merck glanced toward the kitchen. "Wonder where the food is."

She put her hand over his. "What's going on? Can I help you?"

He continued to watch the kitchen door as if he prayed for a food reprieve, but he didn't remove his hand from hers. "We never agreed to discuss me as a part of helping you."

"You're right. We didn't, but I'm worried about you."

His ended his vigil on the kitchen door. A myriad of emotions passed through his eyes.

"If you're not ready to talk about it, then that's okay. You're complicated. I get that." She squeezed his hand and let go.

"I have to walk my path alone. That's the way it is."

"You're not alone, at least not right now." She cracked a small smile.

Merck cleared his throat. He scratched his forehead and rubbed a thumb across one eyebrow. "You've been under a death sentence for what? A few weeks? My pink slip on life was handed to me eight years ago. The end for me is coming up real soon."

"What?" *Merck was going to die?* "No. No, no, no. You can't die." The permanent knot that had taken up residence in her gut the moment she learned of her own death date, tightened. To have known for years that life was limited must've devastated him.

His face softened. "I get what you're going through more than you can imagine. I lived through the fear, the anger, and the denial. I still have all three, but we can't outrun the gods' plans."

"Good Lord, you've known this for *years*?"

He looked haunted.

She hopped up, scooted around the table, and hugged him tight. His arms loosely looped her body, probably a reflex to the unsolicited hug.

"I'm so sorry. What I've been going through is awful, but for you... God, Jason...I mean Merck, I'm..." *Stop babbling*. She resumed her seat. A glance around showed she'd attracted more attention than intended, even though they were in a far corner.

They stared at each other in a silence filled with kindred understanding of the peculiar territory they tread, facing their own deaths.

He said, "You're handling it a lot better than me. I went a little crazy with drugs, drinking, and women for a long time thinking I'd enjoy life. I planned to go out on a high note or some such bullshit." He took a long sip of tea. "I didn't enjoy any of it, either during or after. So, if you decide your quest to find the Trident is futile and want to enjoy your last bit of time, then think hard on what's important."

"What'd you decide is important to you?"

"I want to leave the world a safer place because there won't be anyone left to do what I do when I'm gone, at least not until the next schmuck who gets this soul stuck into him. Might be fifteen or sixteen years before the next guy can handle all this. That's a hell of a lot of time without anyone to police the magical community of those who threaten people."

Oh, my. That broke her heart. All he had to live for was his job. No family. No love. She wanted to hug him all over again.

He ran a hand over his eyes. "Stop looking at me like I'm some sort of hero. I'm not. Never have been. Never will be. I do what I vowed I'd do. It's not fun, but it's my job." He threw a few bills on the table. "Let's get out of here. Neither of us is hungry."

She nodded and followed him outside. The ride back to her house was quiet. He parked and walked around to open her door.

An audience of six druids sat on the porch.

"Do you have anything else you could suggest I try to get information?" She fingered the wilted camellias, planning to get them in some water.

"I've got someone in Savannah I planned to chat with today about it. I can't take you with me this time, though." He reached around her to the glove box, opened it, and pulled out a business card. "If something else comes for you, call me. This has my cell phone number. In the meantime, stay with your protection."

Chapter Twelve

Shannon faked confidence as she walked to the porch, hyperaware of the druids staring her down. Her mother's words about these men echoed in her brain, "*They're woven into the fabric of our lives, dedicated to be Pleiades protectors. Yet they're not just guardians. They're people. Each and every stubborn butthead. Details, honey. Never forget the details.*"

She smiled at the men who would die for her in a heartbeat. Committed, trained, and compassionate. To deny them their job, even if they suffocated her with their *protection*, wasn't fair. She hugged the one closest. "God, I've missed you guys. We should've organized more get-togethers since Mom died. How's your wife?"

"She's good." The tall blond stepped away, but his eyes misted over.

Shannon forced a bright smile. "She must miss you. I'm sorry you have to be down here."

"It's what we do. You know I'd do anything for you ladies."

She gazed up at him, realizing she wasn't the only one grieving her mother's death. "I know. Thank you. All of you."

She greeted the others, asking about their lives, remembering how grounded each man was, how many birthdays they'd celebrated together, how many funerals, and all the weddings they'd attended. This was her family. This is what was important. She couldn't let them down by getting herself and all their other wards killed.

She glanced around at the guys smoking on the porch. "There's been a lot going on, a lot to figure out." She forced another brave smile. "Give me a few minutes to change and I'll whip us up some food."

Air-condition-cooled air bathed her body, raising goose bumps on her arms and legs at the stark change from humidity to dry air.

Her father was nowhere in sight. Right now, she didn't have the energy for a renewed fight about Merck. She hadn't fully processed everything that had to do with Merck for herself.

She needed time alone to get her thoughts organized on Merck.

There was no sense of calm as she ascended the curved staircase toward her room, past the familiar oil paintings. She moved fast. The thought of Eli or her father appearing drove her speed.

She sat hard on her mattress and stared sightlessly at the framed photo of her and the Quarter Horse she'd had years ago. The room needed upgrading. She'd grown out of four-poster beds and sparkly purple throw pillows long ago.

Her mind whirled. Merck wasn't all she thought about, but there was a lot of him in her head.

"*When everything is bad, it's time to cook. Pie helps everything.*" Her mother's words popped into her head. Maybe her mother's ghost was speaking to her, giving her nudges.

Pie. But Pie wasn't just pie. It was always cooked for someone. Merck. He deserved pie for everything he'd done to help her.

***

"Reevo's in town," Danny announced as Merck walked into the office. "He's keeping his distance, but I heard he's in Savannah recruiting."

Merck dropped the heavy tactical vest he'd slung over his shoulder to the floor and massaged his pounding temples. *Great. Another demented warlock to deal with before Friday.* "We'll be hearing about more dead people in the news if I don't get to him first."

"I guess he figured he'd join the party and wasn't too concerned about your threat to deep-six his ass the next time you saw him." Danny clicked through a few screens on his laptop. "There was another girl who washed up."

All the Pleiades goddesses were now dead. Not good.

Merck collapsed into a chair. "How're Chad and his daughter?"

"Fine. There's more bad news."

"Let's hear it." He grabbed a box of ammo off his desk, removed empty mags from his vest, and started loading.

"Owen Campbell boarded a private jet out of L.A. a few hours ago with an itinerary for Savannah. Maybe just coincidence, but I don't think so."

Merck paused, reloading for a moment, but then resumed.

Bad. But not unexpected. "Anaïs will be with him."

Danny leaned way back in his desk chair and covered his face with his hands. "Why is Armageddon kicking off right here?"

"I'm working on the answer to that. You're going to research something while I go deal with Reevo." *And talk to a Wiccan for Shannon.*

"Reevo isn't a do-it-yourself project. You almost lost your arm the last time you tangled with him. I'm going with you."

Merck shook his head.

"I can keep up with you. I know a lot of your tricks. I'm not scared of death."

"That's the problem. I need you to stay alive. When I die on Friday, you'll wait for me to get back the next time around. A favorable judgment from the gods isn't looking good, which means I'll be shuttled into a new body. Who knows how long it'll be before I remember any of this. Fifteen years? I hope I'll remember you and here. You'll need to help my juvenile future self."

"You're shitting me. You want me to sit here with my thumb up my ass until you're new body gets with the program?"

"Yes."

"The gods won't kill you. They can't. There's too much going on right now for you to suddenly disappear."

"I have no control over any of this and I hate it."

Danny resumed his gaze on his computer screen. "All of this has to do with Sleeping Beauty, doesn't it?"

"Pretty sure it does. I don't want you to worry about her right now. She's at her house. Safe with her people. I need you to find everything you can on Poseidon's Trident. I don't want the CliffsNotes from a high school Greek mythology textbook. I need the old stuff. The stuff translated off parchment. I need to know its powers. I particularly need to know who can touch it." Merck strode to the oversized Greek painting behind the desk and pulled it away from the wall to expose the safe. He keyed in the ten-digit code and removed a centuries-old text. "There should be something in this."

Danny flipped through the browned parchment pages. "It's in ancient handwritten Greek. This'll take me days to translate."

"You don't have days. You have twelve hours. I'm relying on all the time you spent with Rosetta Stone last year."

"That was Greek speaking, not reading. It's a different alphabet."

"I know."

"You can do this twenty times faster than me."

"I don't have time. I have to police deviant magical bastards." He grabbed his tactical vest off the floor and shoved the newly loaded mags into a pocket.

"I'm going with you. This ain't optional."

Merck appreciated the loyalty. Two was better than one, even if he would spend part of his time keeping Danny safe. "I prefer you here. I need you to work on this."

"I can translate in the car." Danny flashed his stubborn face.

"Fine. Let's go."

Danny researched online during the drive, occasionally spouting random unhelpful facts to point out the messed-up psychology of the Greek gods. "This is useless."

"The secrets that matter probably aren't online."

"Are you looking for something in particular?" Danny unwrapped a protein bar. "Want one?" he asked with a full mouth. "Got a new flavor yesterday. It's chocolate walnut."

Merck shook his head. The last time he'd tried one of Danny's bars he couldn't get its pasty taste out of his mouth for hours. If he chose to eat overprocessed carbs in a bar, he preferred a candy bar.

Merck parallel parked up the street from the only witch bar in Savannah. Even though it was early afternoon, it'd be busy. The bar specialized not only in booze and drugs, but also had a back room where one could purchase potions, ingredients, spells, and some totems. The items, although costly, weren't top quality or unique. It was the Target of the witch world, good for basics but not for high-end items.

He placed a few items from his tactical vest into the inner pockets of his leather coat. "What would be a better use of your time than be here is to go plant a bug in Owen's rental car."

"Great idea. I sent Chad a few hours ago. He thrives on pseudo-spy shit like that. He already texted me he hacked the rental car service to find out which car they're using, and it's done. He's going to hang around to be sure Owen doesn't upgrade his car choice."

"Great." It didn't come out enthusiastic.

"You're not getting rid of me that easily. Lead on, boss." Danny waved toward the club's entrance.

The bouncer's eyes widened as they approached. In a thick Southern accent, the meatloaf said, "Merck. Unusual for us to see you during daylight. We don't want no trouble, now do we?"

"I'm not here to create it, but to head it off. Your people don't want this one around."

"When you find whoever you're after, you do your business away from here. You make trouble in there, and I'll be forced to hurt you."

Merck shot him a *go-ahead-and-try-it* grin. The fear in the bouncer's eyes communicated he knew he couldn't take Merck, but it didn't stop the guy from posturing as if he could.

Merck pushed through the scuffed wooden door into the spacious multilevel club. It reeked of hookah smoke. He despised the flavored tobacco odor. It reminded him of his mom's parties with "friends" who usually ended up naked, but who should never be seen without apparel in public. Hip-hop music blasted from deep inside, from downstairs on the basement level. He glanced over the railing into the sea of grinding leather-clad bodies. The sensation of threat slid down his spine. He got an image in his head of Reevo lurking nearby. Guess he'd be spending his time in the bar with Reevo instead of getting answers for Shannon.

"He's here. You search the lower level," he told Danny. "Don't confront him if you find him. Text me."

"On it." Danny slipped away.

Merck ordered a gin and tonic at the bar and sipped, but didn't sit. At least the place served top-notch liquor.

A redhead slid onto the stool next to him. Her skimpy top barely covered her medically enhanced cleavage. An ultra miniskirt had ridden up her thighs when she sat, leaving nothing to the imagination. A slow tongue swipe across her puffy lips was more than blatant. Actually, the most apt description was *dirty*.

The redhead was a low-level, nonthreatening magic dabbler—a witch wannabe. Her eyelids drooped and lips pursed as her gaze dropped down his body. Maybe she was a professional. He wondered what it'd be like to pay for time with her.

Whoa. This is wrong. He couldn't believe he'd even entertained the notion of paying for sex or considered anything with this girl, especially when working. She was too young for him and probably had a master controlling her behavior.

He sniffed the air. Damn it, this wasn't just hookah smoke. It was an enticement spell, meant to induce him into something, probably her. He glanced to the other side of the bar and found its source. With a scowl directed at the female bartender, he flipped over the bowl housing the simmering brown contents.

The bartender shrugged, unapologetic. She provided what was paid for. An enticement spell this powerful wouldn't come cheap.

He turned fully to face the redhead, not missing the concealed, probably poisoned blade in her palm. He locked the girl's hand under his against the counter. "Where is he?"

The girl's lips compressed and her eyes darted toward the busy tables to his right. "I don't know who you're talking about."

"Reevo will kill you when he needs an easy death to power one of his spells. You're nothing special to him." He crushed her hand until she released the blade. It hit the floor.

The redhead's eyes widened. "Fuck you."

"Not interested." He slapped cash on the counter for his drink and pushed away from the bar. As he stalked toward the corner the redhead's gaze had traveled he noticed more than a handful of humans sat amongst the witchy clientele. Didn't they recognize the danger for wannabes? They ran the risk of being manipulated and used, possibly enslaved through enthrallment, or killed.

He passed sofas with writhing bodies and a few indiscreet wall grinders. As he neared the corner, a body shoved him from behind, pressing him against the wall with a knife at his throat.

"Merck. I'm so glad you're predictable," hissed a gritty male with a New Orleans Creole accent. To onlookers they were another couple getting it on. Evil poured off the warlock with the sulfur odor reminiscent of a decaying mudflat.

"We need to chat, Reevo."

"Not in the mood."

Merck knocked the knife out of his hand, elbowed him in the stomach, and whirled to jab the warlock in the throat. Reevo wheezed, shifted his balance, and lodged a blade deep into Merck's side. Reevo began muttering. Here came the spells.

Stupid of him not to check Reevo's other hand. The blade burned as if someone set his muscles on fire.

He plucked out the switchblade, which hurt worse coming out than going in.

With a knee-to-crotch crunch, he destabilized Reevo. Taking advantage, Merck forced him back against a wall with the same blade that'd hit him and pressed it tight to the warlock's jugular. The muttering continued. Merck pressed him backward until Reevo was against the wall.

"The spell won't work." Merck show-and-telled the Hexenspiegel hanging around his neck. The small, triangular mirror guaranteed whoever tried to cast a spell on him would only end up hurting himself when the spell was reflected back on the caster.

Reevo's muttering stopped. On the street most would pass by the average height, receding-hairline warlock without a second thought. Many might assume he was a twenty-something meth addict with his stringy hair and reddened eyes.

"Why are you here?" Merck demanded.

Reevo's eyes flashed the kind of nastiness that made killing assholes like him easy. They glared at each other for a few long, hostile seconds.

Finally, Reevo said, "My job is done."

Merck flinched at the guy's rancid breath. "What job?"

"To get rid of you." He leered yellowed teeth. His eyes darted downward.

"I'm immune to poisons."

"Not this one. It's going to drag your ass straight to hell." Reevo cackled. "They're coming for her and there's nothing you can do. Not now."

Reevo wiggled and popped a pill into his mouth. Dark foam formed on his smiling lips. Convulsions wracked his body. Within seconds Reevo slid to the floor. A pulse check confirmed he was dead. To be thorough Merck should incinerate the body, but he couldn't haul a dead man out the front door in the middle of the day without drawing attention.

To top it off, he'd left Shannon unmonitored to come down here, the pinnacle of stupid. Now he had to contend with whatever toxin had been on the knife. He'd been the victim of many poisons over the years. Although most concoctions hurt for a half hour or so, they never killed him. This was different. None before burned as if half of his body was under a blowtorch.

Deus Mortem poison? If it could kill a goddess, then he was toast. He needed the ocean.

His side felt sticky, but the small knife wouldn't have left a large wound. The bleeding would be over soon. His dark clothes hid the blood well.

Merck walked away from the body, snagging Danny's arm to propel him toward the exit. "He's gone."

"What do you mean gone? As in not here?"

"Don't speak," Merck ordered. "We're leaving."

Outside, Danny asked, "You okay? You're walking stiff."

"I'm fine." *Liar. One foot in front of the other. Make it to the car.*

Once they were in the car for several minutes, speeding home, Danny exploded, "What happened?"

"He's dead. Suicide."

"Why?"

"Distraction? Don't know for sure why he lured us here." Bit of a lie, but Merck didn't want to chitchat. He needed every bit of concentration to speed through traffic. He had to make it home and get to the ocean to heal. Then he'd check on Shannon.

That was too long. He should send her a note or a call or something to warn her to be on alert. Danny could go.

Muscles twitched up his injured side and scorched as the poison's sting spread. He compulsively swallowed to fight back nausea.

Thirty minutes into the drive he concluded this wasn't a typical poison. Given the fog clouding his mind by the time they hit the Port Royal city limit, if he didn't get to the ocean fast, the poison barreling through his body might succeed in killing him. He had to get home.

Danny asked, "You think someone went after Shannon while we were down here?"

"I hope not." Merck hadn't felt his phone vibrate with a call or text from her, not that she'd necessarily have time to send him a message, depending on what went after her. He worried, but had to trust her army of druids to do their job. Or she could pop away to her other dimension. "I'm going to drop you off at the office to start translating, but before you do that can you call Shannon's place? You can look up the number online. Call and make sure she's fine?"

"Why don't you drop by? You live next door and all?"

"I've got something to do. Gotta go."

As Danny hopped out at the office, he frowned. "You sure you're okay, man? You look off."

"Tired," he forced out.

Danny's forehead crinkled. "You wouldn't lie to me, would you?"

"I have something at home I've got to do. You call Shannon's place and then get to work. Call if you get anything good in translation." He put the SUV into gear before Danny had fully shut the passenger door.

By the time he pulled into his driveway, his vision blurred. His hands shook. Hell, his arms were trembling. He shut off the car and stumbled up the few stairs to the front door. His hands couldn't coordinate to fit the key into the front door lock. Finally, it opened. He dropped his keys and shuffled through the house, ping-ponging off furniture and walls on his way to the back door. A hundred or so feet into the backyard, and too far away from the dock to invite the water near him, his mind shuttered. Lightheaded, he wobbled. He wasn't going to make it.

Chapter Thirteen

"Can you give me a ride somewhere, Eli?" Shannon found him typing on his laptop on the sun porch. It seemed ages ago when he and her father had argued with her outside of Merck's car, but it'd only been this morning. Cooking helped her forget the stress, if only for a while.

Danny's check-up phone call, although seemingly sweet, set off warning bells. Something was up with Merck. It was odd he wouldn't call himself.

Eli's gaze shot up from his screen. His eyes narrowed, suspicious. "Where to?"

"Next door to see Merck." She held up the pie in her hands as if its existence answered all questions.

"To take him pie?" Eli's eyebrows slowly rose.

"He's had a rough few days and he did save my life twice. That deserves some pie."

"Pie..." Eli nodded and silently stood. He led her out of the house. As he started the car minutes later, he asked, "You okay?"

Her grip on the pie plate tightened. "I'm fine."

"You don't look fine." The concern in his gaze threatened the dam she'd erected while cooking, the one holding back her emotions. She kept a wall of confidence in place for fear of losing it in front of him or any of the other guys. She didn't know what she was doing taking Merck pie. She only knew something prodded her to go to him, pie or not. The impulse had intensified into a must-do over the past hour.

"Maybe I'm panicking a bit with the clock counting down. Merck is the only one who's offered sensible options to find answers."

Eli rubbed his chin. She should've made Eli pie too. For being here. For caring so much.

The trip around the corner was short. Eli cut the engine in front of Merck's house. She'd never been on this forbidden property. Never seen the house's lawn with its impeccably maintained landscaping down to the wisteria creeping up an ancient fence. The white clapboard house had been well maintained. It wasn't as large as the one on their property, but exuded Colonial-era charm. The raised foundation spoke of years of hurricanes and flooding that this structure had survived. Everything about it was beautiful, down to the black-shuttered windows. They were real shutters, which meant they functioned and weren't the decorative crap used on newer houses. The gardens, the landscaping, the house...all of it was the opposite of the hard edges of Merck.

The one time she'd ventured across the creek, they'd met by accident in the woods. But she'd never seen his house, which was well off the main road, like hers. He'd never had a birthday party. There'd never been neighborly borrowing. She'd never been allowed to trick-or-treat here.

"Thanks for driving me over. I'll be good from here." She reached for the door handle.

"How do you know he's home?" Eli gazed at the front door.

She pointed at the SUV. "That's his car. I texted him that I was coming over." She hadn't gotten a reply, but the presence of his car gave her confidence he was home. The nagging feeling she needed to be here pressed her with its urgency.

"Your father wouldn't want you here." Eli shifted to face her. "This goes against everything I am to drop you off and leave. How do I know you can trust this guy? Are you really *with* him? Is he your destined?"

"I don't know. I don't have answers. I only know what's real. Being here with him feels like where I should be. I jumped dimensions with him, which means something. We've known each other a long time. And I trust him."

"All right. Level with me. What is he? I don't mean what he is to you, but what type of magic does he have?"

Shannon slowly turned toward Eli. "I'm safe with him."

"That's not an answer. He's not druid. He's something else, isn't he? What?"

The stubbornness etched into Eli's face meant the easiest path was to answer. If she didn't, he'd accompany her inside, which was guaranteed to be awkward, or he'd drive her home.

She cleared her throat. "This is between you and me. No sharing, not even with Dad. Merck is half god. Poseidon's son."

"What?" Eli's eyes went wide. "First generation? A demigod?"

She nodded. "So, you can see his Poseidon connection makes him important in figuring out my dilemma."

"Uh-huh. What about the fact he's a witch hunter? Your father wouldn't stop reminding us after you left with Merck this morning."

"I'm sorry about how I handled this morning. Thank you for...well, you probably got him rational again. Merck fights evil beings who use magic and are a threat to humans. That's his job. It means he does technically hunt witches sometimes, but only the really bad ones. I don't know the extent of his abilities. What I do know is he's never hurt me."

"I can't let you go alone. You understand that, don't you?"

"Please, make an exception right now. I know this is hard for you." She squeezed his forearm. "I don't detect any evil auras here. The place feels protected. It's probably like ours and he's done some sort of spell or something on the property. I'll be okay. If there's trouble, I'll pop away. I promise. If I need you, I'll text or call, and you can arrive with guns blazing. It takes two minutes to get here, maybe less. I need to do this alone. He's our only hope."

"All right. I'm going to trust you. That doesn't mean I trust Merck, though. If your father asks, I won't lie to him about your whereabouts." Eli picked up his vibrating cell phone. "It's him. He wants a group meeting to discuss security protocols." He met her gaze. "Shannon, your father lost his wife. We all know Charlotte wasn't only his wife. He might've fought tooth and nail with her, but he loved her to the depth of his soul. There'll be no replacing her for him. She ran his house. She ruled all of us and led all the other Pleiades ladies. He almost lost you as well on the day his wife died and he still might. His sons are dead. The man is unreasonable right now. I'm trying to stay neutral, but I think he shouldn't be involved in you figuring out what's going on with the Trident."

"I agree, but he is...well, he's Dad. If it was my daughter doing crazy stuff, I'd probably be a bit over the top too."

"The pie you left in the kitchen will only buy you so much time." He smiled weakly. "I'd say you've got a couple of hours, but you need to be visible by dinner."

"How'd you know I was distracting him with pie?"

"I'm not stupid. Your mom only brought out pie when she wanted something. I went along because, God knows, whenever any of you make pie, it's not to be turned down. Trust me, your dad isn't stupid either."

"Thank you." She squeezed his hand and made a mental note to bake him a pie. With a hop, she left the shelter of his truck and navigated the brick walkway to the front door. She balanced the pie plate in one hand to ring the bell. Nothing. Eli, who was still waiting, looked indecisive on leaving.

She reached for the knob. Door open. Not a good sign unless Merck had some precognition ability and anticipated her here.

With a last wave, she went inside. Eli's truck rumbled down the driveway.

Something wasn't right. A person like Merck didn't leave the front door unlocked. He seemed like the kind of guy who believed in safety and security. No alarm went off as she entered. A glance to the alarm control box on the wall in the hallway by the door indicated it to be inactive.

She'd told Eli she didn't detect evil auras. That much was true. But she also didn't feel Merck's aura as strong as it usually was. She peeked through the window beside the door to see Eli drive away. Maybe she should've asked him to stay.

Her feet caught on a set of keys on the floor.

"Jason...Merck?" she called out as she slid the pie onto the kitchen counter.

No reply.

The back door, which exited the kitchen, hung open. Spots dotted the floor. Dark-red spots similar to dried blood. In a tearing rush she raced outside and burst into the wide-open space of his backyard.

Oh no. He lay sprawled, facedown, on the lawn. One of his arms stretched in front of him as if trying to get to the water, which was too far away.

"Merck," she moaned. Nothing emanated from his aura, which could mean he was passed out or dead.

She knelt next to him and pressed two fingers into the side of his neck, not feeling anything. Then she saw his chest move. *Thank you, thank you.*

"I'm here." With a lot of tugging she rolled him onto his back. A dark stain saturated his stomach. She shook him. "Wake up."

A few shakes later, he still didn't stir.

The water slapped against a small dock hundreds of yards away as if angry. She couldn't drag him that far. Even if she did get him close, his healing power might not work if he was unconscious. Using her ability to move water to him seemed impossible. It was too far.

"You're not allowed to die, Jason Merck. I need you here." He looked vulnerable, not the imposing man who'd threatened Lola. Her heart clenched so hard she experienced physical pain. She rubbed her chest.

Lifting the hem of his shirt and peeling it away from areas where it stuck to his skin revealed a blackened area on his stomach. The discoloration emitted a dark energy as if it, itself, was a living evil. Poison? Magic, most definitely.

Even passed out his face didn't look peaceful. She wished she could reach him and find out what he fought in his mind. Whatever internal battle he waged might not be pain free.

"I don't know what to do." She breathed hard as she glanced around. Her gut knotted into lumps. Should she call 911? They wouldn't know how to deal with this. Maybe Eli? She could beg Eli to use his magical healing skills on Merck. Instinct dictated Eli couldn't resolve the evil of this particular poison. Something that knocked out a demigod had to be supremely powerful and dangerous.

"You can heal the man destined to be your soul mate." Another of her mother's lectures to prepare her for a life as a Pleiades blasted through her mind. Could this man be *the one* for her?

She yanked out her cell phone and called Jen. When Jen answered on the second ring, Shannon rushed to say, "Oh, God, Jen. It's a crisis again. I'm sorry to only call you when it's bad."

"Just lay it on me. It's why I have a cell phone."

"I saw you do that healing thing on Nikolai when he was almost dead. You did something to bring him back from the brink. I need to know how you did it."

"What? Whoa, back up. First, you think you found your soul mate? The Merck guy? Second, he's dying?"

"Maybe."

"Maybe what? You found your guy or he's dying?"

"Both, maybe."

"The full-body healing only works on your Gods'-chosen, meant-to-be forever man. No one else."

"Did you know for absolute sure your now husband was it when you tried to heal him the first time?" This was wasting time she didn't have. She needed information fast.

"No. I had a strong gut feeling about Nikolai, but you're right. I didn't know for sure. Guess you won't know until you try. Then you get to live with the freak out of knowing for sure he's probably your it if the healing does work. On the other hand, if it doesn't work and he dies, then you know he wasn't."

"Merck's down, unconscious, by what I think is some sort of magical poison. What do I do, Jen?" Panic clawed her throat, threatening a monster explosion.

"You've got to try it on him."

"How?"

"This is a *you-must-believe* moment. Ask the Goddess to help you. When I say goddess, I mean you think about your descendant goddess. Then you make circular motions over him. When the power revs in you, give in to it. Let it work through you."

"That's it?"

"It's all I can say to describe what it felt like. Let your heart guide you. It knows what to do"

"That's it?"

No answer. The call had been dropped. She didn't have time to waste calling back.

Let the power rev? Let her heart guide her? She stroked hair back away from his forehead, not that she needed to since it was so short. The act calmed her. She was linked to this man. She didn't have answers on why or how. She barely knew him or at least who he'd become. Yet all those years since she last saw him, living so far away, she'd never really looked for anything special from a relationship. Maybe she wasn't so different from him. Both of them bounced from one person to the next. That didn't mean they were meant for each other, nor that he'd been waiting for her or she him. Their lives intersecting now was too coincidental.

He was her it. That she believed. She had to save him.

"Pleiades goddess, help me. I don't understand any of this, but help me. Please don't let him die. Not now or in a few days." She closed her eyes and made circles over his chest, feeling silly but wanting to do this the right way. Warmth tingled inside her and spread outward, down her arms. Energized. Electric. Good Lord was it draining.

She kept moving her arms until it'd been several minutes and she was so exhausted from the energy depletion that she the circular motion felt like she was pushing them through drying cement.

With a final silent plea to the goddesses, she rested her head on his chest. "Come back to me, Merck."

***

Merck faded in and out for a while until he realized he still lay in the backyard. He blinked up at the orange-hued sky. Sunset. Near eight-thirtyish. A few pelicans flew overhead. Egrets squawked from the marshes. Waves beat against the dock in a steady rhythm, assuring him all was calm. The ocean called to him as it always did, but this time she wasn't screaming for his help to fix something hidden in its depths. It communicated reassurance and a plea for him to recover.

He wasn't dead. His side no longer hurt. The whacky, horror-filled dreams were gone. But he was so weak, he could barely move.

Pressure compressed his stomach as if something lay on top of him. A body?

He looked down his front.

Shannon. Not moving.

She couldn't be dead on top of him. His breaths came labored until his brain registered the soft movement of her chest. Up and down. Regular. Consistent.

Her face looked peaceful, not pained. Had she done something to him? Something to save him?

He lifted a shaking hand to touch her golden hair. She was so beautiful with her flawless skin, now pale from too long spent up north and indoors. She would tan if she spent more time in the sun.

He used his index finger to trace her nose. He liked its slight sloping and how it crinkled at the top when she concentrated. Too tired to speak, he thought to her, even though she couldn't hear. *"You must survive. I can't imagine a world without you in it."*

Her shampoo smelled good. It reminded him of fresh and clean, and all that was good.

There were so many things he should've said to her before now. He'd run from their connection, even though he'd recognized it as something unique. Staying away from her hadn't been entirely about his worry of the Enforcer job spilling into her life, although he'd tried to convince himself of this over the years. It hadn't been about her father intimidating him. His reaction to her panicked him. It still did.

He'd faced off with the scariest of the scary without a second thought. Yet, this woman terrified him. The moment his lips touched hers each time he was sucked into a haze of longing and sexual need so intense he forgot everything but her. It'd blown his mind the first time and again the second time. The details of their long-ago moment that led to him pressed tight against her with her back against a tree were hazy. What he recalled was fear she held the power to control him and to hurt him. Losing the upper hand was against his mantra.

He didn't need a shrink to untangle the web of why he needed control. He'd been smacked around by his "mother" and her friends when little until he got old enough to punch back. He'd been forced to do things he didn't want to remember.

Their first kiss when he'd lost his mind, she never tried to manipulate him to the degree he worried. Sure, she'd used his weakness to get away from him yesterday, but not to hurt him or coerce him into doing something ugly.

So much time wasted. Now they had no time left. Although she'd stopped his immediate death today, she didn't have the power to change the gods' minds.

Her eyes blinked open and met his. "Hi."

"Hey," he croaked out. He wanted answers, such as why she was here and how she ended up on top of him, but right now in the wake of his relief that both of them were alive, all he had the energy to do was to sling an arm around her waist and close his eyes. She didn't complain, but burrowed into him. With the Armageddon shitstorm descending on them and their death countdown clocks ticking away, he should get in motion. He should ask questions and figure out the mysteries.

What mattered was her here. Them together was the only right now he wanted. The concerns pressing on his mind faded away as he relaxed.

Later when he opened his eyes, it was dark. "We should go inside."

"Hmm?" She punctuated her drowsy question with a stretch.

He smiled. "We should go in."

"Yeah." She pushed off his chest to sit up, but the movement was gentle. Her gaze in the moonlight was filled with worry when it found his. "You think you can make it inside?"

"I'm fine." He sat up, instantly dizzy. Maybe not as fine as he thought. His back ached, but it was more of a complaint from lying so long in one position with her on top of him. Even though the stab wound might be improved, possibly gone, he was nowhere near ready to jump up for a ten-mile run. Hell, he wasn't sure he'd make the walk into the house.

He managed a kneel and staggered to a stand. She grabbed his biceps to help him balance as best she could considering she was so much smaller than him.

"Easy there." She slung an arm around his waist. "Lean on me."

Their progress inside was slow. He almost nose-dived on the six steps into the house, but she caught him.

"The den is good." He chin-pointed to the sofa. Their progress to the sofa was slow. When within hopping distance, he angled to land on the soft surface, ending up in an inelegant sit-sprawl.

Head spinning. Stomach rolling. Yep, he wasn't moving from right here with a plan to remain still.

"Hold on." She walked out of the room.

The sound of her walking though his house made him realize how empty it normally was—and also how quiet. Usually there was only the sound of the waves lulling him or calling to him from a distance. There wasn't any street noise in this rural part of Port Royal. No late-night traffic, no sirens, and no neighbors too close.

He liked his solitude, but liked it even better with her here.

She returned with the pillow and comforter off his bed. She patted the pillow. "Lie down."

No argument from him, not with his brain hazing in and out. He lay back and stared at the ceiling. The room still spun. With his eyelids shut, he focused on deep breaths.

Her shampoo teased him as she leaned in and placed the comforter over him. "It's cold in here. Do you keep it set at sixty-five or something?"

"Need it cold to sleep."

"Naturally hot-blooded. Got it." Her fingers touched his forehead. "You're burning up." She pulled up his shirt. "The skin looks better, though. The black-and-purple parts are gone." He thought he detected a bit of awe in her tone, but was too tired to open his eyes and interpret her expression to figure out the nuance behind her words. Also too whacked to see how good the stab wound looked, although he was curious.

Her fingers drifted over the area he'd been knifed. He expected pain but felt only the softness of her touch.

Her voice came out as a whisper when she asked, "Who stabbed you?"

"Poisoned blade...warlock."

"Lucky I found you, then. Do you need anything right now? Water or something else to drink?"

"Orange juice." It came out slurred and sounded more like *orig ju*.

She disappeared again. Questions over what she'd done to him needed asking, but they blurred together. He'd been on his way to meet Uncle Hades two days early. Maybe she wasn't the source of his incredible recovery. Maybe his body had done some sort of miracle healing. Maybe Hades had denied him entry into hell. Gut instinct said it'd been her. On the upside, he might be weak as shit now, but he still breathed. A bit of sleep and he'd be recovered soon.

She returned with a tall glass of juice and sat next to him on the sofa, her hip pressing into his side. "Should I call someone for you? Danny or Chad? I can run you to the hospital or something if you want."

"No. No need to concern them or anyone else. I'll get through this." He pushed up to a sit, ignoring the mental whirlybird, and rubbed a hand over his eyes in a futile attempt to dull the burgeoning headache.

Her face pinched with worry.

"I'm okay. Really." He managed a smile he was sure looked pathetic. He took the juice and drank. His stomach might not be ready for it, but he needed the hydration and the sugar.

"If you say so." She chewed on her lip. "I've got to go home, at least for a bit. I haven't chitchatted with my father yet. But maybe I should stay. I don't think you should be alone right now."

"I'll be fine." He put the empty glass on the end table and laced his fingers through hers. With a gentle pull he brought her close. The smell of those golden strands was pure, clean heaven. "Thank you."

She leaned away and met his gaze.

"Go home. Don't want the old man getting bent out of shape with you gone. Don't worry. I'm just going to sleep this off." He tried to infuse flippancy in his tone like this happened all the time. An injury this severe was a first.

"Okay." The worry didn't leave her eyes. "I'll come back when you're feeling better."

She leaned in and planted a light kiss on his lips. While her mouth lingered there, her hand touched his jaw. "Take care, Jason. You sure you don't need anything?"

He nodded, forcing out a strained smile. "Thanks. Please, turn out the light in here as you go."

Her footsteps echoed in the hall toward the front door. A part of him wanted to call her back. Her presence soothed him, but her leaving was a good thing. He couldn't watch over her like she needed while weak as shit.

The last thing he heard before he gave in to the darkness pressing on his brain was the open and shut of the front door.

Chapter Fourteen

Shannon hadn't left. She should've, but he didn't have anyone she could call. No one should be alone when like this.

Facing her father needed to happen. She was a coward when it came to her dad. She didn't want to hurt him or see him disappointed in her.

Her phone buzzed against her hip. She slid it out of her skirt pocket. Dad had texted twice. Eli once. Jen three times. All messages were versions of *Where are you?* That was a whole lot of it-can-wait. She slipped the phone back in her pocket and tiptoed back to Merck. For a long time she stood outside the entry of the den, listening for noise to determine if he was sleeping.

She didn't want to intrude, especially if he wanted to be alone. A triangle of moonlight spilled across him in the dark room. Merck was lying on his side, breathing deep. He hadn't moved much from when she'd left several minutes or more ago. A small snore came out every third breath.

Seeing Merck like this—vulnerable and passed out—was much harder, even stranger, than she could've imagined. She hadn't known his hardened, grownup persona long, but he still seemed the strong and confident guy she remembered. She moved toward him, drawn as if an invisible magnet drew them together. The comforter had gotten tangled in his legs to the point it'd pulled off his upper body. Untangling wasn't worth the risk of waking him up. The cushy chair across from him encouraged a lazy curl while she watched him.

Her phone buzzed again. Another text, this time from Jen: *Your father called. Didn't tell him anything. He's P.O.'d.*

New text from her father: *Let me know you're ok.*

The one from Dad meant he'd entered resignation she wasn't coming home tonight. The guilt piled on that she'd made all of them worry. She texted both, but not as a group message: *I'm fine. Back soon.*

She scanned through Facebook and news feeds. Nothing interesting had been missed in the world. She clicked off the dopamine-addictive screen and dozed. Something woke her up. A click of her phone said it'd been roughly three hours. She glanced around, wondering what had disturbed her.

Merck wasn't on the sofa anymore. Where'd he gone? The hall light clicked on. He padded back into the den, his shoes now gone.

"You okay?" he asked. All wobbliness seemed resolved. He looked good. Better than good, to the point of energetic. His T-shirt showed off the tattoos she hadn't taken time before to really notice. They went all the way up to the short sleeves and didn't end. Gosh, that was sexy.

She nodded. "You?"

"I'm good." He ran a hand over his hair. "Embarrassed."

"No need. It's okay."

He shook his head. "Shouldn't have happened to begin with. Why're you here? Didn't you have to talk with your father?"

"I didn't want to leave you alone."

He shifted on his feet. "Well, thanks I guess."

Okay, now she felt awkward. She stood and grabbed her cell phone off the armrest of the chair. "I guess I can go now since you're looking better."

He caught her in his arms as she passed him, pulled her against him, and lowered his lips to hers. Tangling his fingers in her hair, he locked her to him and cupped the back of her head. He tasted so good.

Her body melted into him, and her arms twined around his neck. She loved the inherent strength in his arms, his shoulders, and even his stance. Everything radiated power.

He grumbled, "I don't want to stop this time."

"Then don't."

***

He wouldn't. Old vows be damned. No more excuses. Years of fantasy what-ifs involving her and his current wants collided. *Boom.*

"Know what I'm thinking?" His voice came out hoarse.

She shook her head. "Does it involve a bed?"

"A shower." No way was he taking this anywhere while covered in blood with the stench of Reevo's poison still swirling in his nostrils.

"Okay," she whispered. Her phone buzzed. And buzzed again. She pulled it from a pocket at the side of her sexy sundress, typed a quick reply and clicked it off. "My people are worried and persistent."

He took her hand and led her through the master bedroom to the adjoining bathroom. The sunken tub beckoned, but he didn't have the patience to wait for it to fill. Maybe later.

He flipped on the shower and stripped off his shirt. A glance down found a lot of crusted blood on his lower abdomen. The knife's entry point, now closed and healed, didn't have residual bruising. None of the expected blackened skin from poison. Not even a scar. He was okay with whatever she'd done, but that didn't eliminate his need to get questions answered. When there was magic involved, he needed to know exactly what transpired.

His gaze met hers.

She blushed and chewed on her lower lip. Her wide eyes reflected worry.

"Thanks for whatever you did." He waved at his side.

She glanced away. "You looked pretty bad when I found you. I wasn't sure you'd make it." Back to lip chewing. Whatever happened had shaken her and she wasn't ready to hand out details.

Questions could wait. He stepped to her, trailing a finger down her quivering body. "You planning to take this off?"

"I might shower in it." She didn't break eye contact. Her lips twitched into a small smile.

He hooked the hem of her dress. "Probably not a good idea. It looks like a fabric that might not be forgiving of water. Your phone wouldn't like it either." He set her phone on the counter. Slowly he raised the dress's hem higher and higher. She sucked in a breath when his fingers tickled her belly. "You sure you want to do this?"

"Yes."

A thought flickered through his mind, not a reason to say no, but it might cause him to change his approach. "You're not...this isn't your first time, is it?"

She shook her head. "I've imagined this for a long time."

"You imagined us before our kiss in the woods?"

"Way before then. A lot more after." She leaned in and touched her lips to his, at first gentle and then aggressive, pressing her tongue between his parted lips to tangle with his. She pulled back. "I'm ready to experience reality."

"Me too," he breathed out. "I never understood this with you. There's always been something here."

She touched his face. "I think I fell for you a bit the first time we met."

"At the bus stop?"

She nodded.

Same for him. When he first saw her sauntering up the road, it'd been a gut punch. There'd been sexual appreciation for a pretty girl, but also fascination and a hell of a lot of *can't-go-there*. The highlight of each miserable day in high school had been those ten minutes with her

before the bus arrived in the morning. He got there twenty minutes before the bus came just in case she showed up early.

He pulled the dress over her arms. She kicked off the sexy, heeled
sandals. Now only her panties and a lacy bra remained. His gaze
skimmed over the mysterious scar on her body. Dread filled her eyes.

"If I could figure out how to get rid of it, I would. I can cover it up
with a bandage or something."

He touched her cheek, letting his hand slide to the back of her
neck. "We're going to figure it out before time's up. I promise. I don't
find you any less beautiful."

She stepped to him and rested her palm on his stomach. "You sure
you're okay? You're recovered enough and not in pain?"

He was hurting. Big time. But not from getting stabbed. This was
the good kind of hurt. The kind that wrapped anticipation, hope, and
a huge amount of ready to go in one painful package. He managed to
give her an *I'm okay* nod.

She reached for the fastening of his pants and flipped the fly's buttons with a smile.

"Uhh...I'm not wearing anything under there." It was one thing to
borrow Brian Randolph's clothes in another dimension, but quite another to borrow underwear. He also never gave much of a damn for un-
derclothes.

Her eyes drooped to half-mast. "That's all right with me."

He kicked his head back and groaned when her fingers surrounded
his erection. His fingers tightened around her waist.

She released him to skim his waistband. He brushed her hand out
of the way and shoved the jeans down.

Her laugh drew his gaze. "Guess we've both been waiting too long
for this."

He unhooked her bra, pulled down her panties, and crowded her
into the shower.

She jumped when the spray hit her. "Hot."

He switched places, taking most of the spray to shield her. Its heat barely registered to him. He smiled.

"What?" she asked.

"I wanted to kill every single bastard you dated in high school."

"I didn't go on many dates, so your list of potential victims must've been short. I didn't even make out with any of them. Okay, that's a lie. There was the tennis team captain. I kissed him."

"I'll punch him the next time I meet him. He works over at Home Depot in the plumbing department."

"The guy kissed like a drooly dog. It wasn't a very good first-kiss experience." She gazed up and touched his cheek to trace the scars. "My second kiss experience was a lot better." She touched his lips with her index finger. "I hated every girl who bragged about sleeping with you."

"I got around back then. Not denying it. You were too young for someone like me. I knew better than to fantasize about you. I knew better than to give in to fantasy and kiss you." He leaned down, gently kissed her lips, and then moved down to kiss one nipple. "Didn't stop me from doing either anyway. You used to wear a tight green sweater that showed off your nipples. I dreamed of yanking up the sweater and burying my head between your breasts." He nuzzled his nose into the space between her breasts.

She giggled.

"You think I was dirty minded?" he asked.

"Yes."

"You like it."

"Every girl wants to be the star of a fantasy at least once."

"You starred in far more than one. But I swore years ago I wouldn't touch you. I don't break swears on a whim."

"Why when you seemed to make it into every other girl's bed?"

"You're different, and not just because of what you are." She crossed her arms.

"Different as in weird? As in not someone you wanted to take to bed?"

He traced the line of her neck to her collarbone. "There's no girl I wanted naked in bed more than you."

"Then, why not?"

He uncrossed her arms gently and kissed down her neck. "Your brothers would've killed me."

"So this is about the coast being clear now that they're not here to defend my honor?"

"They never scared me."

"You didn't want me enough to go up against them?"

He crowded her against the wall of the shower so she'd have no doubt how much he wanted her right now. "I always wanted you. Always. In high school the mere thought of you in that green sweater would get me so hard it hurt. I could've made a call and had a girl ease it off, but I never did. I'd jack off to the thought of you because all I wanted was Shannon Randolph. I couldn't make it reality, though. My life had become about being the Enforcer. I didn't want you exposed to that. I wasn't what you needed. I still don't think I am."

He wasn't convinced she truly understood that him taking this step with her wasn't casual for him. "When I ran into you on my side of the creek...What the hell made you cross?"

"I *wanted* to run into you. I hadn't seen you in months."

"Got a bit more than you bargained for back then, didn't you?"

Her eyelids dropped to half-mast. "Not nearly enough."

"You weren't ready for what I wanted to do to you. Hell, I wasn't ready for it. But it made me want to try. That was the only time I considered dating."

"Dad scared you off."

"It wasn't him. I let him intimidate me because you scared the hell out of me."

"Me?" Her pink tongued darted out and licked water off her lips.

"You make me lose control." He kissed her again. "I'm going to do it all to you. Shower first, though." He squeezed body wash into his hands and soaped her upper body, his hands lingering on her breasts.

She grabbed the bottle from him and returned the favor, needing to scrub in order to get off all the blood. She took her time tracing the contours of his hard stomach and chest. Her touch made him itch to punch the gas on this.

As she caressed the area where there'd been blood on his stomach, she asked, "Does this happen to you often? You get hurt to the point you almost die?" She touched the scar on his face again.

"Sometimes. Usually, I can make it to the ocean in time. The war-lock today was a top-tier nasty. He was good, but not good enough."

"Was. As in he's dead? Was he here for the Trident?"

"Probably." He didn't want to think about Reevo right now, not when he finally had Shannon naked in his shower. His fingers tangled in her soft, wet hair. He leaned forward and kissed his way down her neck and chest to a nipple, drawing the pebbled peak in to gently suck on it. She grabbed his arms to steady herself.

"What do they think I can do to get the Trident when I don't even know where it is or what I can do to find it?"

"You're so beautiful," he murmured. "More than I ever imagined."

"Stop trying to deflect from the question. You probably know more about it than anyone else on the planet other than your *father*."

"Is the distraction working?" His fingers skimmed down her body, measuring each curve and contour.

Her head fell back against the shower's glass wall on a moan. "Mmm. Yeah, it's working."

"We'll figure it out. Later." He left her nipple to move down, paus-ing at her belly button just south of the scar, and continued to trek low-er. He needed to taste her so badly. He dropped to his knees, never halt-ing the kissing. His fingers teased over the soft folds between her legs, exploring. So wet for him. She spread her legs, giving him more access.

Gently, he eased a finger inside her. So tight. Her internal muscles quivered. She jerked when he touched his tongue to her. Every time she clenched around his finger, he moaned, needing to be there and feel her squeeze around him.

He swirled his finger inside her. She bucked against him.

She rasped out, "I might fall down if you keep doing this. Lying down might be safer."

***

Laughing, he picked her up in his arms and lifted her out of the shower.

Toweling off took seconds. He leaned in and caught her lips, his touch too fleeting.

She gazed at his bed outside the bathroom door—it was large, unmade, and offered a surface that guaranteed she wouldn't fall over.

He smiled wickedly and lifted her, carrying her out of the bedroom. "Not the bed."

She landed on a den sofa. Doable. What was she thinking? She didn't care where. Only that he didn't stop this time.

He settled his head between her legs, throwing a leg over each of his shoulders. His gaze was all about this being his way. The controlling part of her rebelled. She squirmed.

He locked both hands on her hips. Long, broad strokes of his tongue paralyzed her with pleasure. Over and over he stroked until her body arched up to meet him. He kept one hand on a hip and the other caressed her breast. Without warning he squeezed her nipple in sync with sucking. Sensation rippled between the two sensitive areas.

"Oh God, Merck..."

Her brain fought his mastery, but the demands of her body won as sensation overwhelmed her. She met his gaze.

His smile... Holy hell, his smile. Slow and lazy but with an edge. The tension in his eyes made the lazy part a lie. Right now, she wasn't okay with him in the director's chair.

She raked her hands down his neck to his strong shoulders, both tattooed with symbols she didn't recognize. Not pictures, only symbols that were almost stylized lettering. "Don't make me wait. I want you in me when we come the first time. Please."

He stood, lifted her, and sat on the sofa. He leaned in and took her mouth again while positioning her over him. He let her get her knees settled on either side of his thighs. His mouth opened as if to give another command, but she moved first, more than ready and wanting to take the power back into her court. She took all of him as she dropped onto his lap, which was a lot at once. Stretched. Filled. She didn't want to move, perhaps never, for the pleasure of having him there was so great.

His head fell back, exposing his strong neck. She leaned in and kissed him again, playing war with his tongue as he lifted her for a deep thrust. She forgot everything while he led a steady rhythm.

She loved how neither of them tried to hide their want of this. There was no more power play. Just driving thrusts.

"Shannon," he rasped against her.

"What?" she mumbled incoherently, barely able to formulate the word when her world was coming apart.

"Tell me you feel it."

"Feel what?"

"This...between us."

She could only nod. How could he be so obviously in control when she was shivering at the edge and straining to go over?

"This can be more. Do you trust me?"

She nodded again, unsure if he was talking about the moment or longer term. Her brain couldn't function beyond the excruciating rhythm he'd created.

He left her. She moaned denial as he rotated to put her head on the sofa's edge, draped one leg over the back of the sofa and the other on the floor. Open wide. The cool air hit her heated skin but didn't freeze the need for more from him, which burned her from the inside out. God, she was so vulnerable in this position. All worries vanished under the gaze of his unguarded desire. No man had ever looked at her like this. Like his life started and ended here.

He grinned and put on a condom he took out of his wallet. "I gotcha, darlin'. I'm far from done."

He lifted her pelvis, shoving a pillow beneath her, and entered her deep, hitting a spot that sent her mind flying.

"Shh," he crooned. "You will hold on. Feel it. Feel us."

The relentless need for release throbbed within her, but somehow her body waited. Even though she fought to reach the endpoint herself, pressing against him each time he went deep, she couldn't get there as if waiting. For what? His command? His permission? It drew her higher and higher until her mind spun from desperation.

"Now tell me you feel it." His strained plea gave way to a cry and shudder that shook his entire body.

"I feel it. Just...oh God, please," she pleaded.

"This is us."

Pleasure mixed with the unbearable need to reach that denied pinnacle. Her fingernails dug into his lower back as she gripped clumsily and arched under him. "Merck!"

He claimed her mouth right before she could start begging. The pain and pleasure...

"Let go." He continued to thrust relentlessly, drawing both of them into a screaming, clenching release.

Shannon rode it, clinging to him until her trembling subsided. She wrapped her arms around his body and hid her face in his sweaty neck. A lot of his weight rested on her, but she didn't care.

"I'm going to crush you," he murmured.

"No." Her arms tightened. "I like this."

He chuckled against her ear and rolled to the side, still holding her.

Chapter Fifteen

Time passed while she floated. Giving up control had been ah-maazing.

Eventually, she had the energy to say, "I brought pie."

"What?"

"Pie."

"What kind of pie?"

She rolled to face him. "I made peach pie."

"What possessed you to make pie?"

She smiled and touched his cheek. "Sometimes you just need pie."

"Then let's try this pie. I'm a connoisseur of pies, you know."

She sat up, suddenly self-conscious to be naked. He got off the sofa and stalked into his bedroom, returning with his jeans on, and threw her a T-shirt. It covered her all the way down to just above her knees.

He wrapped an arm around her waist to pull her close. "I'd say clothes aren't necessary because I enjoy you without them, but I couldn't give your pie its due if you were naked."

"I'll have to remember that for the future when I need you distracted."

"Only if you want me inside you in the kitchen."

"Or wherever." She bit her lip against laughing when his breath caught. He liked the "or wherever" offer.

"You're a dangerous witch."

"Can be." She sauntered into his kitchen. "Plates?"

He removed two from a cabinet while she found a knife and two forks. She served him a generous piece. Both selected a barstool next to the counter.

He held up a large bite. "The moment of truth."

She gave him a go-ahead nod while she nibbled on her piece. It was good, but she'd known it'd be good. Pie from a witch, especially one of the Pleiades ladies, was baked with... Her sight misted as she remembered her mother's words every time she made pies. "*Made of love, spice, and a little bit of something extra.*" No magic. Just love. She blinked away the moisture, hoping Merck hadn't noticed.

"Mmm," he murmured as he took a second bite.

"How's it rate, Mr. Pie Expert?"

"It's pretty good."

No oohing or aahing?

"Pretty good? That's the most delicious pie you've ever tasted. Admit it."

He took another bite without replying. And another, until he'd finished the entire piece. With a serious face he asked, "You actually baked this? Alone?"

"Yes. I like to bake pie. I can also cook other things. The kitchen and I get along quite well, and I was taught by a Southern cook master. My mom." She bit back a sarcastic remark at his lack of appreciation. Insecurity lodged itself in her mind. Had she messed it up? It tasted right to her.

"You didn't put any sort of potion into it or weave a spell over it?"

"No, I didn't cast a spell. If I tried to mix up a potion, it would probably kill you since I suck at mixing them. My best friend is an expert, though."

"Is that a threat?" His lips eased upward when he met her gaze. "I think the pie is..."

She held her breath waiting for his reply. He broke into a full, toothy grin, which turned into a laugh. She punched him in the arm. "Stop being an asshole."

"Ow." He rubbed his arm. "Yes, it's the best piece of *peach* pie I've ever had."

"But not the *best* pie you've ever had."

"I'm not sure what other pies you have in your arsenal. I'll hold my opinion for best until I taste all that you can cook. I'm partial to key lime pie."

"You're a tough customer." She got up and snagged a glass off the drying rack. "Want some water?" She drank half a glass. "I love the water here. Something about the minerals."

He nodded as he slid the pie plate his way and cut himself a second piece. "Want more?"

She shook her head.

"So, what did you do to me when I was in the backyard dying?" His eyes flickered a deep blue. For a moment she was stunned by the vibrant hue, but then as if the sea had become stormy, the color swirled and darkened. His aura churned with conflicting colors that made no sense. She couldn't gauge his mood or intent.

"What do you mean?" She placed a glass of water in front of him and took her seat again.

"If you hadn't done whatever you did, then I'd probably be having a chat with my uncle Hades."

"I, uh, helped you."

"You did more than help. You took away the poison and healed everything. How?"

She shifted on the barstool to alleviate the sudden urge to squirm. "Sometimes we Pleiades are able to pull someone back from death."

"You can do this death save on anyone?"

She shook her head.

"Can you do this with someone other than me?"

She chewed on her lip. "Only you."

"Why me?"

"We're linked...connected."

"Destined? Isn't that what your father called it?"

"Maybe. I'm not sure." *Yes.* He was her one-and-only. Healing it confirmed it, but she didn't want to freak him out. He wasn't a stayer as the hostess had said. She rested her chin on her hands with her elbows on the table and stared at the stove. "Most of my life I ran from all the destiny crap. I hated knowing I'd have to be the head Pleiades when mom died. I don't deserve to be their leader. I've got the least experience. Then Mom died. I never wanted to jump dimensions and use these weird abilities that I still have no idea how to control. All I wanted was to be normal."

He put two fingers on her chin to pull her gaze to his. "What the hell is normal? Every person in the world faces the death of those closest to us and the burden of responsibility. Our lives come with complications far beyond what most people deal with, sure, but it's nothing we can't handle. The extra abilities are a part of us. They make us who we are. What do you mean you can't control your abilities? What can't you do, or what do you think you should be able to do that you haven't figured out yet?"

"My mom had elemental abilities to control wind, water, and sometimes fire. I think I got those, but I really suck at it. Mom was the turbocharged espresso version of a witch and I'm a weak-tea version."

"I need for you to become good at whatever skills you've got. There are a lot of black-magic shitheads in the area who sound like they're gunning for you. What do you mean by control water?"

"Move it. Change its form."

He stood and filled his glass with water. "Stop the water."

He threw it at her.

Without hesitation, she held up a hand, stopping the water midair.

"Now change it to ice."

She hesitated. The water fell onto the floor in a huge puddle.

"I'm so sorry." She jumped up, grabbed a wad of paper towels, and rushed to sop up the mess. "I suck at this whole magic thing."

"Leave it." He knelt beside her and put his hand over hers. He pulled her to her feet and into his arms.

She turned her head up to his, expecting gentle reassurance. What she got was entirely different. His mouth came down on hers, his tongue sweeping away resistance. His arms crushed her against his tight body. When he lifted his head, her brain fluttered with lightheaded need to continue. She gazed into his eyes, drowning. His hands framed her face.

"What do you see when you look at me?" he asked.

Her breath caught in her lungs. After a slow release of air she moistened her lips.

"Tell me," he coaxed. "Read my aura."

She couldn't look away. Colors swirled around him.

"Do you see disgust? Disappointment?" he coaxed.

She shook her head.

"Tell me out loud. What do you see?"

"There's a lot to see. There's desire." That actually didn't do justice to describe the intensity burning in the depths of his gaze and hovering in his aura. "Lust."

He grinned. "That's a given. Touching you makes me want you. What else? Is there anything negative here? Anything to indicate I think you're something other than a remarkable witch?"

"No. But there's a darkness to you."

"That's a part of who I am. I'm a hunter. A killer. I do it because I can and must. I'm not dangerous to you." He traced one of her cheeks with a finger. "I'll do whatever it takes to keep you safe. It might be something you don't like. Right now, keeping you safe means you learn to trust yourself and your abilities. Hesitation and doubt will get you killed."

"How do I get that confidence?"

"How do you stop the water?"

"I don't know. I just do it."

"That's it, then." He stepped away to refill the cup and slung it at her.

She stopped it midair again.

"Change it to ice. Just do it. No thinking. Do it."

She didn't break her fix on his gaze and focused on the concept of ice. The water changed and hit the floor with a loud clunk. She grinned. "I made a mess again."

"You did." He grinned. "Now clean it up without touching it. Move it to the sink."

"But—"

His face fell to a glower.

She imagined where she wanted the water. No hesitation. Just need to do what might make him smile again. The water moved off the floor to the sink.

"Good." He lifted her hand to his lips and kissed one fingertip. Then he sucked it between his lips, flicking his tongue over her finger. Suggestive. Hot.

He cupped the back of her neck, trapping her for what she expected to be a kiss. But he held her that way, stroking her cheek with his thumb, his gaze searching hers as if all the answers to every problem both of them had to deal with lay inside her somewhere.

If only that was the truth.

"You're going to be okay, Shannon." He stared at her so intently with those eyes as turbulent as the ocean. She wanted to drown in them and forget everything else. Suddenly she became aware of her near nakedness so close to his chest. It'd be so easy for him to push up the shirt and have her on any surface in this kitchen.

Just when she thought she'd melt if this didn't go somewhere, he leaned in. His lips slanted over hers. A breathless moan erupted from her. She clenched his arms. Such strong arms. His tongue took over her mouth until she had to pull away to breathe. He attacked her throat with his lips. His hot breath against her was the sexiest thing she'd ever experienced. His teeth caught her sensitized skin.

Her legs wobbled, and she almost went over with no anchor to buffer her from the intense sensations, but he caught her and fell back onto the barstool. He pulled her to straddle his lap. His hands snaked beneath the T-shirt to rest against the small of her back then down to cup both cheeks of her ass.

"Christ, Shannon," he groaned, leaning his forehead against her shoulder. His hands massaged and soothed.

"Please," she begged as she ground her pelvis into him, rasping all sensitive zones against his jeans while his hands continued their squeezing torment.

"Hasty little thing, aren't you? I've got to teach you to slow down." His fingers teased her, invaded her.

"Slow down later." She wiggled and pressed down against them, seeking and needing. She didn't want to savor. Not right now.

He showed her no mercy, allowing her to angle backward a bit so he could use his fingers deeper. She rocked her hips against him until she flew apart. "Merck..."

His mouth caught her cry as she shattered.

"Now that was fucking beautiful," he muttered.

She buried her face in his neck, not sure if she was embarrassed or overwhelmed. She rolled her head outward to rest it against his chest. Absently, she traced the tattoos streaking down his arms to his hands and over his shoulders like barbed wire with foreign-looking script. "What do these mean?"

"I wish I knew. Every time I kill a deviant magical, a new one appears."

"There are hundreds."

"I've been busy. Never forget I'm not a good person. I've done a lot of things." Softly, he added, "I've killed a lot."

She leaned away to cradle his head between her hands. "Don't say things like that. These people you killed probably murdered more than a lot before you stopped them. They would've killed more. You could die every time you go after one of them. Do the marks hurt?"

She traced a few of the inked lines and rested her head on his chest again, next to his heat, with the thump-thump of his heart against her ear.

"Not really."

"I want a better look at them. How about the bathtub?"

He grinned, lifted her, and carried her to the bathroom. He set her down on the edge of the tub and turned it on.

She could almost feel the electricity arcing between them. A glance up at his seductive mouth, now thinned into concentration on the water tumbling into the tub, and she could almost taste him. His gaze drifted possessively over her face.

Waiting for a full bathtub would take far too long when all she wanted was her lips on his again. She stood and found his mouth with hers, her tongue plunging deep and stroking along his, not giving him time to think. She loved the shape of his lips, their softness and strength. She tugged his jeans down until they pooled around his feet. He yanked the T-shirt over her head and skimmed his hands down her breasts. Then he leaned forward to replace his hands with his mouth. He bit gently on her nipple, and heat flared straight to her legs. A choking cry broke from her, her body shuddering for him all over again.

He backed her up against the wall, pinning her wrists and drawing them over her head while his mouth continued to ravage her. Fingers teased between her thighs. "Darlin', you're so wet for me. I wish I could wait until we're in the tub."

She couldn't talk. Couldn't even plead. She was blind with want for everything the low rasp of his declaration suggested might come next.

"Wrap your legs around me." His voice was hoarse in her ear. He dropped her wrists to support and lift her body. Her legs automatically locked around him. When he was poised to enter her, he paused as if waiting. Was she supposed to beg?

He leaned in and kissed her cheek and then the bridge of her nose. "You make me feel things I never have before."

He dropped her body over his, linking them together. She heard her own shattered cry as he filled her and drove into her ultrasensitive body. The friction, hot and tight, dragged fire over her body.

The possessive glitter in his gaze, which swirled a myriad of blue colors as he continued a relentless rhythm, mesmerized her. Harsh desire etched into every line of his face. Her mind stilled. Everything in her quieted. That wasn't just desire or possession in his expression and in his aura. That was love. This man might own her body and had wiggled his way into her heart, maybe even her soul, but she owned him right back. He might not even know it. He probably wouldn't admit it.

It was too fast for love. It was lust. Had to be. Didn't love take time?

He shifted, slamming against a zone of nerves, and once again she was lost to the intensity of what he created within her. He thrust hard until she shattered. Moments later, with a cry, he came apart. His heart thundered against her chest as he panted. He gently lowered her and they collapsed against each other, held up only by the wall.

"Give me a second and I'll carry you to the tub," he whispered.

"That's romantic, but it's only three steps away. I can make it." She waved behind him.

"If you can still walk, then we're not done tonight. Not even close." A wicked grin spread across his face.

Oh yeah. Totally on board with everything the grin promised.

Chapter Sixteen

Boom. Boom. Boom.

Shannon blinked into the darkness around her. The glow from the bedside clock and the moonlight through the open window mingled to cast a cool light over the entire room. Merck's arm banded her tight against his front in his bed.

Boom. Boom. Boom.

The front door.

"I'll get it. Stay here," Merck grumbled, pushing off the covers. As he rotated to sit on the edge of the bed, the muscles in his back rippled beneath his skin. His fingers scratched through his hair, but did nothing to tame the disheveled look. With an agitated exhale he pulled on his jeans, hooked his knife against his hip, and stomped out of the bedroom.

She buried deep beneath the covers again, using his residual heat to warm her in the super-cooled house. She didn't want to move. She wasn't even sure she could and was shocked at how spry he seemed.

A few seconds of him gone and she already missed the warmth of his body next to hers. Her heart kicked up, worried her father might be the one who'd arrived. The bedside clock read a little after two a.m.

"Hey!" a voice called in greeting. "You in there?" The knocking became more insistent.

She relaxed, silently thanking Eli for keeping her location secret. He just earned himself more pie.

"Coming, Danny," Merck called out. Seconds later, he said, "Come on in. Why're you here?"

"You haven't answered your cell phone for the past four hours. This can't wait."

"I've been busy." Merck's voice came out rough. "What'd you find out?"

Shannon couldn't make out what Danny said. She caught fragments of conversation, but Danny rapid fired, flipping between Spanish and English. Merck replied in Spanish. More back and forth she couldn't make out. Learning Spanish needed to be a priority.

There was a pause and then Danny spoke heatedly, "You didn't. Tell me it's not Sleeping Beauty in your bedroom."

No reply from Merck.

Danny asked, "What the hell is going on? You made her another one of your girls? Every time there's a girl involved this happens."

Every time. Her stomach dropped.

"One thing led to another. Things happen," Merck replied. Nothing was said about her being any different than his normal. "I'm not dead yet."

Them together, for him, was about him dying soon and going out without regrets? Maybe about thanking her for what she'd done for him? She'd fallen into his arms more than willingly. That wasn't his fault. She'd been chomping at the bit for years to get a taste of what it'd be like with him. Every moment more than exceeded her fantasies, but this wasn't as serious for him as it was for her. She'd really thought he had to be her destined guy. Still did. After being capable of dimension hopping and magically healing him, he had to be *the one*. Death date aside, she didn't understand how he thought them together was insignificant. Just another notch on his belt or a simple distraction. Another willing bed partner.

Absurd. She didn't buy it. Their bond was unique, but she didn't have time to sort out his psychology or convince him of fate. Merck would come around, even if it might be too late when he did. Time for her to return home and work on finding the Trident. Maybe her father found someone she could ask. Doubtful, but she had to hope.

She pushed off the covers and hunted for her clothes, finding them in the bathroom. She slipped on her underwear and dress, then stared at herself in the mirror for a long moment, searching for and finally finding the resolve to do what she needed to do.

Her phone sat on the bathroom counter. With sigh she typed out a quick text message: *Can you pick me up at the end of Merck's road in a few minutes?*

She hit send and slid the phone into the side pocket on the dress.

The guys' argument was still going on when she entered the hallway. She did all she could to tune it out. Her heart couldn't handle overhearing Merck explaining away what they had.

After a deep breath, she marched into the fray. The argument cut off when she became the center of both guys' gazes. Merck looked bored, whereas Danny's eyes blazed with anger.

"You two can stop. Sleeping Beauty is taking off. Just pretend none of this happened. I'll go back to my life crisis and you return to yours."

Merck's lips thinned. "All right."

"That's it? That's all you've got to say?" Wasn't he even going to try to stop her from leaving?

"You need a ride somewhere?" he added.

Her heartbreak changed to anger. "I'm good. Probably best if we try to figure out things on our own from here." She froze for a few seconds, her gaze locked on his, unsure what more she could say.

Merck remained silent, his eyes shuttered and hard. This must be his Enforcer side. Heartless.

With emptiness swelling in her chest, she walked out the front door.

***

Shannon's name lodged in his throat. He wished he could ask her to stay, but what Danny had revealed meant anywhere away from him made her safe. The moment the front door latched behind her, his chest clenched so tight breathing became tough.

Let her go. He had few options otherwise to keep her safe.

Shaky from fighting his urge to chase after her and soothe her hurt, he clenched his hands and returned to the kitchen. His eyes caught on a fork with a few pie crumbs that hadn't made it to the sink. She'd made him pie—damned good pie. The best pie he'd ever tasted. No one had ever made him pie or cinnamon rolls before.

As he slumped into a chair, for the first time in his life he considered giving in to self-pity over the shit that drove his existence. He'd never asked for the responsibility of keeping people safe. He wanted Shannon and everything that came with being with her—laughing and eating her home-cooked food. But being with her didn't jive with being the Enforcer.

He cast his gaze out the window to the water, which beat at the docks as if reflecting his inner turmoil. The house was so empty without her.

He didn't want to shake her free of where she'd lodged herself deep in his soul.

This might be love. Hell if he knew. This waxing- poetic shit wasn't the sex talking.

He couldn't—wouldn't—live with himself if she died and he hadn't done everything possible to protect her on his last day of life.

Oh, hell. He only had one more day.

Despair slammed into him. He pictured himself sliding into a puddle of hopelessness. Alone with his misery. Sounded like a sappy country song.

Enough. He put a mental lockdown on defeatism and shoved personal desires into the back of his mind. He had a job to do. On his last day he'd get it done. Doing so might save her life.

He would find the Trident for her. If he couldn't, he'd bargain with his father as his death-day request, even though he had no negotiating power.

Danny glanced up from his phone where he'd been emailing or texting. "You look like pecked-over roadkill."

Yeah, he felt like it. "Owen and his entourage will be coming soon. Daytime most likely."

Danny nodded. "I thought he'd come to South Carolina for her, but the bug Chad planted in his rental picked up a conversation that revealed it's you he's interested in. He wants to find her, but he doesn't know where she's gone. He's got no clue she's here. Why would he want to find you?"

"Owen figured out my parentage back when his father dated my mother. Where best to search for Poseidon's Trident than to start with his son?" The one time he'd visited his "mother" out in Los Angeles when he'd been twenty, he'd gotten into a drag-out brawl with Owen over something stupid on the beach before his "mother", who'd been dating Owen's father, had broken them up. The water had crept up the beach like fingers until it reached him and fixed every bit of injury from their fight within seconds. That was the danger of doing anything close to the ocean. It sought to protect him.

He'd never forget Owen's expression. He'd ghosted white. A conniving expression passed over his face, there for no more than a few seconds, as if filing away the information for future use. If Merck had been after Poseidon's Trident, the first place he'd start was someone he suspected to be a water god's offspring or who had water abilities. Why he'd waited so long after Shannon got stabbed to come across the country and "talk" with him made no sense.

After years of monitoring Owen's activities, him seeking the Trident surprised Merck. Owen might be fascinated by magic, given he was descended long, long ago from Orion, and he might've even dabbled in some magic, but Owen never came across as inherently evil. Merck suspected this had more to do with the necromancer and whatever sway she held over Owen.

"What are we going to do?" Danny asked.

"Let them come."

"They'll kill you."

"Thanks for the faith."

Danny twirled his keys around his index finger, a telling gesture he did when nervous. "I'm worried. I doubt he knows everything about you. I don't even know everything about you. God knows what they're planning."

"I don't want you around when they find me. I suspect he'll be toting a necromancer with him. Anaïs."

"I feel like a dick for hurting Shannon." Danny scrunched up his face and gazed toward the front door. "I'm not sure you can repair this one easily."

"I needed her to leave and stay away from me, at least for now. She should be safer with her people if she stays with them and stays low. Thanks for playing along."

"I don't like being an asshole, especially to a *bonita* sexy *chica*. More so when you've got your balls in a wad over her. I've never seen you so fucked up over a girl. You sure her people can protect her better than you?" Skepticism oozed from his words. "Seems like all of this is about her and Poseidon. Who better to deal with it than you?"

"I'm trying to do the right thing here, which means keeping her far away from Owen and the necromancer. They don't know she's here. I want it to stay that way. And I've got to figure out why she's been targeted for having the Trident when she doesn't know anything about it."

"Women like her don't like it when people make decisions for them. You should call her and tell her what's going on."

"Now you're the definitive expert on women?"

"Unlike you, I was married for six years before my wife was killed. I think I know a bit more than you about relationships. Honesty is always the best bet, especially when emotions and sex get tangled in the mix. Otherwise it'll bite you in the ass."

Merck rubbed at one eyebrow. Yeah, he'd fucked up, but he'd apologize later. He still wanted her far away when Owen and cohort arrived. "What'd you find out about the Trident?"

"Most I found was about its symbology. The trinity of three—the beginning, the middle, and the end, or trinity, unity, and opposition. Or Poseidon has three sons who warred, although he really had four. Well, five if we count you. Or could be about his three weapons of warfare—shields, swords, and spears."

"That's scholarly crap. Anything useful?"

Danny shook his head. "The stuff I translated talked about the Trident as the symbol of his legion, his throne, and a great source of power. I can't find anything on who can touch it or what it could do in someone else's hands."

"Nothing new. All right. I figured this wouldn't be something research could figure out. I want you to keep an eye on Shannon from a distance. Just make sure she stays on the property next door. So, park it at the end of her road, but their property is protected and monitored. If you step foot close to the house, they'll know. If she leaves, text me."

"What are you going to do?"

"Touch base with some water friends."

Chapter Seventeen

"Where were you last night?" Shannon's father asked while he drenched a pancake in strawberry syrup.

Shannon tried to formulate a lie, but functioning on little sleep wasn't conducive to creativity.

"Uh..." She cut a piece of her pancake pile and shoved it in her mouth.

Her father stopped chewing. His eyes narrowed. "You were next door with *him*, weren't you?"

Oh, God. Not the don't-lie-to-me stare. That one look from her father reduced her to an eight-year-old caught midnight snacking on pie. Pie. Focus on pie. She forced her mouth into a smile and asked, "How was the pie last night?"

His index finger shot out to point her way. "Your mother used to pull the smile and ask a question to distract me. It won't work on me this morning."

"So, you didn't like the pie."

"Of course I did. It was excellent, as always. Reminded me of her." His face fell.

"I miss her too. We've never really talked about it."

"She did what she had to do. What she said she'd do. She always told me one day something would threaten you and, if it came to a decision between you and her, well, she'd save you. It was the way of things.

But..." He wiped at his eyes and stared at the ceiling fan. "I love you both."

"I'm sorry. It was my fault. If I hadn't been there, then she would be with us still."

He shook his head. "The gods deemed it to be this way. We had a long run. Thirty-five years together. That's a lot longer than most of you ladies get." He was trying to hide his agony, but it was in his tone.

She jumped up and ran around the table to hug him. "I love you. I'm sorry to make you nuts, but you're driving me nuts too."

He hugged her back and whispered, "She was my soul and you're my heart. With the boys gone..."

"Yeah." She resumed her seat and cut another bite of pancake. A huge weight seemed to have lifted in the air between them.

"The pie was good." He sipped cranberry juice.

Thoughts of pie made it impossible not to remember and obsess over what she'd done with Merck before pie. And after pie. Her mind constantly replayed the experience. She couldn't go there right now, not at the breakfast table with her father.

"Shannon?" He cleared his throat.

"Yes?"

"Last night..."

So he wasn't dropping the line of conversation, even though it'd detoured. She shoved an overlarge pancake bite into her mouth and chewed. Seconds later, when her father didn't offer to change the subject, she said, "You know I'm almost thirty years old. If I decide I want to go out for a while, take pie to a friend or whatever, then I'll do it."

"You took *him* pie?" His look. Oh God, now he was giving her the heart-wrenching, disappointed look.

"Yes." Good. That came out with more confidence than she felt. She took another bite, even though her stomach identified itself as full.

"Eli picked you up sometime after two in the morning. You slept with him?"

"Who? Eli?"

"Don't play dense. Eli doesn't have a real thing for you. You went next door. You brought him pie..."

She covered her face with her hand. "Dad, we're not talking about this. I mean...seriously?"

"It's a conversation we're going to have because I don't trust him. I don't know what the hell he is or his motive for being around you. He's got a bad reputation with women and he's always had a thing for you."

Merck had always had a thing for her? Even as a flattered thrill flooded her, she wondered how many dealings her father had had with him. Had he tried to ask her out more than once and her father blocked?

She put down her fork, careful to avoid clinking it against the plate. "I know this comes from your need to protect me. Mom sent me down here to find help, which I'm pretty sure is Merck. He's a key part of understanding all of this." *Only, I might've messed up any chance of him helping by sleeping with him.* "We don't know if the gods are messing with his life or mine."

"Why would they mess with his life?"

"He's Poseidon's descendant."

"What? That doesn't make him any better. The bastard could be in cahoots with Poseidon. What the hell were you thinking?"

She bit her tongue against giggling. Only her dad would say "cahoots." She touched her father's hand. "Please, calm down. I know you and he had some sort of fight when he was younger, and you don't like him. I'm worried having you down here. There's so much going on. I don't want you hurt."

He sandwiched her hand between his. "I'm here. I'm not leaving. You're all I've got left. If you died and I wasn't here...well, I couldn't live with that."

"Then you have to let me do what's needed to figure this out, even if it involves working with Merck. You have to trust me."

"All right." He nodded. "I still don't like you dealing with him."

"Did Merck really ask to take me out in high school?" She pulled her hand from between his.

Her father's gaze dropped. "You were too young for him."

It'd happened. Merck had marched across the creek, knocked on her front door, and intended something more. So many years lost. If they'd had a bit more time together back then, she might've discovered they were destined. Sure they'd been so young, but her life may have gone differently. Her mother might still be here.

She and Merck weren't over. The horror of both of them on a countdown to death meant figuring all this out had to happen right now. "Why did you call him a criminal? What'd he do?"

"He egged my car. He and his friend Chad. Do you know what egg does to a car's paint?"

She struggled to keep her face serious. "He threw an egg at your car? What'd you do to the poor guy after this dire incident?"

"Poor guy? He was a menace. I hauled them to the police station."

"Did you press charges?"

He shook his head. "I asked the police to keep them locked up overnight so they wouldn't do something worse. It was Halloween, and they were fifteen. I had to save us from the toilet paper and who knows what else was on their agenda." He waved his fork in the air at her. "He was a bad egg." A smile broke across his face. "Bad pun. Sorry."

"Oh my God. He egged your car and you flipped out. You were so psychotic about that BMW."

"The car was one of a kind."

"Isn't that the truth. It was in the shop every other week. Lordy, remember when you turned it on, the exhaust smoked like a rocket at takeoff? A real gem." She burst into laughter.

"You just don't get it," he grumbled.

"It almost exploded that one time when Mom drove me to go shopping."

"Your mother didn't know how to drive a stick shift."

"You're holding a grudge over a kid prank that happened over fifteen years ago?"

He smiled. "Yep."

She released a pent-up breath, knowing her father was willing to let it go. He might not like Merck or trust him, but he'd trust her.

Eli breezed in and loaded a pancake onto his plate from the pile of cooked ones. "Pancakes. I love your pancakes, Shannon."

"Thanks."

"And your strawberry sauce. Bloody hell, I missed this stuff." He licked the spoon after drowning his pancakes.

Her father didn't bark at Eli to leave as Shannon was sure he wanted to do.

Eli glanced between the two of them. "What's on tap for today?"

"Dad said he found someone I can talk to. We're Skyping in an hour."

***

Merck's boat rocked on the offshore waves while he gazed up into the sunny morning sky. The light was so bright it burned his retinas. A few scant clouds lazed high overhead. He leaned over the side and touched the water. All still remained stable. Two dolphins appeared. He recognized their leader, having known the old guy since he was a teenager. The whole pod swam around the boat. He touched the nose of the leader, instantly understanding one of the younger dolphins had an injury. The hurt dolphin bobbed too far away for Merck to reach it.

"I'm not going to hurt you, buddy. If you want help, it's yours."

The juvenile didn't move to get closer.

"Show me what's wrong."

The young dolphin surfaced, exposing his tail and entire backside, which were covered in fresh, deep lacerations indicative of a propeller collision. The leader of this pod kept his group away from all boats except Merck's. This meant someone ventured close, maybe even chased them. He wanted to hit something, but took a deep breath, knowing any outward sign of anger would terrify the young dolphin.

"I'll help you."

The older dolphin pushed the juvenile toward Merck. He kept his hand steady, hovering a few inches above the water. The juvie touched his nose to Merck's fingers. Merck envisioned the wounds healed, and within seconds the dolphin scurried away. It did a flip and chirp before disappearing below. He smiled, relieved to see the damage repaired.

The older dolphin returned to Merck and touched him in thanks. As if the dolphin spoke, he heard a warning in his mind. *Athena. Ericthonians. Onshore and fighting.*

His heart pumped hard as worst-case scenario images flickered through his mind. Stupid of him to think Athena done. What better time to go after Shannon than when he was offshore.

Damn it.

He whipped out his phone. No text from Danny. The Ericthonians must've come in from the shore side then.

He said to the dolphins, "This fight is about more than the Trident. I don't know if Athena understands that." The pod leader blinked up at him, offering help. "I don't want you or your pod hurt. I need to convince Athena this is much bigger than getting the Trident for its power."

He waited for the dolphins to swim away before cranking the boat and pushing her to top speed. It wasn't a speedboat, but she could move when asked. Merck calculated time to shore at fifteen minutes. The bow slapped against the water. He wove through the familiar buoys into the coastal channel and toward the Randolph property dock.

He hoped he wouldn't arrive too late.

Chapter Eighteen

Merck tied the boat to the closest piling and hopped off, but paused, detecting a disturbance in the water. Water bubbled on either side of the dock.

A green ichthyocentaur rose from the water as if propelled from a cannon to land on the dock. Seconds later a blue ichthyocentaur alighted next to him. Both transformed to human form immediately prior to landing, clad in leather battle gear.

"Bythos?" Merck asked of the used-to-be green ichthyocentaur.

"This is Aphros. My brother." Bythos waved at the other guy who towered above them both by at least a foot or more.

"Are you guys here to help or dissuade me?" Merck asked.

"You think we'd miss out on a chance to kill some Athena underlings? We'll even settle for a decent fight, which we haven't had in ages." Bythos tossed his huge sword from hand to hand.

"Good enough. Try not to scare the straights too much, though. There's bound to be a few druids around," Merck said.

"All right." Bythos stretched while Aphros gazed toward the forested area ahead.

"I'll get to Shannon." Merck palmed his knife.

Bythos grinned. "You like her. That's progress."

"You're a real pain in the ass," Merck mumbled.

A deep sound rumbled from Aphros's belly and erupted into a laugh. "I like this kid. He's a hoot." He leaned down from his ultra-tall height to ruffle Merck's hair.

Merck rolled his eyes and pulled his head away from the hair ruffling. "We're in a bit of a hurry here."

"Are you going into battle with that toy?" Aphros nodded to Merck's knife.

"It'll get the job done."

Aphros pointed at Merck's face. "That's why you got those from them in the past. These things must be fought at a distance." He handed Merck a huge sword off his back. Merck accepted the blade, expecting it to weigh too much to be useful, but it felt no heavier than his knife. Magic.

"Do us proud and you can keep her."

"Thank you." *I'm better with a knife*. But one didn't scoff a god's gift.

Merck sprinted in the direction of the house. No noise other than the impact of his tennis shoes breaking sticks echoed around him as he tore through the forest. Eerie. Not even a bird or the wind. Not a peep from the now-absent Ichthyocentaurs. He'd lost sight of the two during his dash and didn't see them anywhere.

He pulled up at the tree line and viewed the chaos. Ericthonians and snakes were everywhere. Six or seven druids were fighting on the porch of the house and around the lawn. There was a lot of blood, but he couldn't tell whose. Two druids were down, possibly dead, but neither was Brian Randolph or Eli. More than twenty dead snake men littered the lawn. Kudos for the druids.

Weapons were up and firing round after round into snakes and snake men in a snowstorm of bullets. Bullets didn't kill these guys, although it might slow them down. These things only stopped when they bled out, but there'd be more. It was an endless army. Getting rid of them required giving Athena what she wanted.

He sighted Shannon at the far edge of the porch using her preternatural skills to keep the creatures off her, pushing them away with wind. Pride filled him as he watched her manipulate the air like a pro. Powerful, directed, and effective. No hesitation. No doubt. God, she was spectacular. Her face showed strain though.

His senses worked as fast as possible while he ran toward her, but he felt as if he were underwater. He dodged free-flying bullets, his movements so quick that the bullets appeared to move at a snail's pace, as if they were hovering mosquitoes. He leapt, hurtling over the bodies of dead snakes and a few live ones, to strike the snake creature threatening Shannon. With a whirl, he sliced off the head of a lunging snake. The borrowed blade's sharpness impressed him.

The creature fell. A second snake man sprang at him. He was too close for a sword swing. He rammed it as hard as he could. It rocked back, but not very far. Damn these things were strong. It swiped at him with its ultra-sharp nails, nearly tagging his shoulder.

"Behind you!" he yelled at Shannon. She spun, but too late. A snake creature swiped Shannon's side. Direct hit. She had an hour or so before the change to snake creature started and one to two hours before the change was permanent. This entire shitfest needed to end so he could get her the antidote.

She dodged another strike, whirled, and lodged a small blade into the snake man's neck. Good for her.

It got her again as it went down. Shit and super shit.

He threw himself back at the creature leaping for him. It ripped down his chest with its nails and jumped out of range of his sword. He gasped, his gaze lifting to the sky. The Ericthonian was coming at him again. No time to dwell on pain. He lunged forward, his blade striking its target in the neck this time. The snake man hissed in pain, gripped its neck, and struck out again, but missed. Finally, blood loss too great, it collapsed.

It wouldn't be down long. Snake creatures resurrected themselves after about ten minutes, like a hydra with its many regenerative heads. Bleeding out paused them for much longer than hacking them to bits, but nothing killed them since they were the creatures of Athena. The druids couldn't defeat an immortal army.

A new Ericthonian approached him, flanked by two serpents.

Shannon's father fought alongside two druids at the opposite end of the porch. They were covered in bloody scratches. All of them would need the remedy to prevent the change. He had a small bit at the office, probably not enough for this many people. No time to fly to the one shaman in Greece who could brew the right healing potion.

This had to end. He protected people. It's what he did, who he was. Above all, he protected Shannon.

This entire business with Poseidon reeked of gods fucking with his life. His fault. His responsibility.

Merck pointed the sword at the approaching snake man. In Greek, he said, "All of this needs to stop. Take me to Athena. I am the only one here who knows about what she seeks."

The creature halted, cocking its head as if considering his words. It gazed at the blade he held and then nodded.

Shannon grabbed his arm. His gaze met hers for an instant and then resumed his stare on the snake man.

"I'm going with you," she said. "This is about me."

"We don't know exactly what this is about." He met her father's gaze over her head. "Stay with your father right now. I'll deal with this."

"You can't stop me from going with you."

"I might not make it, darlin', but I need for you to live. You still have a chance to survive all of this." His breath came out a harsh rasp. "Please. I need for you to be somewhere safe while I speak with Athena. Go." He nudged her toward her father. All the Ericthonians looked to be backing out of the fight.

Her gaze darted around the yard. The breeze carried the stench of blood. Streaks of red painted the front of the white house, and the porch rails like a B-grade horror film.

"The only place I'm safe is with you." She took a step toward him, but her father caught her arm.

"He's right. Stay here. With us," Brian ordered.

Merck wished he could keep her close and promise her the safety she asked of him. Right now he had to deal with a goddess he'd never met face-to-face. If everything went south and Athena killed him, then Shannon would be safer out of view or with the druids in a renewed fight against the snake men. He gazed at Brian for a few seconds, silently pleading he keep her safe, before jogging after the Ericthonian.

He approached the black-haired woman at the water's edge. Not a woman, he amended in his mind, a goddess. Serious goddess. Everything about her appearance was perfect and toned with dark Mediterranean skin and catlike eyes. Intelligent eyes.

He'd lost sight of Bythos long ago. Right now, it'd be nice to have the brothers as backup.

He bowed when Athena's attention focused solely on him. "It is an honor to be in your presence."

"Give me the Trident," she ordered in an echoing voice that ricocheted painfully between his ears.

Merck's spine went rigid. Athena's tone and glower demanded fear and deference. What was the worst she offered? Death. He may not want it today, but he wasn't afraid of it, even if she could probably dream up a painful way to ensure he died eternally screaming. He'd accept it if the outcome protected his water friends and kept Shannon safe.

He asked, "Why do you want the Trident?"

She frowned as if he was an idiot to question her. "I do not answer to you, but I detect your father's stubbornness should I refuse to answer. To take Poseidon's power and kill him, of course."

Merck shook his head and pinched the bridge of his nose. He released a long sigh. Athena didn't get the big picture. "This is about revenge for you, then? For something he did a long time ago?"

Athena scowled a promise of impending pain, but the slight widening of her eyes was a clear *yes* on Poseidon being a shithead at some point in the past.

Merck said, "Assuming I could get the Trident for you, which I'm not saying I can, and I give it to you, what then? Will you steal all of Poseidon's power and rise over him, humiliate him, possibly even kill him and ascend to his underwater throne? Then what?"

Athena's face lit up. Her lips curved into a jubilant, scary smile.

The hairs on his arms stood as chills skirted along his skin. "Are you ready to take on his responsibilities? Do you love all of the ocean and her creatures to the point you would devote the rest of your existence to their welfare? To mediate the battles amongst them and against humans? To fight pollution? To pick up after natural disasters? To heal their injuries?"

"Who are you to question me?" Her voice echoed inside his skull to the point his ears hurt.

"So you want his throne without responsibility? Perhaps you plan to delegate the responsibility of sea life and ocean welfare to someone else. Someone who won't understand them? Someone equally power hungry?"

"You want this job." She smiled superiorly as if she had him figured out.

"No, ma'am. I've got enough to deal with, thank you. I don't want all that. That's an insane amount of responsibility. Without Poseidon or a similarly powerful ruler, there will be chaos underwater. I have visited a world, a dimension actually, where Poseidon doesn't exist. The animals are scared and hurting. They need what only he can offer them: the assurance of his presence and control. If you swear to me on your soul and the soul of the children you love that you plan to dedicate all that you are to care for those who need their water god, then I will find this Trident for you."

He and Athena gazed at each other in silence. He expected her to rip off his head or deliver an extremely painful hit now that he'd revealed he didn't have the Trident and had thrown down an ultimatum.

"I want him to hurt," Athena finally said. Pain transformed her beautiful face.

Merck said softly, "Poseidon did some dickhead thing to you? He probably doesn't even remember it or didn't think twice about it. I'm sorry. He's a guy and sometimes, honestly, we just don't get women or we're so wrapped up in our own shit that we do things without thinking." He shrugged. Been there, been guilty of it too many times, and may not have even recognized it when he'd done it other times. "Words from me won't help, but destroying him and the balance of his underwater world won't help either. Sure, it'll feel great for about a minute. Then it'll heap a load of extra duties on you for the rest of your existence. Have you ever told him to his face what he did that pissed you off?"

She tapped a long, silver-painted nail against her teeth. "I don't like your arrogance, but you're smart. He violated my temple with Medusa. It's why I turned the bitch into a monster. Poseidon refuses to meet with me to discuss matters." Her eyes darted over Merck's right shoulder. "Isn't that right, Bythos?"

Bythos bobbed in the water, back in his half-merman, half-horse form. "I don't recall you submitting a request for an audience recently. If he refused, then perhaps he doesn't think you mean to meet peacefully. The previous two times he agreed to meet with you there were traps meant to hurt him."

Merck took a step toward Athena. The snake men around her tensed for attack. He said, "If you require death to end this vendetta to take a throne you have no plans to rule in the manner which it will need, then kill me. Kill Poseidon's son. But first, vow you will stop attacking Shannon and her family who have nothing to do with any of this. If the Pleiades goddesses have been assassinated, then she and the others related to her are the last of the Pleiades bloodlines. They need to remain alive."

He stood tall, ready for the deathblow but confident it wouldn't come. He'd never felt so certain a threat wouldn't kill him as right now. The gods who would preside over his live-or-die judgment in the next twenty-four hours would never let him out this easily.

"To his face, I would hear you call Poseidon a dickhead." Athena savored the last word as if highly entertained.

"I can do that."

She gazed at Bythos. "He is ready."

With a wave of her hand, she and all her snake men disappeared.

What did that mean? Ready for what? His meeting to determine his fate? Anger slid through his mind. Damn it. Was all of this some sort of elaborate test?

All these people hurt, possibly killed. His ocean in chaos. And it was a fucking game. He hated the gods and their bullshit.

Bythos clapped a hand onto his shoulder. He flinched. Bythos was now back in humanoid form. "That could've gone very differently. Glad you understand the gravity of the missing Trident."

Merck threw off Bythos's hand. "What the hell was all this about?"

Bythos held out a glass bottle. "This is for the *straights* who got scratched by the Ericthonians. A drop or two on the scratch should do the job, but it's got to be within the next hour."

"Thanks." He took the vial, relief settling into his chest that he wouldn't have to run to work to get what little he had left to help Shannon. "But it doesn't answer my question."

"There are things I can discuss and things I can't." Bythos grinned as if he was thoroughly enjoying this.

Merck held out the sword. "Tell Aphros thank you. She's really a remarkable weapon."

Bythos shook his head, rejecting his offer of return. "The ever-sharp blade is meant for you and no other. A gift from your mother."

"My mother?" He palmed the beautiful blade. The intricate hilt and etched blade were not human made. The sword exuded a rich energy. Old magic. "Who's my mother?"

"You're no bastard."

His eyes shot to Bythos, shocked. "Amphitrite?" The true wife of Poseidon.

Bythos nodded.

"Why'd she give me up?"

Bythos glanced out to the ocean. "I shouldn't tell you this, but you showed grit today. That I respect. To have another child your mother had to bargain." His deep gaze returned to Merck. "The goddesses who govern children and childbirth forbade Poseidon more after his first few were disastrous. The only way Bendis and Aphrodite would allow your existence was to have you submitted to scrutiny. Your mother had to give you up for your younger years and let you be judged. Trust me when I say the negotiation was long and bitter."

"They wanted to test me?"

Bythos nodded. "To see if any catastrophic issues arose as did with your brothers."

"Do you think I'll pass?"

Bythos's face fell. He shrugged. "The judgment is not just about you. It's political and complicated."

That's what he'd suspected. It meant he could probably do whatever the hell he wanted and it wouldn't matter. "When will this judgment take place?"

"Today or tomorrow." Bythos shrugged again. "I'm not sure."

"How did someone get the Trident to begin with and why is Shannon involved? What did Athena mean by *he's ready*?"

Bythos grinned. He dove into the water, disappearing.

Chapter Nineteen

Merck imagined ways to kill Bythos to invoke the most pain while staring at the spot he'd disappeared underwater. He pivoted. Ahhnd...oh, boy. Another Brian face off coming his way.

Shannon, her father, and several other men stared his way. Maybe they were shocked. Maybe they were preparing to attack him. He couldn't tell.

Brian held Shannon to him by her arms as if she'd been trying to break free, only they now stood frozen. Brian was the first to move, releasing her and stepping toward him.

Brian held out his hand. To shake? *Uh, okay.*

The second Merck's hand touched his, Brian pulled him into a bear hug. The bone crusher made him realize his wounds weren't superficial. They hurt.

Wincing, Merck put his arms around Brian and patted his shoulders. "What'd I do?"

Finally, Brian stepped away. "I misjudged you, son. I'm sorry. I owe you my life. Our lives. Those fuckers were going to rip us to shreds. Nothing we had was stopping them until you and your friends came along."

Merck blinked at Brian while his brain blanked. "Anyone would've done it."

Brian's forehead wrinkled. "No. Not anyone would've confronted a goddess and offered his life in exchange for us. For my daughter. That took balls. Athena could've leveled your ass. You proved there's a hell of a lot more going on between you and them than even I can understand. That was some top-notch hero shit we just witnessed."

Before Merck could respond, Eli stepped up. Hug number two. More pain. All he needed was a few steps backward to the water, then he'd be healed.

Eli stepped away and asked Brian, "What about this guy, huh? Some kind of kick-ass for Shannon, isn't he?"

Parallel-universe time. Brian looked at him as if he were a superman of sorts. A hell of a long way from the hostile who'd faced off with him yesterday and called him a criminal.

"Come on. Let's get you taken care of," Brian said.

Merck opened his mouth to say he'd be fine. If he backed up a yard or two, all would be resolved. He only needed a few moments with the water. The openness on Brian Randolph's face strangled the refusal in his throat.

The ocean screamed her offer of help behind him. He met Shannon's gaze, indecisive.

"Eli can help you," she said softly.

Even so, he didn't relish the trek to the house. The Ericthonian had done a job on his side. "All right. I need to treat everyone who got scratched to prevent the transformation into one of those snake creatures."

Twenty minutes later, everyone had been treated, except Shannon. He pulled her into the downstairs bathroom and shut the door. "No more delaying. It's your turn. Shirt off."

She tugged off the T-shirt, exposing several huge slashes. He allowed a few droplets from the vial to fall into the scratches. He found himself wanting to touch her all over, as if there were other injuries she hadn't shown him.

She flinched. "Burns."

"Sorry. Has to be done."

"I know." She turned her head away from him, but it didn't hide the tears running fast and furious down her cheeks.

"Are there any other spots they got you?"

She shook her head.

"It hurts that bad? I wish I could prevent it from hurting when I put the drops on, but I can't. It sucks. I think you'd make a pretty snake woman, but I'm not really into that kind of girl. Those pointy teeth and slitted nose. Their mindless need to kill..." He shuddered.

She shook her head and grabbed a tissue. "Sorry, I'm kind of emotional right now."

"You did good against those guys."

"It's not that. You offered your life for all of us. I found out I'm just one of the hoard of women who parade through your bed. It's a lot to take in."

"Look, Shannon, you and I..."

"We aren't. I know. I wished for more, but I'll respect your decision to be alone. This doesn't have to be uncomfortable. You can go." She waved at the bathroom door.

Shit, he'd zoned, and she'd gone the wrong way interpreting. "We are."

"What was that?" Her forehead crinkled.

"This...you and me, it's real. I let Danny run his mouth because I needed you to be away from me for what's coming later today. I'm sorry. It was an assholish thing to do, but I told you I'd do whatever must be done when it comes to keeping you alive."

"So you don't have flings with whatever girl you're working with?"

"No. I haven't been with anyone in a long while. That's not saying I'm not good at anything that might be longer term. I'm not really sure how it's done. All I know for sure is you're not a fling. We've been involved in some sense ever since we met."

She chewed her lip.

"I need to get you fixed." He waved at the scratches. "They'll scar if we don't do it now."

She touched his marred cheek. "Like this?"

He nodded. "If we wait too much longer, they'll be permanent. You're too beautiful to have that carving up your skin."

Her cheeks flushed. "I'll get Eli to do it."

"No. I want to do it."

"He's a lot closer than the ocean."

"We can go to the creek since it's closer than the ocean. It'll work. Any natural water source works."

She frowned at the door.

"What's wrong?" he asked.

"My father... All right, we go to the water and you do your thing, but then we have to hurry back. He got the drops of that stuff, but he hasn't accepted healing help. He's—"

"Like you?" he interrupted. "Sees to everyone else first?"

"They all did so much for me. I can't stand thinking of any one of them in pain. Two of the guys almost died today."

"It's what they signed on to do. Give them at least that much respect."

"You're right. You impressed him. A lot. You did what each of us would do for each other. If there's a way to end a fight and save the others, even if it's our own death, not someone else's, we'll do it. We're a family. You're a part of that now." She touched his cheek, the cool pads of her fingers sliding along his scars.

Didn't that just give him a case of the warm and fuzzies. Family. He cleared the sudden congestion in his throat. "I'm not real sure about what it means to be a family. I know friends like Chad and Danny. I guess we're family in a way."

She shifted, her knee bumping his injured side. He winced.

"You're hurt too?"

"Yeah."

"Let's get to the water right now. Then we'll come back and force Dad to get help."

The second she had her shirt on he tugged her outside and toward the creek. Healing both of them took moments. She yanked up his shirt as soon as he was done to run her hand along his smoothed side, now blood free. "How does it clean you up too?"

He shrugged. "It just does. Magic."

"Unfair. I need a shower. Let's go back. I'll convince Dad to get Eli to take care of him. Then I'll shower."

"Then I'm taking you out on the water." He stroked her hair and ran his fingers down her spine.

"Why?"

"Today's my last day. Official judgment comes down sometime in the next twenty-four hours. I'm sorry we didn't come up with an answer for you on the Trident. I'll ask Poseidon when he shows up to judge me. Not sure how I'll get you the answer, but I'll try to text you or something before I..."

She touched his forearm and squeezed. "It won't be your last day. You're a badass. Badasses don't die."

"I don't want this to be over." They were right for each other. Got the memo and on board the train. He wouldn't fight it anymore.

Chapter Twenty

When Shannon came out the front door after her shower, Merck almost told her to go change. How the hell did she expect him not to peel the flowy halter sundress off her before they even made it to the dock? It molded to her body, leaving little to the imagination. Of course, he already knew what lay beneath, so his brain easily filled in details of every curve.

She grinned and did a spin. Her blonde hair lay loose down her back, hitting her shoulder blades. But that wasn't what made him lose all train of thought. The dress had almost no back, which meant no bra. The missing part of the back didn't go all the way to her butt, but ended high enough to discreetly cover the scarred area. Still, it showed off her otherwise unblemished skin. He wanted to kiss the indentation of her spine as it traveled south. His throat tightened up, as did other parts of his body.

"Nice dress." Shit. Could he be any more lame?

"Nice enough to rip it off?" She leaned in close, fisted the front of his shirt, and whispered, "Because right now I want to yank this off you. We've got an audience, though."

She pulled away with a hooded smile. Naughty witch.

She patted a sunhat down onto the top of her head. Her delicate fingers laced through his. "Dad, Eli...they think me going out with you is a waste of time, but I'm not seeing any answers coming my way. So, let's go."

She led down the porch stairs. Her scent teased his nose, something floral he recognized as her shampoo mixed with the coconut essence of sunscreen. Somehow he managed to walk them to his boat and even untie it, although he barely remembered. As he navigated out of the No Wake Zone, she squeezed in next to where he stood at the wheel. He wrapped an arm around her slim body, cataloguing the curves pressed against him. She chatted about how she loved the birds and the beautiful weather and some other mundane topics. He managed a few coherent small-talk phrases, but seconds after he said something, he hoped she didn't quiz him. He couldn't remember a single thing that came out his mouth. All he could focus on was the feel of her pressed against him out here, on his boat, and in the world he loved. He wanted her fully his out here.

"Hang on," he warned when they hit open water. He shifted the boat into a higher gear.

Shannon squealed and grabbed her hat to hold it on when the bow pounded against the water, throwing spray around the sides. With a wipe she removed a few drops of salty water from her face and squeezed closer to him in the sheltered area around the wheel. The brilliance of her smile punched him mid-chest.

He headed for a sandbar he knew well. The tide was low. It'd be perfect for walking, even though what he planned involved not getting off the boat for a while.

"Why'd you want me to leave your place? Is it you want to be alone for your judgment or something else?"

Damn. He hadn't thought she'd let him get out of that one without an explanation. "What's coming at me is going to be dangerous."

"The gods' judgment?"

He shook his head. "Owen Campbell is here."

"What? How'd he find me?"

"He's looking for you, but I don't think he knows you're here. He's here to talk to me. He probably thinks he or his necromancer girlfriend can coerce me into giving up info about the Trident or recruit me to find you."

"Why would he link the two of us?"

"I don't think he's linked us together. He knows a bit about my water abilities."

"Ah. Then, you'd be a good starting place to find the Trident. I thought the same."

"I don't want you hurt in the crossfire of whatever he has planned. It's safer for you to stay away."

"If he's down here why are we out joyriding and not preparing?"

"This may be it for us. Not bringing you out here at least once would be a big regret." He gazed over the bow, lost in thoughts of this being his last ride on the water. He'd never again feel the salty spray on his skin, see the pelicans, or visit with the dolphins.

She took his hand and held it in silence for a while as the boat smacked its bow through choppy water. She leaned into him and rested her head on his shoulder. "It won't be it. It can't be. You know, I might've listened if you'd been honest at your house."

He snorted out a sarcastic *yeah right*. "You wouldn't stay away. You think Owen knows more about the Trident than we do, which I don't."

Her cheeks flushed. "I might have a few questions for him."

"Let's keep you being down here to ourselves."

She sighed deeply and rested her head against his shoulder. "Maybe we can strike a bargain about my whereabouts during this confrontation."

"A bargain?" He slowed in the waters near the sandbar and raised the motor in the shallow water. "Want to get off and discuss this bargain?"

"Not yet." Her eyelids grew heavy as she looked up at him, hooding her blue irises. She kissed his jaw and throat while her fingers traced the stubble on his face he'd neglected to shave.

Damn it, he should've shaved. He hadn't anticipated doing this again with her. "What kind of bargain?"

She smiled a true, wicked-witch smile. "I want to have you out here."

"What else do you want?"

"Everything. I get you and I want this." She rested her hand over his chest. "I want the one thing you never gave to anyone else."

"How do you know I loved someone else?"

"I already have your heart." She smiled when he frowned. "I knew you loved me the moment you said my pie was pretty good."

"What more is there, then?"

"For today, possibly the last few hours of your life, I want everything that's you."

"My soul?" *But you already have it.* Looking into her pale eyes, he felt a jolt of something close to fear. From the first moment he'd met her so long ago she'd been the woman in the back of his mind. He couldn't imagine a world without her and didn't even want to know what it would be like. This must be the hell Brian was living through if he felt something like this for Shannon's mother.

Somehow Shannon had been roped into the game the gods played with his life. He couldn't control that. He couldn't predict the outcome. Yet he had to figure out how to keep her from being collateral damage.

She nodded. "Everything."

"I give you everything and you'll stay away when Owen and his friends arrive?" He cradled her head and claimed her mouth. She drew him in deeper, but he was still in command of the kiss, giving her everything he had until she clung to him and whimpered.

He pulled away. "Well?"

"You drive a hard bargain. I don't think you'll walk away from us right now if I say no."

"I might walk. This is important. They can't know you're here." He leaned in as if to kiss her but didn't make contact.

She groaned in frustration. "Okay. Fine. I'll go home after this."

He reached for the clasp at the top of the halter top. "I've been imagining this since the second you walked out the front door." The yellow fabric collapsed to her waist. Coherent words failed him as he skimmed his fingers from her collarbones to her breasts. He bent his head and curled the tip of his tongue along one of the pebbled pink tips. She arched into him and grabbed on to his shoulders.

"God, I want so much..." She trailed off.

"Don't worry, darlin'. I'll give you everything you want. Just tell me how you feel." His mind should be cluttered. He should be running through eventualities and preparing for today's confrontations. Making plans fell into the background. Only she had the ability to stop his brain from analyzing and plotting. It felt pretty damned great.

"So little time." She moaned when he nipped at a nipple.

"We'll make it enough."

***

Shannon's world tilted as he continued to kiss her breasts, curling his tongue against her skin. His breath teased her before he straightened and pulled away. She whimpered complaint. "Merck?"

"Shh." He cupped her face, then he stepped away and placed towels from a storage box on the floor of the bow. She would've thought her dress and panties disappeared by magic if she hadn't felt him swipe them off. He lowered her to the boat floor.

Merck teased her with his touch, sliding his fingers through her folds. Lightly at first but enough to make her squirm. When she tried to push closer, he moved his hand away, denying her. He caged her with his arms, his body not touching hers. "Tell me what you want."

"You without clothes is a start." She plucked at his T-shirt.

He didn't make any motion to remove his clothes. "Then what?"

"I need you to want me so much you can't stand it."

He leaned in and whispered, "I already do."

"I want you wild. I want all that you keep caged."

"You don't know what you're asking for."

"You don't trust who you are. You keep yourself too much on lock-down. For me..." She intoned as if weaving a spell, "Let it go. You've got nothing to lose."

Merck's mouth slanted over hers with intense kisses. It was hunger, pure and unadulterated. Unchecked, it spilled out of him without finesse. The trembling clench of his fingers on her drowned her in the truth of how much he wanted her. Good Lord, she needed this man.

He trapped her arms above her head, caught one nipple in his mouth, and sucked hard, the edge of his teeth scraping her flesh. Everything about him surrounded her, overwhelmed her. When the world began to swim, he drew back. He said some compliment she barely heard. He released her hands. His fingers grazed through her sensitive folds, his fingers slicking back and forth in an intense rhythm until blood pounded in her ears. Her vision blurred.

"Merck." She rasped his name as his rhythm quickened. She scratched her nails across his back with a shiver.

"Jason," he corrected. "Out here. You and me. It's Jason. Say it. Say it while you're coming."

"Ja—" Her body exploded.

"Shh," he soothed, keeping her on edge with clever twists of his fingers. "My beautiful witch."

He lifted his head, giving her the full impact of his blissed-out eyes. She skated her fingers around his rib cage and down to the bulge in his pants. With a gentle tug, the zipper of his fly opened. His body tensed beneath her touch when she freed him. He groaned.

No more teasing. With one hand holding her down and the other angling her hips upward, he pushed into her. He felt huge. Her head spun.

"Does it scare you to know you're stuck with me for however long that may be?" He pushed a little deeper, a little harder.

"No." Pleasure spiraled as she sought that edge again.

He angled her pelvis to hit all the right spots. "It should." Every thrust got a little harder, a little rougher as if his self-control was fraying.

The sparkles in her sightline multiplied.

"Is this what you wanted?" he rasped out.

Yes. The word didn't come, but she did. His entire body shook. Rumbling started in his chest, giving way to a string of words bitten off between fast jerks of his hips. His forehead dropped to rest on her chest as he panted.

She tried to soothe him, but her arms felt too heavy to move.

His lips brushed over her forehead before he rolled the two of them to the side. "You okay?"

"I can't move."

"Me neither," he said, even though he did.

His hands were gentle as he eased her panties back into place and pulled her dress closed.

"You won't die. You can't," she whispered.

"Too many reasons say I will."

"None of this means anything if you're not here."

He cradled the back of her head. "I wish I could promise what you want to hear, but maybe all I can give you is me right now. If we're destined, that means maybe I'm just supposed to give you whatever kid you need and that's it."

"That's not what I want. I love you. I've always loved you."

He shuddered where her hands touched him.

She said, "If you can't be here, then neither can I. I need you." She fanned his face with her hands and kissed him. "You're not an evil person. The gods will see that."

"You name a sin, any sin, darlin', and I've done it. I've lied, stolen, and cheated. I've treated women and men like shit. I've killed so many I can't even keep count anymore. With those deaths came collateral damage. I've caused too many to die, which was my fault especially in the beginning when I first became the Enforcer."

"Are you trying to scare me away or convince yourself you deserve to die?"

He gazed upward. Birds flew in lazy circles above them, looking for a meal on the exposed sandbar. The wind carried the sound of the sea as the boat rocked with the small waves. "I've been rationalizing my impending death for a long time. Me dying makes sense. Your dying doesn't. You haven't done anything to deserve this kind of end."

His aura swirled with sadness. "I think you being forced to find the Trident is about me."

"You think it's your fault someone a continent away shoved a bespelled sword in my stomach which somehow linked me to the Trident?"

"I'm beginning to think it probably was."

"Whether or not it does, right now, this feels right." She snuggled closer to him.

He slid his hand over her nape to twine his fingers in her hair. "It is. This is where we belong. If I could give you every day like this, I would."

She fell back against the boat with a grin. "You're so stubborn."

"What?" His forehead wrinkled, confused.

She rolled back toward him, smiling. "Those three little words won't kill you."

He grinned.

"God, you're annoying." She punched his shoulder.

"I'm not sure we're at a three-little-words point in our relationship. We haven't known each other like this long enough."

They rested in silence for a while.

He suggested, "Let's walk on the sandbar before the tide comes in."

She hopped off the boat, her feet landing in the soft sand and knew deep warm water. As they walked in silence, the warm, dark sand squished through her toes.

"I might not be here tomorrow. This is as real as it gets."

She didn't reply. Couldn't. No Merck. For her. For anyone, anymore.

Him gone? Her palms sweated. Her heart beat so hard she thought it'd bounce right out of her rib cage. A world in which he didn't breathe or laugh or fight...

This was worse than someone showing up on her doorstep to inform her he'd died. At least there was finality with that, even though no less devastating. This was letting him go like sending a soldier into war, only the outcome seemed certain to be a coffin coming back.

"Okay?" He squeezed her hand. His bright blue eyes trapped hers. The hard expression that tightened his face reminded her he wasn't just Merck the man, but he was the Enforcer. Tough. Stubborn. And totally ready to face whatever manner of weird magic might be thrown his way.

"Okay."

No, not okay. Not even close.

Why couldn't she have a normal life? Two people love each other, get married, and then everything was all roses, puppies, and happy days.

This was real life. It sucked.

"Before I go, I'm going to try to negotiate about the Trident for you with whomever presents my judgment." Birds squawked overhead. He glanced upward. "It's time. We have to return to shore."

The ride in was quiet. The closer they got to land, the more her nerves drummed up. She held his hand tighter, although she wanted to wrap her arms around him and never let go.

Merck tied the boat to his dock, smooth and efficient. Not a wasted movement. He helped her onto the dock. Her arms wound around his neck to kiss him as if it were the last time she'd get the chance.

"I love you," she said, getting lost in the deep blue of his eyes.

"I won't forget it." His mouth turned into that annoying grin. He enjoyed torturing her. She'd get the words out of him eventually.

He turned toward the house but held out his hand to halt her.

"What is it?" she asked.

His sudden stillness sent her natural alarms shrieking.

"Run for the trees. Go as fast as you can. Don't look back. Get across the creek. If it's too high where you end up, then run toward the ocean and it'll get shallower." He glanced down at her. "Hurry. You promised."

Her heart beat hard as she gauged the distance to the trees. "What's here?"

"Something evil."

Chapter Twenty-one

Shannon charged for the tree line. She'd promised to go home. Maybe she should she pop away to her alternate dimension.

No. It was a crapshoot she'd end up somewhere familiar and then be able to travel back to South Carolina. With her luck, she'd end up in another country when she returned.

She'd already made up her mind not to allow Merck to face whatever came with Owen Campbell and his necromancer fiancée alone. The druids would help. That meant getting across the creek or... She plucked her cell phone out of the pocket in her dress, halting next to an ancient oak tree in order to text Eli.

Something flew by her ear and hit the tree. Black and purples swirled in the air, heralding an evil aura nearby. Texting could wait.

She ran flat-out in the direction of the creek and then along its edge, searching for where it looked shallow. Her lungs burned, and her legs ached from stumbling on uneven ground and tripping over branches, but she didn't stop. She batted sweat out of her eyes and off her forehead. The canopy overhead darkened as the forest became dense with old trees. And maybe not just from canopy but whatever approached from behind.

Something slammed into her back, thrusting her forward and to the ground. She landed hard. The world around her settled until there was only the sound of the creek, the narrows within sight about a hundred yards ahead. Over the creek's roar came footsteps crunching leaves and sticks. She struggled to breathe through the pain ripping through her. Another knife? A gunshot? Something worse?

She got to her knees and stood slowly while rotating to face whatever was coming. Alone and trapped—bad odds. Time to pop away. She closed her eyes to concentrate, willing herself back to the Hawaiian beach. Nothing happened. She willed harder.

Whatever she'd been hit with must dull her magic or prevent interdimensional travel.

A medium-height man with stringy brown hair sauntered her way. His aura swirled with the worst colors possible. Dangerous evil.

"Perfect shot, wasn't it? Hot damn. You're coming with me." He laughed out a low, raspy sound filled with arrogance. Power buzzed off him. Not godlike abilities, nor anything on the right side of nice, but something slithery.

She glanced up at the trees her mother always loved. Her mother's words slid through her mind, *"No harm will come to you in this forest. Trust the elements."*

"What do you want?" Her voice came out far calmer than expected, given the *oh-shit* going on in her mind.

"You. Shannon Randolph. I can't believe I'm the one who found you. She's going to be so pleased." He rubbed his hands together.

She was terrified, but stillness, almost an acceptance of what needed to be done, settled over her. No more running. No more being afraid of what she was. The gods may deserve her fear, but a human with pumped-up evil skills? Not so much. A sharp buildup of energy surrounded her as if an electrical current flickered through the ground. The trees swayed when the wind picked up, heralding an approaching storm.

The guy glanced around. "What are you doing?"

The wind increased, twirling into a spinning wind funnel.

Shock, horror, and utter terror spread over her attacker's face. He stood frozen as the tornado sped toward him. With a scream he ran. The miniature tornado increased speed and sucked up its target. The funnel disappeared upward into nothing, leaving behind a gentle breeze. Where the evil man had gone, Shannon didn't know. She didn't see him, but sensed him gone. As in forever gone.

She'd done that. Her. No one else. Her.

In the aftermath, the steady motion of running water of the creek calmed her.

There was also pain. She touched her back, her hand coming away with blood. No knife, but it might've fallen out. Or was it a bullet? The guy hadn't been carrying a gun. Either way, she was hit.

She glanced toward the narrows of the creek and then back in the direction of Merck. Wiped out from the energy output required to build the tornado, she stumbled against a tree. She wasn't going to make it across alone. Even if she did somehow cross the stream, she'd collapse on the opposite shore.

A body pushed her from behind into the tree. Her hands were gripped behind her and cuffed.

"No disappearing. Let's take a walk." The man leaning into her gripped the back of her neck, spun, and propelled her forward.

She butted her head backward, intent on his nose, but he ducked. He punched the side of her head. Dazed, she fell to her knees.

One glance up and she froze. The familiar blue gaze of the host of *Extreme Survivor* glared a command of compliance. Owen. Everything about the buff, blond man was angular and beautiful as one would expect for the host of several popular reality TV series.

"Behave, Shannon, or I'll knock you out. Then we'll have to cut the Trident out of you. No one here's a surgeon. So your chances of surviving aren't good."

"You're saying my chances of living are higher if I go with you willingly?"

He yanked her to her feet. "Can't say it looks good for you either way."

She wobbled, light-headed from the punch.

"Move." Owen pushed her forward.

She stumbled, catching herself on a low-slung tree branch whose bark burned her palm. Her legs buckled.

He wrenched her back up by an arm, slung her body over a shoulder, and trudged up the hill back toward Merck's house. Each jarring step shuttled pain through her body.

She focused on breathing to ignore the faintness in her brain. Breath in. Breath out. *Slam.* She whacked against Owen's back and gasped. New breaths. *Slam.*

Owen dropped her to the ground in the backyard. She blinked through tripling vision, relieved to no longer be moving. A scan of the yard for Merck found him statue still on his dock as if he hadn't moved from where he had told her to run. He didn't glance her way or deviate from his fixation on the stunning woman with a kid-in-the-candy-store grin. The grin was directed at Shannon.

Anaïs. The necromancer.

"Good job, sweetheart," Anaïs said to Owen. "Where's Reevo?"

"Don't know. He got a direct hit on her, though."

"Reevo died in Savannah," Merck said.

"Oh, did he die? Haven't you heard of fake-death pills? Azalea-induced coma?" Anaïs shot Merck a condescending smile.

"He's dead now," Shannon said, but it came out slurred.

Anaïs tugged Shannon to her feet, gripped her neck, and pulled her head backward. "Does it hurt, Shannon? Do you feel the black poison's spread as *Deus Mortem* destroys your body and works its way to your mind?"

"Go to hell." She struggled against the necromancer's abnormally strong grip.

Anaïs dragged her closer to Merck, throwing her onto the dock at Merck's feet. "Get the Trident out of her and give it to me. If you don't, she'll die."

"What'd they do to you?" Merck's gaze darted down to meet hers. This was the Enforcer again. No warmth lit his eyes. Stone-cold scary. This was good. She needed him focused on business, and deadly.

"Shot me with something in the back. Burns."

Merck stared silently at Anaïs.

Anaïs said, "Something you're familiar with. I'm impressed you survived when those Pleiades goddesses went down so easily. Seems I'll have to come up with something special for you next time. Nothing of this world can counteract the poison, though. But I can. Give me the Trident and I'll give you the antidote."

Merck knelt and rolled Shannon over to view her back.

"I'm sorry. I ran toward the creek. I swear." Shannon found the confidence in his gaze calming.

"This isn't your fault. I shouldn't have sent you away when I knew they were here. The mistake is on me." Merck addressed Anaïs. "What assurance do I have you'll give me the antidote should I give you what you want?"

Anaïs gestured to Owen, who removed a syringe from an abandoned backpack Shannon hadn't noticed in the backyard. Anaïs pointed at the first piling still far enough away from Merck to keep Owen out of danger. Owen set the syringe on the piling. His aura swirled with the colors of deceit.

Merck gazed at the syringe filled with clear fluid.

Shannon whispered, "I don't think whatever's in that will work."

***

The syringe had to be bogus. Highly unlikely she could've stolen both *Deus Mortem* and its antidote from Circe. He saw only one way out of this.

Merck's addressed Owen. "How do I know the syringe isn't filled with more poison or just ordinary saline?"

Owen didn't answer. His gaze remained fixated on Anaïs in an oddly robotic way.

Anaïs shrugged. "You've got to believe in something."

"Why are you with her, Owen?" Merck asked. "You might hang out with some magical assholes from time to time, but you're not like her."

Owen acted as if he hadn't heard him as he stared moon-eyed at Anaïs.

Anaïs reached out with her talonlike, blue-painted nails and touched Owen's square jaw. "We're in love."

"Uh-huh," Merck grumbled sarcastically. "More like spellbound or bewitched. Why did you kill the Pleiades goddesses?"

Anaïs smiled broadly. "Their souls have made me invincible. I can wield the power of the Trident now."

"Why those particular goddesses?"

"Rick wanted them dead. I needed their power. Win win for all of us, even if Rick got killed. Win win for me, I guess." She grinned. "Get it out of her."

Shannon released an almost silent moan. The small noise tore through him, killed him. "All right. I do believe in something."

Shannon whispered, "Don't. They can't have it."

"Sometimes, you've got to believe. I'm going to see if I can get the Trident from you. Totally not sure on how to do this. You think you can lie on your back, or does it hurt too much?"

"Will side work?" She rolled to her side, facing him.

He yanked his knife off his belt and cut a hole in her dress over the scarred area.

"Are you going to cut it out of me?" Horror passed over her face.

"No."

"Okay. I trust you. I do." Her eyes settled into a faith he hoped he'd deserve. He didn't know what the hell he was doing, but he was going to try. He cut a small window in her dress and held his hand over the scarred area. Closing his eyes helped him sense the power lodged within her. He detected the ocean and all that was marine in its most organic and primal sense churning beneath her skin.

Come to me, he silently commanded. A strength he'd never before experienced fueled him with energy. His hands closed around something solid. He gasped as his body charged, not with discomfort, but with a vigor that was tempting and intoxicating. When he opened his eyes, he held the Trident. He almost dropped it out of shock. The golden symbol for rule of the ocean was in his hand. It didn't burn him as he'd expected it would with anyone not Poseidon. It accepted him. It tempted him with a boundless power of rule.

It also wasn't impressive for something considered to be so powerful. Three barbed tines on the end of a metal pole. The metal didn't even look like real gold. The thing just looked like a boring fishing tool.

"You can't give it to her," Shannon said, breaking through his fixation on the weapon. "Please, give it back to him."

"You'll die," he said softly.

"This isn't about me. It's about people who shouldn't die for something they had nothing to do with. Worthy people. People I love."

How he loved this woman.

"Give it to me!" Anaïs screamed. She charged toward the dock, but waves picked up as the ocean churned, casting over the dock both in front of and behind Merck and Shannon, hindering Anaïs's trajectory.

"This is about a lot more than either of us or the necromancer." He kissed the inside of Shannon's hand. For years, he'd been fighting for free will. He'd fought for a choice in his future. Now he realized he'd never had a choice.

Fuck free will. He'd believe in destiny. His destiny was about this brave woman who'd die for those she loved. It was about protecting her bloodline and that of the other Pleiades descendants. No matter how much this might hurt in the short-term, fully expecting to lose her to death or be cast out of this life when judged, love had to endure. Maybe in another lifetime he'd find her. Maybe in his next life as the Enforcer he'd remember her. Love was infinite. It could sustain. He would remember. "There's only one way for you to live."

He stood and held the Trident as if he meant to toss it to Anaïs. Shannon gasped. He gazed down and winked at her. With a pivot, he cast the Trident toward the water. His eldest dolphin friend jumped from the water and caught it.

"Return it," he ordered the dolphin. Merck knelt beside Shannon and reached one hand toward the water, praying it could heal her. The water ran up his arm and onto her, around her lesions. Nothing. The darkness was still on her skin. He tried again.

"I can't do it, baby. I can't heal this poison. It's powerful enough to kill a god. She used it to kill all seven of the Pleiades goddesses." Even he heard the panic in his tone.

"Thank you. As you said, this isn't about us."

He smoothed hair away from her face and kissed her briefly.

With a frown, her eyes moved away from his to stare at the churning sea. "What's happening?"

The sky darkened and the water pounded the dock, angry or perhaps excited. He couldn't read the ocean's mood, which was rare. Overhead, dark clouds gathered. Slivers of light peeked around the clouds, glittering furiously. Water sloshed against the dock, growing in height with each new wave. From the water rose a gigantic man with long white hair, grasping the Trident. Vicious blue eyes skimmed over Merck and Shannon.

Poseidon.

All Merck remembered from years of research into his mysterious father were accounts of him being unpredictable and easily pissed.

Merck dropped to his knees, kneeling with head bowed, but made sure to remain protectively in front of Shannon. Heavy footsteps approached. His heart thundered against his ribs as visions of various ways he could die passed through his brain. Doubt hit him. Maybe he shouldn't have given the Trident back.

"Who attempted to steal my Trident?" a thunderous voice demanded.

Merck glanced up.

Poseidon pointed to Anaïs, who stood frozen at the dock's entrance. Far behind her Owen shook his head feeling as if he was coming out of a daze or dream. He glanced around, shocked, and slowly backed away.

"You deem yourself more worthy than I to rule my seas? You see yourself as jury and executioner to destroy several of the sea nymphs?" Poseidon twirled the Trident and scrutinized her.

The necromancer chanted and cast a blast of energy toward Poseidon.

The energy hit him, causing him to back up one step. "You attack me? For the Trident's power?"

"I have absorbed the souls of the seven goddesses. I am strong enough to wield it's power."

He pointed the Trident at her. "Then feel it. Feel the power you so long to have."

Anaïs screamed as her body lit with light. At first, she laughed with glee, but then she screamed in pain.

"May it consume your tainted soul and return those souls you stole to their owners." Poseidon's expression didn't alter even when Anaïs's body fractured with light and combusted into nothing. He pointed at Owen. "You are free of her enthrallment descendant of Orion, but you should run or I will destroy you as well."

Owen fled.

In the silence that followed, Merck lowered his gaze again. "I'm prepared to die, but please let Shannon live. Clear this poison from her. She deserved none of this."

A large hand landed on his shoulder. Solid. Heavy. Then a painful squeeze. A good squeeze or a you're-going-to-die squeeze? Shit, he didn't know.

He peeked up, but tried to remain deferential. Not easy when the eerie blue of Poseidon's eyes penetrated straight to his soul.

"You do not need me for this request, my son." Poseidon's voice thundered inside his skull, as powerful as Athena's, but a lower resonance.

"I tried. Nothing happened when I asked the ocean to help."

"You have been judged."

"Take me, then. Please. Not her. Heal her."

Danny strolled onto the dock. He knelt before Poseidon. "My time as watcher has ended. Anything more you need from me?"

"Danny?" A loud *what the hell* pinged around in Merck's brain. Danny here didn't make sense. What did he mean by being a watcher? Merck shot to a stand. "Why are you here?"

"I'm sorry, Merck. My job was to watch and provide unbiased information needed for your judgment."

"I trusted you. And you spied against me? To him?"

"You still can trust me, man. Sorry about the spying. But when a god asks you to do something, it's not like you can say no." He shrugged.

"You can if it involves throwing a friend under the bus."

Poseidon swept his arm to silence them. "Judgment is done."

Merck swallowed hard against panic. Sweat slid between his shoulders. He glanced down at Shannon, who'd curled her body into a C and clutched her middle. He didn't want her to die. Not like this.

Shannon struggled to unbend her body. She reached out and grabbed Merck's hand. He clasped her smaller hand in his.

"What does that mean?" Merck demanded.

Poseidon's angular face looked pinched. He waved a hand. "I've already explained."

"You've explained nothing." He bit back more demands when Poseidon cast him a deadly glower. *Athena wants me to call you a dickhead.* But he didn't say it out loud.

"I heard that," Poseidon thundered. For a split second, his lips tilted into a smile. His eyes creased out and softened. "Impertinent, just like she said you were. I like that."

Now he'd get struck down.

"Bythos can deal with you and your questions." Poseidon pivoted and disappeared into the ocean, which calmed almost immediately upon his departure. The old dolphin jumped out of the water into a back flip, followed by three other members of his pod, including the juvenile Merck had helped.

"What the fuck did he mean?" Merck yelled. "Danny, what'd you tell him or them or whoever the hell you reported to?"

Danny backed up a few steps with his hands in the air. "Whoa there. Had your back, man. Only good stuff to report. You worked hard, played hard, believed in good shit."

"Then why is this happening?"

"I swear I only reported good things." He made a cross sign over his chest. "Always said I'd be there for you and I meant it."

Shannon's eyes locked on the sky and darkened. Death was coming, but not for him...for Shannon.

He shook her. "You stay with me...stay. You're not going to die."

"Oh, God. I'm not going to make it."

"You hang on. Damn it."

She whispered, "I love..."

"No!"

Chapter Twenty-two

"Are you going to continue acting like a baby or are you actually going to do something?"

Merck's head snapped around to stare at the end of his dock. Bythos calmly strolled his way wearing a flamboyant Hawaiian shirt and linen pants. His bare feet made no noise as he approached.

"You here to kill me this time?"

Bythos held his hands away from his body to demonstrate no weapons. "I'm here to clean up the mess, as usual."

"I tried to heal her. Nothing happened. Can't you do something for her?"

"Not my thing. You were judged."

"What does that mean?"

"It means stop being a dumbass and try again." Bythos crossed his arms and stared.

"But I'm still here."

"Yes. You are. You were judged."

"They're not going to send me to Hades?"

"Guess not."

Try again? Maybe he needed to be in the water with Shannon for it to work. He scooped her into his arms and paced to the end of the dock. He met Bythos's gaze for a moment, finding no confirmation

221

this was the right move. Bythos looked simultaneously entertained and bored.

As he passed Bythos, Merck muttered, "I really don't like you right now."

"I know, but you'll like me even less if you keep flapping your lips and she dies." Bythos leaned casually against a piling and picked at his nails.

"Shannon, you with me?" Merck jostled her.

Her eyes blinked open, but then drifted shut.

"I need you to hold on. Take a deep breath. We're going under."

***

Her body lit on fire, jolting her to consciousness. A scream crested, but Shannon quickly closed her mouth when water flooded inside. Something held her underwater. Drowning her.

Her head broke free of the ocean's surface. She thrashed, coughed up water, and gulped in air. Her toes couldn't touch ground. Whatever tried to drown her still restrained her.

"I've got you. Stop struggling. Here..." The cuffs around her wrists magically disappeared.

She grabbed at Merck, panicked in the water.

"You're fine. I swear." His hands cradled her head above the water, allowing her to breathe.

"Why are we in the water again?" His dock sat a hundred yards or more away.

"I thought I'd lost you," he whispered. "But I didn't."

"Your healing worked? I thought you couldn't..."

"Yeah, me too, but second time's the charm." In a blink, they were on the dock.

"How'd you do that?" She shifted in his arms since he still hadn't let her go.

"Not sure." He dropped the cuffs on the dock. His gaze met that of the water god who he'd spoken with after the Athena encounter.

The god smiled at her, his eerie, pale eyes swirling. "I'm Bythos." He took her hand and kissed it. "You're more beautiful than the ocean at sunset in the spring."

Merck knocked his hand away. "Stop hitting on her. You're not her type. Besides, that was pathetic."

"I thought it was nice imagery." She caught Merck's glower. "Maybe a bit cheesy."

Bythos shot Merck a smug smirk. "I told you I could be her type."

"Push it and I'll castrate you," Merck warned.

Bythos shrugged. "You passed their test. Means they granted you your full status."

"A full god?" Merck asked.

"Yes and Poseidon unlocked all your powers. You still have responsibilities, though."

"What am I the god of? I know there has to be balance between all the gods."

Bythos shot him a *you're an idiot* glare. "What are you best at when it comes to the ocean?"

"Fixing its issues."

"There you go. God of water healing. Able to heal it and use it to heal others, but your primary duty is as protector to the Pleiades."

"And be Enforcer? Triple duty?"

"Never said it'd be easy, although being a god might make the Enforcer business easier now that you're resistant to black magic. I hear the Pleiades descendants are a handful." He smiled again at Shannon. "Their bloodline must persist. If they all die, their ability to bridge dimensions will crack and fracture reality as we know it." Bythos clapped him on the shoulder. "I'm proud of you, kid. Now I'm out of here. I'll be back, but fair warning, it's far more interesting to attack you at random than deal with this type of minutia." He granted Shannon a slow, sexy smile. "If he cannot satisfy you, I'm available." He leaned in and touched her cheek. "I love all sea nymph descendants."

Merck pulled her away from him. "Watch it, asshole. I've got a pretty kick-ass sword now. I know how to use it."

"I don't see it on you." Bythos winked at her as he dove into the ocean, shifting to merman form seconds before hitting the water.

"I think he likes you," Shannon said.

"He's a total pain in the ass."

"He's sweet. You're a full-blood god? As in Mom's a goddess and Father's a god? Is that why your face is fixed? No more scars." She brushed her hand over his now-smooth cheek.

He touched his face. "Seems I'm not a bastard. I just had to pass some asinine test, no thanks to Danny." He tossed his chin at Danny, who stood at the entrance to the dock, silent and shocked.

"Now that it doesn't look like either of us are going to die..." Wickedly, Shannon pressed her body against his, her hand sliding provocatively over the ridge in his pants. "Maybe you can use your new godly powers to grant us a little privacy from Danny?"

"I heard that," Danny yelled from the entrance edge of the dock. "Yeah, yeah. I'm outta here. Later, Merck." He waved and stalked out of the yard.

Merck made a sound somewhere between a groan and a sigh. He slammed his mouth against hers. She moaned at the contact of his tongue, kissing deeper and deeper until she couldn't tell where she ended and he began. He ducked his head and rested his forehead against hers. "I can't do that again."

"Merck?"

"I can't watch you almost die."

She twined her arms around his neck. "I'm not going anywhere."

"It would shatter me."

"Look at me. You're not going to die today or tomorrow." She cupped his face and encouraged him to look into her eyes. "There's an us. For as long as we both exist there will be an us. You as a god means you might live longer than me. I don't know how that'll go."

She closed the distance and kissed him softly.

He whispered, "I've never done an us thing before."

"Me either. I've never really tried to be with one person. We can figure it out. But you and your job... I'll always worry about you and what you're going after. I can't promise I'll always sit on the sidelines. I think you could teach me a lot and I'd be pretty helpful."

"I don't want you near some of the filth I have to go after."

Shannon smiled. "We can figure it out together. All I know is it won't be much of a life if I don't have you in it."

He searched her eyes for a long moment. His gaze dropped to her lips, and when it rose back to hers, his pupils dilated. His breathing picked up. "I have a condition."

"What kind of condition?"

"More pie." His hands tunneled into her hair, pulling just enough to tilt her head back and get full access to her lips and down her neck. He pressed her against a piling. His hands slid up her thighs to dip between them. He nudged aside her soaked panties and stroked where she was pulsating. She gasped.

"I can do pie. Take my dress off," she begged.

"No. I like it on you out here. No one else sees you naked. Only me."

"There's no one here."

"Bythos might be peeping. Fucker can get an eyeful, but not everything."

She slipped from beneath him and snagged the cuffs off the dock. With a grin she dangled them from one finger. "I think you've been a very bad boy." She slapped them over his wrists.

"You're a wicked witch," he whispered.

"I can be, but only for you." She kissed him again, but this time there was no rush to it. No desperation. She kissed him like she'd been doing it forever and planned to keep on doing it the same way. "I'm ready to hear those three little words."

He dropped his cuffed hands around her neck, placing the weight of his arms on her shoulders, and pressed her back against the piling. "You are mine?"

She scowled.

He grinned. "I love you. For however long we've got, I love you."

"You're going to marry me."

"Was that a proposal? Because if it was, I think you need to work on your delivery, darlin'. It sucked." He chuckled.

She placed her hand against his chest. "This belongs to me. It's always been mine."

"Ouch." He rubbed where her hand had been. "What'd you do?" He plucked the T-shirt away from his neck to peek down it. "There's a mark."

"The tattoo means this is the real thing. You and me. We Pleiades can place that mark on the guy chosen by the gods to be our soul mate. It's you. It means you're stuck with me. Forever."

"I already know this is the real thing."

She unbuttoned his pants. "If you even start to think about bed hopping, just remember, I can be a very wicked witch."

Acknowledgments

With immense gratitude to my readers who welcomed my characters into their lives and imaginations. This book is for those of you who requested one more in the Keepers of the Veil series.

Sasha Knight, your insight and tough editing were invaluable.

Nichole Severn, thank you for being fresh eyes in a time of need.

A huge shout out to Quincy Marin for her graphic art expertise. You are magic on the computer.

None of this would be possible without my husband, family and friends. We lost a beloved furry member of our household while writing this book, a cat who left a hole in our hearts but filled our lives with love in the short time he was with us.

About the Author

Award winning author, Zoe Forward[1] is a hopeless romantic who can't decide between paranormal and contemporary romance, so she writes both. Her novels have won numerous awards including the Readers' Choice Heart of Excellence, Golden Quill, Carolyn Readers Choice, and the Booksellers' Best.

When she's not typing at her laptop, she's tying on a karate belt for her son or cleaning up the newest pet mess from the menagerie that occupies her house. She's a small animal veterinarian caring for a wide range of furry creatures, although there has been the occasional hermit crab.

She's madly in love with her globe trotting conservation ecologist husband who plans to save all the big cats on the planet, and she's happiest when he returns to their home base.

***

---

1. http://www.zoeforward.com/home.html

Sign up for Zoe's NEWSLETTER[1] to keep up with the latest in books, events and news.

***

Also by Zoe Forward...

IN THE KEEPERS OF THE VEIL SERIES:
Protecting His Witch[2]
His Witch to Keep[3]
Playing the Witch's Game[4]

***

OTHER PARANORMAL ROMANCE TITLES:
The Way You Bite[5]
Dawn of a Dark Knight[6]
Forgotten In Darkness[7]

---

1. http://www.zoeforward.com/contact.html

2.   http://www.zoeforward.com/book4-Blurb.html

3.   http://www.zoeforward.com/book5-Blurb.html

4.   http://www.zoeforward.com/book6-Blurb.html

5.   http://www.zoeforward.com/book7-Blurb.html

6.   http://www.zoeforward.com/book1-Blurb.html

7.   http://www.zoeforward.com/book2-Blurb.html

<u>Darkness Unbound</u>[8]

---

8.   http://www.zoeforward.com/book3-Blurb.html

24937737R00137

Printed in Great Britain
by Amazon